Heart Land

Center Point
Large Print

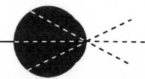

**This Large Print Book carries the
Seal of Approval of N.A.V.H.**

Heart Land

KIMBERLY STUART

CENTER POINT LARGE PRINT
THORNDIKE, MAINE

This Center Point Large Print edition
is published in the year 2018 by arrangement with
Howard Books, a division of Simon & Schuster, Inc.

The text of this Large Print edition is unabridged.
In other aspects, this book may vary
from the original edition.
Printed in the United States of America
on permanent paper.
Set in 16-point Times New Roman type.

ISBN: 978-1-68324-952-8

Library of Congress Cataloging-in-Publication Data

Names: Stuart, Kimberly, 1975- author.
Title: Heart land / Kimberly Stuart.
Description: Center Point Large Print edition. | Thorndike, Maine :
    Center Point Large Print, 2018.
Identifiers: LCCN 2018030105 | ISBN 9781683249528
    (hardcover : alk. paper)
Subjects: LCSH: Man-woman relationships—Fiction. |
    City and town life—Fiction. | First loves—Fiction. | Large type books.
Classification: LCC PS3619.T832 H43 2018b | DDC 813/.6—dc23
LC record available at https://lccn.loc.gov/2018030105

To my parents,
two Iowa kids who have built
something beautiful

Heart
Land

one

No one had said anything about farm animals.

Three minutes to midnight in a cavernous Manhattan loft, dark except for the lights we'd brought in for the photo shoot, and my view was entirely taken up by three leggy models holding *sheep*. Sheep. As in woolly coats and blank expressions and a reputation for being daft. There were three small ones, lambs, if we were being technical, and each of the models clutched her own. I wasn't sure who looked more terrified, the animals or the women.

One of the lambs bleated loudly, and Akeyo, the model on the far left, startled, causing the photographer to bark for neutral faces.

I shifted in my boots, a glorious pair made of the softest charcoal suede. They were a complete indulgence, a splurge from a month prior when I was finally allowing myself to believe I could soon be vacating my position as a design assistant at Milano, one of the premier fashion houses in New York, and heading at last into the designer role that had my name on it. The final edict would come down tomorrow, and in a moment of pre-promotion hopefulness, I'd tugged on my new boots in the early morning hours. Turns out, I'd been suiting up for an interminable workday. And turns out, these boots with the three-inch heel, so perfect at nine a.m., eleven a.m., even three p.m., were spawn of Satan every minute after eight.

I checked the clock on my phone again and bit my lower lip to stifle the groan. We had hit the nine-hour mark into the Photo Shoot of Doom.

Taking a deep breath in, I let it out slowly, reminding myself again that tonight would mark the end of long days without purpose and that tomorrow held the promise of something entirely different. *Slow breath in, slow breath out,* I thought as I watched the assistant to the photographer's assistant rush up with a bottle of water and a pack of chewing gum.

Isa snorted quietly next to me. "I think we passed the point of cleansing breaths when the first model broke out in hives."

Isa had started her job as a junior visual merchandiser at Milano the same week I had been brought on as a design assistant. We had gone to the Fashion Institute of Technology together, both of us finishing at the top of our class, and we had struck up a fast friendship over our love for vintage Dior and our disdain for sensible shoes.

"Remember clogs and how we hate them?" I whispered, sucking in a sharp breath as I moved too quickly and felt the sting of a new blister.

Isa raised one perfectly plucked eyebrow. "I do remember. A sister never forgets."

I shook my head, my whisper rising in volume. "I'm leaving the sisterhood. I love clogs. I want them. Big, ugly ones with arch support and horrible, thick leather soles that make me look like a chef. Or a Midwesterner."

Isa tsked. "You can take the girl out of—"

Her words stopped abruptly when Javi, the senior designer in charge of the shoot, threw a clipboard across the room.

"Iowa!" he shrieked, shielding his eyes from the glare of lights.

I jumped and headed toward him, dodging the art director, the creative director, and an impossibly tall makeup artist who was beelining for Akeyo with a tube of lipstick, deep wine color already bared. I walked across the room cringing at the nickname Javi had christened me with for the photo shoot. In general I tried to forget my state of origin. In general I found others much less willing to forget. Doing my best not to shuffle or whimper with every blistered step, I picked through the electrical cables snaking around the photographer and her crew.

"How can I help, Javi?" I asked, bright smile in place.

"Grace, thank God you're here and not one of those other idiots in your department."

My smile remained fixed. I knew two things:

first, that Javi thought we were *all* idiots, me included, and second, that he had given that same faux compliment to every person on our team at one time or another. "What do you need?" I looked at the models, itching to try my hand at these shots for Milano's newest ad campaign. The women were perched on an elaborate assemblage of wooden crates draped with the sumptuous fabrics Milano would feature in its upcoming fall line. The models wore beaded bralettes over wide-legged, high-waisted trousers. The cut on Akeyo's top needed different tailoring, and I knew just what to do to make it beautiful. My fingers twitched involuntarily, willing Javi to ask me what was wrong and how to fix it. *Ask me how to fix it. Ask me what's wrong and how to make it right.*

He took an indulgent pull of his umpteenth espresso of the day before pushing the empty cup toward me, the person nearest to him who occupied a low rung on the totem pole. "Put your 4-H skills to good use and take that animal," he said, nodding to the sheep held by Akeyo. "The sheep is tired and starting to sleep. I need his eyes to be open."

I bit my lower lip, feeling my pulse quicken and recognizing both an exhaustion and a disappointment familiar enough to make me nearly burst into tears. I stared for a moment at Javi, who already had his back to me and was engaged in conversation with the creative director on the possibility of changing the ad's font at this stage of the game. Gripping Javi's empty espresso cup, I considered saying all the things I'd wanted to say over the years to so many of those higher up in the pecking order. I could, for example, return his empty cup and point him toward the trash bin a few paces away. I could ask him (again) to refrain from mentioning geography when ordering me around. I could, most thrillingly, march right up to the models and start rearranging, redraping, redoing all that was done wrong and then amaze and delight everyone in the room when I resurrected an ad campaign that was in desperate need of inspiration.

I sighed. Every one of those options was unthinkable, so I tucked the empty paper cup into a pocket of my pants and held out my arms to Akeyo. Her eyes were large, a brown so deep it bordered on onyx. She trained them on me with pity before erupting in a hoarse coughing fit.

"Sorry," the model said, quietly enough to keep it between us. "I'm getting over a cold." She glanced out of the corner of her eye toward Javi, and I did the same. He was, mercifully, now yelping at the creative director, the two of them gesticulating forcefully at the images of the shoot displayed on a computer.

"We shoot tethered so we can make these changes!" Javi shrieked. "This is why we connect the camera to the computer, Giles, so that we can change directions as needed, in real time!"

"Exactly no!" Giles said, his French accent becoming more pronounced as his face reddened. "We cannot change at this juncture. The font and placement shall not be moved!"

Akeyo coughed again, her eyes betraying nerves. She and I both knew that there were plenty of women not struggling with a hacking cough who could be summoned for her place in this campaign. I rummaged in a deep pocket of my trousers and slipped her a cough drop.

"Thank you so much," Akeyo said softly, her eyes filling with emotion. She lifted her chin toward the sheep wriggling in my arms. "And I am so sorry that you are in charge of the livestock."

My smile was tired but sincere. "Looks like the livestock is safest far away from cameras and computers right about now."

Akeyo giggled, and I made my way toward the makeshift pen at the back of the room. I must have been muttering because Luca, suddenly next to me, said, "Baby, conversing with the animals makes you one slippery step away from a place you don't want to visit."

I put down the sheep and turned to face my friend. "The fabrics are perfect. You nailed it again."

Luca narrowed his gaze at the scene lit up

before him. "I really did," he said, nodding slowly. Luca was Milano's technical designer, a transplant from our Rome office, and he was a mastermind at putting designs into action. He was able to take a vision and make it a reality, from sourcing hard-to-find fabrics to determining just how many centimeters lay between each button on a cuff. He watched the scene before him, his eyes darting back and forth between the models and the posse of folks staring, not directly at the models, but at the images appearing on the screen. "The fabrics are sublime. But there's something off about Akeyo's top."

Isa joined us and handed me a glass of cucumber water. She nudged me gently and said, "There's totally something off with that top. And I'll bet Grace knows how to fix it."

I sighed. "I sure do," I said, not bothering to detail it to the friends who didn't need me to prove anything to them. I sipped the water and turned to check on the sheep. I shook my head at the absurdity of my life. No little girl grew up with this version of The Dream. I was sure of it. And not only because I'd taken stock of The Dream countless times throughout the last decade, checking its pulse, wondering if it would still stir to life if I poked it with the toe of my favorite (and only) pair of pointy-toe Louboutins. I'd had plenty of practice looking in on the original dream, but even the casual observer would have been able to tell you that tonight's version of events was a far, far cry from how this whole thing had been meant to play out. *One more night,* I thought as I scooped a clump of sheep poop into a bag and turned to my friends.

"Who said the fashion industry in New York isn't glamorous?" I said.

"Ew," Isa said, making a face. "You act like this is normal. We don't have poop like that in the Bronx. Rat poop and roach poop, yes. But that stuff is so . . . big." She shuddered at the bag I was tying off.

I rolled my eyes. "Iowa is not exactly the sheep capital of the country. Pigs and cows are more our thing. Their thing," I corrected, the reflex kicking in. "And I only learned to pick up poop in a bag after moving to New York and walking with you in Central Park." I pointed to Luca. "Yolo the Yorkie is the mistress of poop in bags."

Luca straightened. "Do not compare Yolo to these savage beasts. Yolo is a sophisticated animal who loves foie gras and deep-tissue massage. She does not *bleat.*"

I caught Isa's gaze and saw her biting her lower lip—Isa who could not keep a succulent alive and who once screamed bloody murder when a butterfly brushed her cheek, claiming there were no butterflies where she grew up and that all animals should have the decency to just stay in the zoos the city provided for them.

Javi shouted from the other side of the room. "We need the sleepy sheep, Iowa! Let's finish this up and get out of here before midnight, shall we, people?"

I leaned over to pick up the squirming sheep, who much preferred to be gnawing on the very expensive wheatgrass someone had purchased for its pleasure. "These sheep are better protected for their working conditions than we are," I huffed as I gathered up the animal in my arms. "Did they unionize or something?"

Luca and Isa were uncharacteristically silent after what I thought was a very funny joke. I turned and bumped straight into the chest of James Campbell, my painfully good-looking boss, who had, if I wasn't mistaken, taken to passing by my desk more than was strictly necessary in recent weeks. He cocked his head first at the sheep, then at me.

"Miss Kleren, are you interested in filing a complaint?" He wasn't trying very hard to hide a smile. "I'm pretty sure there's a form for that somewhere." His light blue eyes sparkled with amusement. I realized I was staring at those eyes when Isa cleared her throat.

"No thanks." I straightened and tried for some dignity. I sidestepped as elegantly as I could while holding a sheep, and walked toward an increasingly impatient Javi. James followed me, and I stole a glance at Isa and Luca as I walked

17

away. Isa raised one eyebrow, and Luca smirked. Their ears were likely still ringing with a particularly spirited monologue from earlier in the week, when I had dissected, not for the first time, whether James was actually flirting with me at work or if he was just being friendly. Just when I'd thought the verdict was definitely in one direction or another, James would leave me guessing once again.

I completed the sheep handoff to Akeyo and retreated to the shadows behind the lights. James followed me.

"Love those boots," he said, nodding appreciatively at my feet. "Those are boots that should be seen outside of this depressing warehouse."

I fixed my eyes on the shoot, determined not to show my cards just because he had elevated taste in footwear. "Yes, well, even my feet are committed to doing well at this job. I'm all in."

"So I've noticed," James said, a smile in his voice. Of course he had noticed, I quickly reasoned. He'd reviewed my work for years, and he knew I was overqualified and underpaid but that I was sticking it out at Milano because I was one break, one quick promotion away from a designer position and the chance to finally do what I was wired to do.

We watched the scene before us in silence, laughing together when Javi took a blush brush out of a makeup artist's hand and did an impromptu demo on his own face, jabbing his finger at an image on the screen. "This woman just returned from a shoot in Barbados! Near the equator! How is it possible your makeup is causing her to look sun starved?"

I startled when James took my hand in the darkness.

"Hey," he said softly, and I turned to look at him. "Listen, I hope I'm not out of line saying this, but I like you, Grace. And I think you like me."

My eyes widened and he laughed.

"Don't look so shocked. Certainly I'm not the only one who's been thinking along these lines?"

His boyish grin made me stutter a response. "Yes. No. I mean, you're not the only one who has been thinking."

"Good," he said, amused. "I like a girl who thinks. So," he said, leaning closer, voice lowered to protect the privacy of our conversation, "let's get out of here, grab something to eat. I'll cover for you. Javi's a total pushover when it comes down to it, and he's distracted anyway. We can unwind, you can tell me about your day, and those shoes can get some of the attention they deserve." He looked suddenly hopeful, maybe a bit nervous, and I felt a part of me undo itself a bit with his vulnerability.

But I gently removed my hand from his grasp.

"Thank you. It's a lovely offer, James, but I'll need to decline."

James made a face. "Rather polite, aren't we? That's not the Grace that banters with me in the coffee room."

I met his gaze, wanting to tell him there was more to me than a good banter, that he'd been right to think I was interested, but not knowing how far to push this conversation, especially the night before I was to finally have my chance to speak up and be heard by James's boss, my boss, the woman with the power to change everything for me. At the mere thought of Nancy Strang, the formidable head of design at Milano, I stood straighter, returning my eyes to the shoot, on firm footing again. "I'm so sorry, but I need to get plenty of rest. It's open-call day tomorrow, and I present first thing in the morning."

James came to stand in front of me, blocking my view. "I know that, silly girl," he said, his eyes alight with amusement. "I might have put in a good word for you to get that prime appointment time."

"You did?" I said, hating how my voice had taken on a neediness I definitely felt and desperately wanted to hide. I cleared my throat. "I mean, thank you so much. I'm sure I can take all the help I can get."

"So just come with me." He linked his fingers in mine, slowly rubbed the inside of my palm with his thumb. "I promise I won't keep you out too late. We can just stop by my apartment."

I raised one eyebrow.

"Just for a bit," he hurried on. "Noemi left *pasta e fagioli* in the fridge and I know for a fact she baked homemade focaccia today. Even people with presentations in the morning have to eat."

I rolled my eyes. "Most people with presentations in the morning don't have personal chefs," I said, but my stomach was rumbling at the thought of a rich, hot soup and fresh-baked bread. Plus, the idea of seeing James's Upper West Side digs was a temptation that sounded decidedly more interesting than a rigid campout on the high road. "A personal chef sounds distinctly foreign to a girl like me."

"Well, then, it's good you know someone who can introduce you to the finer things." James's voice had lowered, so I needed to lean toward him to hear his words.

I could sense Isa and Luca watching us. The responsible thing to do was to clarify what James was up to, what I was up to, after so many of these flirty conversations that week and so many other weeks throughout the last six months. The responsible thing to do was to stay at work until Javi called the shoot. The responsible thing to do was to fish out my latest overdrawn account notice that was burning a hole in my bag and hold that notice like my favorite stuffed animal, a near-and-present reminder that I had no business taking cabs from the Upper West Side to my tiny apartment in Harlem, much less wearing shoes that could pay for things like food and shelter.

The responsible thing to do would have to wait one more day.

I shook my head but smiled the answer to his invitation. "You make it tough for a girl to say no."

He laughed. "That was the plan, anyway. Shall we?"

James's penthouse apartment was a thing of beauty. I heard my breath stutter when I entered the spacious foyer that opened into a perfectly appointed living room and a wall of French doors that led to the balcony. I set my bag carefully on an inlaid wood table in the front hall, unable to toss it down roughly as James had done with his car keys, a quick, careless shedding onto a table so elegant and refined, it would have made my mother swoon. I followed James through the pristine living room, barely letting my full weight settle into the plush carpet as I stepped. We reached the kitchen and he directed me to a stool alongside a sprawling marble island. I perched gingerly and took in the soaring windows, the backsplash made of a glazed tile that screamed "imported and rare," appliances that looked untouched and prohibitively expensive. The thought came unbidden that I was a long way from the kitchen of my youth, with its Formica and lemon dish soap and copious amounts of tater tots and hotdish.

"I wish my mom and dad could have had soup in a penthouse apartment in the Upper West Side," I said, and immediately regretted it. My guard must have dropped and I scrambled to pull it back up over my face and my feelings, but James looked at me with curiosity in his eyes.

"Are they fond of New York?"

"Something like that," I said, busying my hands with the linen napkin James had folded and set before me. I pushed away the image of my mom as she talked about her dream to travel, her hope to visit all the most fascinating cities, New York at the top of that long list, and to take me and even my begrudging homebody dad along. I swallowed hard, not wanting to think about plans cut short and words cut short, midconversation. I cleared my throat, too loudly in the quiet room, and I did what I'd long ago become a master at doing: I switched the subject.

"Can I help?"

He shook his head, a smile playing at his lips. "No, but thank you for offering."

I watched as James turned down the burner under a bright blue Le Creuset, and stifled a grin at how awkwardly he held a wooden spoon. This was a man who had been raised with nannies and personal chefs and all the perks old, independent wealth could offer. A wooden spoon, I was sure, was not a familiar weapon.

I smiled as he stirred, feeling a sudden tenderness toward a man who usually projected the confidence that came with all the framed diplomas and signed celebrity photos hanging on his office walls, a silent, powerful witness to stories he could tell.

"Thanks for asking me over," I said, inhaling deeply the intoxicating smell of garlic and tomatoes. "You were right. I needed to eat and to take a break."

James shook his head. "Tell me about it. This week has been crazy. I've clocked in far more hours in the office than out."

"The fall campaign has to be sapping you as much as it is us underlings." I winked.

"Ah, but you're an underling on her way up, right?" James left the stove to dim the overhead chandelier and reached to light three candles on a hammered bronze tray sitting on the island between us. Dishing up two bowls of soup, he set them on plates and tucked generous slices of bread next to the steaming bowls. He placed my dinner in front of me before lowering onto the bar stool next to mine. We ate in silence for a bit, the warm soup filling my mouth with heat and comfort and a riot of flavor. I murmured my approval and James nodded. I looked at him. The candlelight flickered, casting soft light on his face.

James shook his head and sighed. "This brings me back," he said, pointing to the soup with the end of his spoon. "Growing up, I had this phenomenal nanny, Amelia. She was with our family from the time I was a toddler to when she left to go back home to Italy when I was twelve. She made a soup just like this, and she would let me sit at the kitchen counter while she cooked." He took another slurp, and I had to bite back a smile at seeing him so lost in a good memory that he forgot his normally particular manners. "I've been trying to get Amelia's food back in my kitchen since the day she left. This is pretty close." He smiled at me, suddenly bashful. "Sorry. Little detour down memory lane there."

I shook my head. "Not at all. It sounds like Amelia was beloved."

"Absolutely," he said after draining his bowl. "She was like a second mom to me. First mom, maybe. My own mother is very, how should I put it?" He tilted his head in thought. "Efficient? Professional?"

I winced. "Sounds like the perfect administrative assistant."

His laugh was wry. "She certainly employed a slew of those over the years, and most of them left before she could commit their first names to memory." He sounded more amused than embittered. "But my mom did do an exceptional job vetting nannies, and Amelia was a total gem. In fact, she's the one who inspired my interest in fashion and design." He sliced two more pieces of focaccia and set them on our plates. "Amelia loved well-made clothes, beautiful things, rich color. We would make things together on her sewing machine: costumes, forts, you name it. She helped me realize I wanted to work in the fashion world and that I would need to be the black sheep of the Campbell family." He grinned and lifted his slice of bread to toast Amelia's wisdom. "My mom wasn't quite as big a fan of Amelia after that."

I laughed. "Well, one can hardly blame her. We didn't exactly choose the stablest of professions."

He leaned toward me, dabbing his napkin on the corner of his mouth, excitement in his eyes. "Speaking of our dubious career choice, tell me about tomorrow. I'm assuming this is your last night as an underling?"

I inhaled a deep breath and let it escape, feeling the butterflies revisit my stomach when I thought about the next day's event. Each year Nancy held an open call for junior designers to present their work and ideas to her for upcoming lines. I'd presented in previous years, and I'd received positive feedback, but I knew this year was different. This year would change everything. I could feel it in a way I hadn't before. And after six years working a job I could do with my eyes closed, the emotional stakes felt weightier than ever. "Yes," I said. "I hope. I mean, I'm sure." I sat up straighter in my chair. "I'm totally ready. I've been prepping for months. Years, really. I'm going to walk in there and show Nancy what I've got."

"Tell me. Spare no detail," James said, his focused attention pushing a shot of adrenaline through my veins. James knew about The Dream because he nurtured a similar one. He was much further along in his pursuit than I. In fact, considering his pedigree, he was probably further along than I when he was still in diapers and jiggling to the Wiggles with his nanny. He'd attended Harvard Business School as a nod to the three generations of Campbell alumni before him, but James knew from the start, despite rumblings of concern from his father and grandfather, that he wanted to work in the fashion industry. Even with his cushy legacy, James was a hard worker, having made head of department at Milano just one year out of HBS. And he wasn't stingy with his success. He was very encouraging to me and to the other employees under him. Isa had been quick to train a wary eye on James, certain a man with his background could never understand the plight of an average girl working her way up. She'd certainly told me so on multiple occasions. But I'd found him to be generous with his success, the boss who was eager to share the glory with his team, the type who cheered others on instead of tripping them on their way up.

I took stock of his face, his interested gaze, and I settled into my chair. The soup, the warm bread, the coziness of the candlelight were making me feel relaxed and perfectly at home, within a shelter from my rough day and from the gathering chill of an early spring evening outside. A slow smile forming, I started in with a description of the line I was going to present the following day. I was midway through explaining an evening gown for our Met Gala line, ridiculously perfect in emerald satin with hand beading along the waist, when I realized James wasn't listening anymore. He was staring at my mouth but I knew it wasn't in an effort to understand my reasoning for dropping the neckline on the gown.

"You look stunning," he said into my ear, his lips brushing my cheek.

A shiver made slow and steady progress from my neck downward.

"I should go," I said quietly. "I need to be up early tomorrow."

"I do too," James said, moving slowly toward me as he closed his eyes.

I pulled away. "James," I said, one hand on his chest. I marveled at how sure I sounded when I was having to make a Herculean effort to stop looking at James's lips. *Your boss,* I reminded my head and my heart and my lips. *This man is handsome and charming and he fed you home-made focaccia, but he is also your boss.* "This could get complicated."

He looked at me, long enough for me to feel studied. "We have feelings for each other," he finally said. "That feels pretty uncomplicated to me."

I swallowed hard. "Thank you," I said, my hand pulling back from his chest. "For dinner. It was everything I wanted my first personal chef experience to be." My smile was sincere. "I've wondered about this." I pointed to him, to me. "About *us.* Believe me, I have." I shook my head slowly, my eyes on his. "But I think we'd better hit the pause button. Tomorrow might be just another day for you but it isn't for this girl."

I waited while he ran a hand over his face and saw the reluctant smile that was appearing there. I pushed my stool back from the counter. "Let's plan to celebrate tomorrow. After I knock it out of the park and Nancy begs me to be a lead designer at Milano and gives me a raise that will make me tear up every time I see my paycheck."

James took my hand. He kissed it slowly but stood up. "That sounds just about perfect." He pulled me to him, my hand still at his lips.

My heart was galloping fast enough to make its pulse heard in my ears.

"Tomorrow, then," he said, his voice low.

I nodded and moved back, taking my first steps toward the door. "Tomorrow." I smiled and felt his eyes follow me as I walked to the door and into the quiet of the hallway. I was shaking slightly as I turned. I shook my head, laughing at his exaggerated forlorn expression, framed in the doorway where he was still leaning. *I could get used to this,* I thought as the elevator doors closed on the view of James, his eager attention, a framed view of luxury and marked success. My stomach fluttered as the elevator rushed me down ten floors to the city I knew and, I decided anew as I stepped under the tailored black awning and onto the sidewalk, the city I was finally poised to conquer.

two

My phone alarm must have been ringing forever because it was close to six when I forced my eyelids open and realized *NSYNC wasn't actually singing "Bye Bye Bye" at my thirteenth birthday party, as they had been moments ago in my dream. I fumbled around until Justin and Joey became louder and I located the phone to shut it off. After a few moments of silence, the inky blackness of the room beckoning me back to deep sleep, I sat up with a jolt of recognition and remembered: today was Nancy Day.

I threw off the covers, my feet hitting the worn wood floors of my studio apartment. I groped in the dark, fingers outstretched, until I found the bedside lamp. The light cast long shadows in the room, and I rubbed my eyes, still swollen and heavy from sleep. My meeting with Nancy was scheduled for eight sharp, and I pushed myself up to a wobbly standing position, mindful that there would be no fuzzy socks or coffee over the *Times* this morning. Straight to the shower and straight to the rest of my life.

A half hour later, showered, makeup on, and

31

hair coaxed into long waves, I rounded the corner to my tiny kitchen and tapped my feet impatiently while I waited for the coffee to brew and a bagel to toast. Still munching on the bagel, I tiptoed across the cold floor to my closet, pulling my robe tight around me as I walked. I passed the framed black-and-white photo that stood on the bookshelf near the kitchen, and I stopped, unable to ignore the image. I picked up the photo and felt my heart rise in my throat. My mom and dad, laughing at something the little girl in their laps said or did the moment before the shutter snapped shut. I closed my eyes, wishing for the millionth time I could call them, talk with them, relate to them every detail of what I was about to do and hear them cheer me on. I set down the photo gently, a thought lingering that I could call Gigi, that she would likely have the right words to say or at least make me laugh while she looked for them. *No time,* I assured myself, and instead I reached for a new dress I'd just finished working up a few days prior. I unwrapped it gently from the hanger and felt the black fabric run through my hands before slipping it on. I tugged up the exposed side zipper and took a step back, narrowing my eyes at my full-length reflection. I nodded, satisfied. It was perfect. Stunning and chic with just the right amount of edge. And it did what great clothes were meant to do: it made me feel beautifully ready for anything.

Pleased with myself, I threw on a red lip and grabbed my bag, still holding the overdrawn account notice within.

"Not for long," I said out loud, squaring my shoulders before letting the heavy door swing shut behind me.

The waiting atrium for Nancy Strang's office was roughly eighteen times larger than my entire cubicle five floors below. I sat on the edge of one of the midcentury modern chairs that lined the wall and tried against all odds to relax. I'd been waiting close to a half hour, and all the cool and confident self-talk I'd been spouting in my head all morning (and out loud during the empty elevator ride up) had dissipated into fragmented, nervous thoughts. Did I have all of my notes? I checked again. Yes. Design boards? Yes. USB for the digital part of the presentation? Yes. Index cards in my pocket with bullet points in case I got lost or panicked? Yes, yes, yes, and yes. I took in a deep breath and let it out slowly, my eyes on Buckley, Nancy's admin. He sat at a circular desk in the middle of the large room, his blank gaze trained on a computer screen.

"Busy day?" I said aloud. I was dying to ask just how many hopeful designers were presenting to Nancy today, but I didn't know if Buckley would appreciate such a direct question.

He didn't even look away from the screen.

"Not any busier than the other three hundred and sixty-four."

"Right," I said. "I'm sure you see plenty of traffic up here. All sorts, probably. The hopeful, the shamed, the stylish, the dowdy looking for inspiration. Maybe a celebrity or two." I stopped abruptly, Buckley's disdainful expression making me bite my lower lip to stop the flow of words coming out of my mouth. It was the stress. Stress made me revert to my roots, chatting up the people around me as if I were not in a Manhattan fashion house but instead still in the farmers' co-op in Silver Creek, Iowa, sharing bad coffee and town gossip over a linoleum-topped table. I tried smiling at Buckley and biting my lip at the same time but was fairly sure the end result was more like a grimace.

He spoke quietly into his headset and then looked at me. "Ms. Strang will see you." Turning back to his screen, he added, "She prefers a less-is-more approach when it comes to words. Maybe tuck that little hint into your back pocket."

I nodded and stood, gathering my presentation materials and new resolve. I pushed open the towering white door into Nancy's office and was struck immediately by the expansive windows offering a stunner of a Midtown view. I hadn't seen this much of New York from an aerial perch since I was a tourist on the top of Rockefeller Center. I cleared my throat and walked toward the view and Nancy, who sat behind a long Lucite desk.

I offered my hand. "Ms. Strang, it's a pleasure to see you again."

She offered a small smile. Nancy was a petite woman, seemingly at odds with such vaulted ceilings and expansive views. She did not compete but she sure did fill the space with her direct gaze, not to mention a formidable reputation. This was Nancy's twenty-fifth year at Milano, and the years before those had been spent resurrecting Gucci from a post-eighties slump. Nancy Strang was a force, and to the outside world at least, it appeared that everything she touched in the fashion industry turned instantly to retail gold.

"Grace," she said. Her close-cropped black hair was a trademark, as were the round, colored frames on her glasses. The color changed with the season, and today the frames were a bold spring green. "Welcome. If you don't mind, we'll just skip the chitchat and get right to the business at hand. I'm sure you are well prepared for this meeting."

I stood in silence for a beat before realizing she would not be saying any more. I cleared my throat and spread out my design boards on the easels provided. Turning back to Nancy, I began my rehearsed intro.

"Winter. A blanket of fresh snow, the stark

beauty of leafless trees, the long angles of early twilight . . . Winter is a distinct mix of minimalism and indulgence. Clean lines and long hours. The pale winter sky and the raucous palette of the holidays. Milano's winter line should reflect this unexpected harmony." I stopped, my heart racing and making my voice shake. I wet my lips with my tongue and began again, willing my voice to be less timid. "I've designed these pieces as a nod to our long tradition of exquisite, clean tailoring and luxurious fabrics while also bringing a fresh burst of color and modern lines to the silhouette."

The boards were perfectly executed, my digital files loaded without a hitch, and the longer I spoke, the more comfortable I felt. I never even touched the cheat sheet index cards in my pocket, much less consulted them. I knew it all by heart. My designs were on trend, clean, and completely fitting with the long history at Milano. The shapes, colors, textures: everything *screamed* Milano. I felt my shoulders relax, confident I was hitting the right notes at the right times.

I finished my presentation and stood in silence, waiting for questions. I felt my smile grow a bit as I waited, so happy with the result of all my effort. Images of late nights doing grunt work flickered through my thoughts, all the times I'd been overworked and underappreciated, all the moments when I'd wondered if it had been worth it to put up with the order forms, the photocopying, the sewing of individual sequins on an accessory that was soon to be discarded by the designer in charge anyway. It *had* been worth it, just to get to this point, just to finally have the chance to show one of the most powerful women in the fashion industry, face-to-face, what I could do.

The silence began to stretch, and I shifted slightly in my heels, the blisters from the day before starting to pinch. After what felt like ten minutes of silence, Nancy looked up from the designs I had laid before her.

"Grace." She said my name as a declaration.

I smiled.

She fixed her large brown eyes on mine. "I appreciate all the time and effort you have put into this presentation. It's clear you are conscientious, thoughtful, responsible . . . all the things that make a great assistant.

"However," Nancy said, folding her French-manicured fingers over her desk, "I'm afraid I'm not catching the vision here."

My mind started to spin. Catch the vision? The vision was straight-up Milano! The vision was *Nancy's* vision!

"Grace, I believe in being direct. No one does anyone any favors by being nice. Lying is not nice. So, Grace, I'm sorry but I just don't see you having a design future here at Milano. I wish I had better news."

I froze, my eyes becoming dry before I remembered to blink. When I tried to swallow, I realized my mouth was slightly open and I shut it, hard. *No design future?*

I cleared my throat, my thoughts starting to ricochet. "You're looking for something different? I can change it. Is it the jacket? Maybe it needs to be cropped—" I shuffled the boards, looking for the jacket that was probably too long, but Nancy interrupted me.

"This is not a matter of one hem that can be tweaked." Nancy remained still, her face composed, the apple green in her glasses frames the only counterpoint of color against her black-and-white long coat. "I know you've been here a few years—"

"Six," I said, more roughly than I intended. "I've been here six years."

One of Nancy's eyebrows rose slightly. "Indeed. And you've done great work in your current position. Perhaps you should stick with what you know. Grace, not everyone can be a designer."

I shook my head slowly, slowly, back and forth, willing my thoughts to stop spinning. "I graduated first in my class at FIT. People were scared of me there . . ." I cleared my throat after realizing I was mumbling. Raising my voice, I continued, "I was offered all sorts of jobs that last year of school, but I picked Milano. I picked you." I pointed to Nancy, my fingers trembling. "I picked you because you're Nancy Strang! You're brilliant! You're a legend! I wanted to work at a legendary house for a legendary woman!"

I saw Nancy shift in her chair, but I barely paused to breathe. "I came here because I thought after putting in my time, clocking in at the bottom of the ladder, the very bottom rung, I might add, I knew I would move up. I knew it because I'm a good *designer!* I am not a photocopier! I am not an errand runner or a coffee maker or a sheep holder! I *am* a designer!"

By this point, I had reached a shriek. I knew this because my final words rang back at me from the soaring glass, and I heard the pitch. The pitch was definitely a shriek.

"Ms. Kleren, perhaps you should—"

I matched Nancy's measured tone with a good, old-fashioned yell. "Perhaps I should *not!* Perhaps I'm sick of doing what I should and getting absolutely nowhere for it!"

When the room stopped throbbing, I realized Buckley had, at some point, opened the door to Nancy's office and was waiting at the threshold. I looked at him, disoriented.

"Thank you for your presentation, Ms. Kleren." Nancy's tone was cold and dismissive. She turned in her chair, away from me, toward her laptop and her bazillion-dollar view.

I stood, rooted to my spot. My limbs felt heavy

39

and numb after the sudden rush and release of adrenaline. Buckley said my name softly, and I dragged my gaze from Nancy's back to his face. Spidery lines creased his typically smooth forehead.

"This way, please," he said, propping open the door as wide as it would go.

"Thank you," I said, so quietly I was sure no one heard but the carpet. I gathered my boards from the floor and walked through the door Buckley held for me. When I heard him shut it quietly behind us, I turned to him.

"I probably could have edited some of that out," I said, still shaking.

"Probably, yes," Buckley said, striding ahead of me to push the elevator down button. "I believe I did mention less was more. You appear to have chosen a different tactic."

My shoulders slumped as I shuffled into the elevator, holding my design boards so tightly, I could feel them cutting into my hands. The doors closed on Buckley and opened a moment later on my floor. I kept my head down as I walked to my desk, dropped my things onto my chair, and hurried as quickly as I could manage to the small restroom at the back. Mercifully, it was empty, and I collapsed against the door as I locked it. The sobs came easily and with a vengeance. I jumped with both blistered feet into what my grandma would have called a "pity extravaganza." I had blown it, had squandered so much precious time, not only on my presentation, which I had thought was phenomenal, but also on the last ten years of my life. It was a total waste, I thought as I cried bitterly. One long, exhausting, unfulfilling waste.

Hot tears fell as if racing each other down my cheeks, and I sat down hard on the floor, shame and embarrassment flooding me. What kind of person had an emotional meltdown in front of one of the most powerful people in fashion? Promotion or not, I had a job to do, and indulging in my hissy fit had likely knocked me back to the bottom of the Milano totem pole. A rough sob escaped when I realized that for once I was glad I had no parents to tell. I wouldn't have been able to stand their disappointment in me.

Slips of rough commercial toilet paper were my only tissues, and as I used them to blot my tears, I could feel my cheeks getting raw. I cried through the paper, through the raw, through the knocks on the door from Isa, who sounded increasingly concerned. When I'd spent every tear immediately available to me, I stood shakily and turned toward the small mirror above the sink. My eyes were puffy and an angry red I hadn't seen in years, since a time of my life when tears were a constant companion. My dress, so fresh and innovative an hour before, looked rumpled and ridiculous, like something a little girl would wear while playing dress-up in her mommy's closet.

Maybe it's a metaphor, I thought as I swallowed the bile creeping into my throat. I splashed water on my face in an effort to resurrect some part of my appearance. Maybe I looked like I was playing dress-up because I was a total fake. Maybe I didn't belong in this industry after all. I'd had ten years to try and this was where I'd ended up? In a cramped bathroom, crying like a toddler and dressed like one too?

"Grace, please. Open up." Isa sounded a little frantic, though she had the kindness to continue using a muted voice. I shuddered, thinking about all the people at work in the room beyond that door and how Isa was sparing me their inspection.

I swallowed hard and opened the door an inch. I could see Isa's trademark cat eye through the crack.

"Grace, honey, open the door." She sounded like she was part of a hostage negotiation. "Come on out. It's going to be okay."

I sighed and opened the door. I took a step back when I saw James next to Isa. He looked very uncomfortable. Beyond our little group, I glimpsed people standing at their desks, paused in their work to watch the three of us.

I lifted my chin, scrambling for any semblance of self-possession. "I'm fine," I said, a bit too loudly. "Just a rough morning. We can all get back to work."

I took a step forward but James stopped me. Following Isa's gaze, I looked to the floor. Next to James's polished, custom lace-ups sat a cardboard box.

Filled with all the contents from my desk.

I looked up at James's face, disbelieving.

"I'm sorry," he said, avoiding my gaze. "When Nancy makes a decision . . ."

"Wait," I sputtered. "James, you know me—"

He shook his head quickly. "There was nothing I could do. Grace, you're fired."

three

Here's something I appreciated about New York: no one really cared if you were a total loser. Sure, it stung to lose my job. Sure, I needed a shower and a break from my sweatpants and hoodie, particularly after the red sauce incident of three (four?) nights ago. Sure, I would have been horrified if anyone had popped by for a visit to my apartment and had seen the tornadic state of both the space and its single occupant. But that was the thing: people in New York didn't pop by for visits. Popping by was a veritable art form in my hometown. I'd popped by with the best of them in Silver Creek, knowing how late was too late, how early was too early, how long to stay (as long as the conversation flowed), when to bring banana bread (new neighbor) or a casserole (death in the family) or cleaning supplies (new baby, family illness, prolonged grief).

Popping by in New York, however, just didn't happen. I had never been so grateful to live in a city where civilized, happy self-absorption reigned supreme, where people had the decency to meet at restaurants or bars or museums or coffee shops but not on my couch. Because I loved my couch. I'd gotten to know it well in the two weeks since Nancy had crushed my dreams. I squeezed one of my throw pillows with renewed affection, watching the credits roll for *Splash*, a satisfying end to a Tom Hanks marathon on TBS. I reached for the remote, pushing aside mostly empty take-out containers, a single sock, and a cup of cold coffee to get to it. Slouching back against the cushions, I clicked through the channels slowly, pausing to watch the end of *The Price Is Right*, a classic scene with Rory and Logan jumping without parachutes on *Gilmore Girls*, and an infomercial on a sleeved polar fleece blanket that briefly had me considering another segment of the textile industry. I clicked up a channel and stopped.

The camera panned slowly across the faces of earnest singers in choir robes, and the strains of "Great Is Thy Faithfulness" filled my apartment. I stared, my hand stilled on the remote. A lump constricted my throat and without my permission, my eyes brimmed with hot tears, remembering the last time I'd limped through the words of that familiar hymn. I'd been standing next to my grandmother in the front pew of our church, gripping Gigi's arm for dear life as we endured the joint funeral services for my mom and dad. The ice storm had happened three days before, and the marks from their mangled car still mocked me on the road just beyond our house.

I was a junior in high school. I was too young to know how to face suffering head-on and keep singing through the tears. Gigi took me in with open arms and I lived with her while I finished my last year of high school. I'd left for New York the morning after graduation.

The hymn ended, such hopeful words marred by the anguish of that moment. I remembered Gigi's trembling voice next to me, how she'd sung with tears rolling down both of her cheeks.

Gigi.

I groaned, leaving the church channel on, though I found the monotone of the balding pastor less riveting than the choir number. I reached for my phone with a feeling I had seen an unanswered text from Gigi within the last day or so. I scrolled through and saw I was right. Gigi had sent a message two days prior, and I hadn't even opened it, much less responded.

Hi, honey, it read. *I hold you are hippy. Been thinking along you. When are you complicated home for a visit?*

I smiled. Gigi, as a general rule, resisted all forms of technology. Her VCR was still doing a valiant job for her infrequent movie nights. She maintained an active landline with an accompanying answering machine (tape, not digital). And while she tolerated having a laptop in her home, she always looked like she wanted to spit to the side whenever she discussed it.

So a cell phone had been a tough sell. During my first Christmas visit home after moving to New York, I'd presented her with one that I had already tricked out entirely, from its enlarged print on the screen to a troubleshooting tutorial I'd laminated and put near her answering machine. Gigi had scowled, but her love of her only grandchild had won over her disdain for tech. When her best friend, Goldie, showed her how to use the text function, Gigi had grabbed on immediately, thrilled at the efficiency of typing or speaking a message while not having to stop her work in the house, in the garden, at the town library, in the serving line at the fellowship hall. Too busy to bother with details, most of Gigi's messages were cryptic, some of them completely unreadable. I'd become a pro at interpretation, though, and I did my best to reply promptly, holding to the only remaining connection I still had with my childhood, my hometown, my family.

I held the phone in my hand, wondering how to respond to Gigi's request for a visit. I didn't need to look into my little dining area to know the late payment notices were piling up on my cluttered table. Getting fired made my fragile financial situation tremble like a house of cards, so close to a fall, it took my breath away. Billing statements were getting pushier in their language, printed now on colored paper with threatening exclamations on the envelopes. I looked around at the disaster of my apartment, feeling my stomach sour as I realized I had no way to pay the next month's rent, due in only five days.

I clicked off my phone, unsure of how to respond. Gigi lived a thousand miles away, but she was still able to sniff out a lie from that distance. Better to say nothing at all, to not even tiptoe in the direction of "I lost my job, I'm broke, and I'm not coming to Iowa forever and ever, amen."

I pulled myself to my feet, taking a moment to breathe deeply when the sudden change left me light-headed. Padding to my closet, I stood before it. I'd felt a little jolt of happiness the first time I'd seen this closet, moments before signing the rental agreement. Completely atypical of a sublet of this size, my apartment had a delightfully large closet. And I had filled every inch of it, top shelf, hanging rack, floor space, wall space—every bit was filled with beautiful clothes, shoes, bags, and belts. I paged through the hangers and felt my heart become heavy with a knowing dread. The vintage Chanel bag, the Dior skirt I'd found on deep discount, the Armani jumpsuit that had cost more than I cared to remember now but had made a stunning impression at Milano's holiday soiree that year . . . I let the textures of all those perfectly designed and woefully expensive garments pass through my fingers, wishing I didn't know what I had to do.

My entire net worth lay before me. If I was going to stay in New York—the New York I loved, the New York that was the center of the fashion world, the New York that would demand a very large rent check in five days—I needed quick access to cash. I clenched the muscles in my jaw and reached for an empty shopping bag. I would rebuild, I assured myself, starting on the left side of the closet and working right. My hands shook a little as I folded the chosen items and placed them carefully in the bag. This bag was my ticket to a new job, a new resolve, a fresh start in the only city I wanted to inhabit. I filled one bag and started another.

A girl had to do what a girl had to do.

After a cumbersome train ride down to the Upper West Side (no cab for me today), I paused on the sidewalk that ran in front of Second to None, the best consignment store in the city. The first time I'd visited, I'd been wide-eyed and in ferocious love, so thrilled to step between the topiaries by the front door and into the quiet of the store, just in from rubbing shoulders with women in that neighborhood who were wearing clothing I wanted desperately to inspect and take apart, to learn by dismantling how such beautiful clothes came to be. I had built the beginnings of a great wardrobe in this store, most of those pieces long gone but some of them lying hopeful in the bags at my feet.

Standing on the sidewalk, I remembered with sudden force how I'd longed to call my mom after my first visit here. She would have loved to hear every detail, I just knew. She'd loved clothes and fashion and would have shared my delight in finding such a gem in the middle of this strange, exhilarating, enormous city. She would have wanted a complete recap, listening to everything in a way only a mom can listen, all attention paid to moments unimportant to the outside observer but singularly important because the moments belonged to her daughter.

The memory hit me in the chest and I pushed it immediately away, a skill at which I'd become very adept over the last decade. Inhaling sharply, I gripped my heavy-laden bags and jostled them successfully through the front door. The store was nearly empty on a Tuesday morning. I navigated awkwardly through the racks and approached the front desk, catching a glimpse of myself in a mirror as I walked by. I stood straighter, forcing my spine into an assured position. If there was one thing I'd garnered from the last ten years, it was how to fake it until I made it. I'd taken extra care before leaving my apartment, applying my makeup precisely, choosing a stylish but classic look that would appeal to the Upper West crowd. My hair was smoothed neatly, precisely, and the auburn highlights brought out flecks of deep green in my eyes. I looked more put together than I'd been able to accomplish in weeks. I just hoped all the effort worked.

"Hello," I said brightly to the woman behind the counter. "I'm here to consign a few items."

She put up one manicured finger as a symbol for me to wait. Her eyes remained on a piece of paper before her, but she didn't seem to be reading or calculating sums. I watched as her eyes didn't move, just stayed focused on one part of the paper, hand still raised to quiet me. She waited so long, I started to wonder if her skinny arms would start to shake with the effort, but then she removed her wireless glasses and looked up.

"Welcome to Second to None," she said, unsmiling. "I am Tatiana and will be helping you today."

"Fantastic. Great to meet you, Tatiana. I'm Grace." I threw her my warmest smile, my Midwestern manners rusty but still putting hers to shame.

"Have you consigned with us before?" she asked, her eyes sharp, as if willing me to try to fool her.

"Um, no," I said, then more confidently, "definitely not. Not that I didn't want to." I added hastily, "I would have. Because there's no shame in it. At all. And this is a great shop. Really. I love the topiaries." I bit into my lower lip to help my mouth remain in a closed position.

She paused a moment, then continued. "We take only items that are on trend and in perfect condition. No stains, no rips, no tears, no fraying. We offer you a lump sum today, based on fifty percent of the profit we hope to achieve with your items. Is this clear?"

I nodded, taking it all in. I began adding up the value of the bulging bags I placed on the counter, watching as Tatiana began to remove the items and lay them before her, eyes sharp, hands moving quickly over buttons, seams, zippers. My internal calculator was buoying my spirits even as she worked. Three, maybe even four months' rent was represented, I thought. Three months was surely enough time for me to steady my shaky feet, follow up on the emails and résumés I had sent out from my couch, and reroot myself in a new job, maybe even find a room-mate.

I felt a catch in my breathing when Tatiana pulled out my Manolo pumps. She noticed and looked up, eyebrows arched in question.

I put my hand out to touch the shoes. "I love these shoes," I said, my fingers on the perfect stitching along the arch. "They were my very first grown-up purchase after finishing school. I bought them for myself as a graduation present."

Those shoes were more of a statement to me than any diploma. My first Manolo pumps. The perfect, tangible symbol that I was running head-long into The Dream and making good time and real progress.

The woman sniffed and pushed the shoes toward me. "You aren't ready to give them up. Better take them home or they will make you a bitter shell of a woman."

I pushed them back. "No," I said with more certainty than I felt. "I'm ready. It's time."

She shook her head but took the shoes. "I've seen many bitter shells in my line of work. You should keep the shoes."

I didn't say what I was thinking, which was that bitter shell or not, a girl had to eat. I decided to turn away and pretend shop for the rest of the viewing. Better to not actually witness the pillage. When I saw Tatiana wave discreetly to me from above a display of hats, I moved quickly to the counter. Three, maybe four months. That was all I needed.

"You have beautiful things," the woman said, her monotone belying the compliment in her words. "We will take everything."

Yessss. I felt flush, knowing that Second to None had a reputation for being very particular. I smiled warmly, waiting for the reveal.

She began folding the clothes into neat stacks. "I can offer you five twenty-five." She continued folding until she looked up to see me waiting for the next sentence. "Do we have a deal?"

I shook my head to clear it of the noise that was beginning to descend. "You mean for the shoes? Five twenty-five for the Manolos, right?"

At this I glimpsed the first smile from the Ice Queen. "No, no, no. I would lose my shirt if I did business that way." She chuckled at her not-funny fashion joke. "Five twenty-five for every-thing."

My thoughts became loud, bossy. Five twenty-five? Less than half of *one* month's rent, much less three.

The woman noticed my reticence. "We sell items at estate sale prices, so you'll be hard-pressed to get a better offer. You could try selling the items individually on eBay, if you have the patience. And a willingness to ship."

I shook my head, trying to gather my thoughts and a viable plan. "I don't have a lot of time . . ." My words trailed off as I felt my phone vibrate in my purse. Distractedly, I rummaged until I found it tucked into the folds of another cursed credit card bill. I glanced at the screen and saw Gigi's text.

Goldie says there are sales on flights to Des Moines. Three hundred dollars for a rind-trip trucker!

Tatiana waited, the silence growing between us.

I stared at the words on my phone and swallowed hard. With one long, last look at my worldly possessions, I typed a quick response to Gigi:

On my way.

four

I leaned into my small window on the left side of the plane and felt the cold of the plexiglass on my forehead. We were descending into Des Moines on the only daily direct flight from LaGuardia, and I could feel my blood pressure going up even as the plane made its way down. A patchwork of brown fields, too chilled to show the riotous spring green of new corn and soybeans, gave way abruptly to residential neighborhoods, long roofs of shopping centers, and the geometric outline of a modest downtown skyline.

I sighed and closed my eyes against the harsh light reflecting off the clouds. I hadn't slept well the night before. All my efforts at creative makeup and my best tricks with lip gloss and eyeliner would do nothing to fool Gigi. She would assume it was bruising city life that caused the circles under my eyes to deepen. I wouldn't tell her that I'd wrestled with sleep and ultimately lost because my body was waging war against Iowa.

The pilot made a bumpy landing onto the tarmac, and a cheery flight attendant welcomed us to Des Moines, the capital of Iowa, home of around four hundred thousand souls, and host to the world-famous Iowa State Fair, where a person could eat both a pork chop and a deep-fried Snickers bar on a stick. The other passengers chuckled appreciatively, which offered a convenient mask to my groan.

It was one thing to come home for Christmas or a long weekend. This time I was coming home on a one-way ticket. The shame of that burned my cheeks as I waited to file off the plane. The woman ahead of me was corralling a passel of young children, each of them tugging his or her own roller bag. I looked around me as I waited, noting again the enduring legacy of yoga pants in my home state. I would have wagered that not one of the women wearing the style had actually ever practiced the sport, but the pants persisted, along with all manner of Iowa Hawkeyes and Cyclones gear, Levi's that were in no way hipster ironic, and a startling number of running shoes.

By the time I'd reached the top of the short escalator leading me down to arrivals and baggage claim, I had to work on composing my face to meet Gigi. She'd been so excited to hear I was coming for a visit, but I just couldn't bring myself to disclose the full story of what was bringing me home. I knew I wouldn't be able to hold out long under Gigi's scrutiny, but I was savoring every minute before I had to come clean.

She saw me before I saw her, and her smile was luminous, even from across the large room. I smiled back, filled instantly with the familiar and deep love I had for Gigi. She stood as close to the bottom of the escalator as possible without hindering progress for other passengers. When I reached the bottom, she pulled me into a hug, and we stood to the side of the traffic, my shoulders slumped and my face turned into her neck. Five minutes on Iowa soil and I was already regressing to the girl I'd been when I'd left.

When Gigi pulled back, her eyes were narrowed. "You look exhausted."

I shrugged. "City life."

She shook her head, taking me in from head to toe. "Your clothes are lovely but something's off." Again with narrowed gaze and then, "Where is your carry-on?"

I cleared my throat and glanced at a businessman passing, his shoes making a sharp percussion on the polished floor. I tried for nonchalance. "Oh, I checked a bag this time. Thought I'd stay for a bit longer."

She froze, gauging the look on my face, which I was fighting to keep neutral. "You're welcome to stay as long as you'd like," she said, her face resolved and earnest. Taking my face in her hands, she added, "You know that, right, honey? That an invitation like that never runs dry or changes or goes out of style?"

I felt hot tears slide down my cheeks. And I hadn't even made it to baggage claim.

I held the white bakery box of treats in my lap. I could feel the warmth of a scone just out of the oven seeping through the bottom of the box, the smell of butter and sugar filling Gigi's minivan. I pushed around the pastries, struggling to show my gratitude for Gigi's gesture. She'd come to Des Moines early in the day and scoped out a new bakery, navigating through unfamiliar streets and morning traffic. I knew what the effort had cost her, but the thought of eating something rich and delicious under the circumstances turned my empty stomach sour.

"So Goldie showed you how to use Google Maps?"

"Shh." Gigi frowned at me before inching out onto Fleur Drive and obeying the reminder from her phone to take Interstate 235 east out of town. "I have to hear Nigel if we're going to get anywhere."

I raised an eyebrow in her direction. "Nigel?"

Gigi nodded, carefully merging onto the interstate at a speed that would have made her a breakfast snack on the streets of New York. "Nigel is the man who helps me navigate. Goldie showed me how to do that too. She said it's so much easier taking directions from a British man. And I do believe she's right."

I stared at my grandmother's profile. Who *was* this woman?

"You are, in fact, the same person who still owns eight-track tapes and a slide projector, correct?"

Gigi snorted. "Of course I do. And my slides from our Mount Rushmore trip of 1979 are available for you to see at any time during your visit."

I marveled at that—not Gigi's newfound respect for GPS, but that she could so casually mention the past, a time when my mom, her daughter, was full of life and laughter and probably making teenage, sarcastic comments about South Dakota and the letdown of traveling all that way to look at rocks. I turned to look out my window, watching the city fall away and the empty brown fields blanket the outskirts of Des Moines.

We made our way toward Silver Creek, letting the first few miles unspool like ribbon behind us. I did my best to maintain the flow of conversation, but Gigi kept clearing her throat and taking quick glances at me while she drove. No more than ten minutes into the drive, Gigi signaled and slowed to a sloth's pace. She put on her flashers and pumped her brakes, looking all the while in her rearview mirror.

"What's wrong?" I asked, my voice tight. "Do we have a flat? Is something wrong with the car?"

Gigi pulled over to the middle shoulder, cars whizzing by and making the hair on my neck stand at attention. I gripped the car handle hard enough for my fingers to tingle.

"Gigi, what is it? Are you feeling sick? I can drive. I mean, it's been a while, but—"

She put the car in park, flashers making a rhythmic click as they blinked on and off. She turned to me. "Nothing is wrong with the car," she said in a relaxed tone more appropriate when *not* sitting on the edge of a freeway with a seventy-miles-an-hour speed limit.

"What, then?" I was getting snippy, but my body was sitting about twelve inches from a semi that roared past.

"I need some honesty before we keep on toward home. Baby girl, you need to come clean. What's the story?" She ticked off the items on her list for evidence. "You look rough, all pale and sallow, which probably means no sleep but could mean a grave illness. You have two gigantic suitcases but not one teeny explanation why. And most disturbingly, you have not eaten one bite of the goodies that would normally usher in all sorts of exclamations and detailed descriptions of what's going on with your taste buds." She took my hand in both of hers and searched my face. "Gracie, honey, what happened?"

I sighed, keeping my hand in hers. "All right, I'll spill, but can we please merge back onto the racetrack? I'm too nervous to think, much less tell the truth."

"Deal," Gigi said, and did a slow merge back onto the thoroughfare.

When we made it to the north of town, where traffic lightened up and my grip on the door handle relaxed, I came clean. "Gigi, I blew it." I spoke quickly to get the words out before any rogue tears could catch up. "I outspent my salary, I didn't save any money, and then I got fired."

She sneaked a glimpse at my face before returning her eyes to the road. She was quiet for a long time before responding. "First of all, I'm glad you are not gravely ill. I can handle spotty makeup application much better than grave illness."

I made an attempt at a smile.

She continued. "I suppose I can imagine the money mismanagement. It happens to the best of us, and you always did have a weakness for shopping." Her tone was wry but gentle. "But there's some sort of mistake with the firing. Grace Kleren does not get fired." I saw her frown deepen. "You're the hardest working girl I know, honey. Is that city run by idiots?" She put out her hand to stop me. "Don't answer that."

The smile worked this time. "Not idiots, exactly. They just didn't like my work. And then, um, I kind of wigged out." I launched into my sordid tale, letting my misery vent in full to another person for the first time. I didn't hold back when tears rolled down my cheeks, and I let anger spill out of my voice when I told Gigi how worthless I felt, how betrayed by the company I'd served for so many years. Gigi listened quietly as I spoke about Nancy Strang, the shame of my meltdown, my weeks of cloistered seclusion in my apartment, and my defeat at Second to None. It felt like a release to tell the entire story start to finish, though my heart felt heavier in the telling, not lighter.

In time we exited the highway and turned toward the few remaining miles to Silver Creek. I ran out of words just as we passed the McCullough farm on the west side of town. The century-old oak tree in their front yard still arched over the wooden swing where I'd broken my arm in second grade. Fully deflated, I felt my spine melt farther into the front seat, especially as the houses started to sit more closely together. Gigi said nothing, just covered my hand with hers as we entered town. The Williamses' split-level, where I saw Michael Jackson's "Thriller" video for the first time, against my parents' wishes, and launched the start of nightmares for a month. The Grays', where Jenna Gray and I spilled a bottle of purple nail polish after Mrs. Gray had told us not to paint our nails on the porch, and we'd had to repaint the entire floor as punishment. The Achenbachs' sprawling ranch, where I'd played spin the bottle for the first and last time and ended up under a fake sprig of mistletoe fending off an overly eager Alex Nichols.

Gigi said nothing as we turned slowly onto the town square. When Nigel barked his disapproval she started punching the phone with such impatience, I took it from her and ended our route.

"Hmph," she said, a frown on her face. "I do not need some man from England telling me how to get around the middle of my town."

The courthouse stood as a proud sentry over the square. The long arms of the clock in the high tower pushed steadily into the next hour, and I heard myself sigh out loud. Gigi mistook my sigh for appreciation instead of the restlessness it really was.

"Town council had to raise all sorts of funds, but they finished the restoration of the clock tower last year. Cleaned the exterior too and replaced all the windows. Looks good, doesn't it?"

I nodded, trying to muster admiration I didn't feel. You could put a bow on a pig, and you could clean the limestone on the courthouse, but Silver Creek was still the same sleepy, tired, uninspired town it had always been. One restaurant, two bars, four stop signs, a library, and a handful of stores that limped along, year after year. My longing for Manhattan was palpable.

"A real nice family moved in last year, after

the Hartsocks moved away." Gigi's voice had become a little thick, and I realized she had slowed the car as we moved two blocks off the square. We were passing 14 Azalea Street, the house where I'd grown up. There was a tricycle on the front walk. Big pots of purple hyacinth, still tiny in the new warmth of spring, flanked the front door instead of the hanging baskets of ferns my mother had favored for that spot. The rest, though, looked the same. Achingly, horribly the same. Buttercream-yellow clapboard still looked crisp and clean against bright white trim, the house numbers, a special-order gift for my dad for Father's Day one year, still gleamed in burnished silver above the front door, and the window above that door still opened to the dormered ceiling of what used to be my bedroom.

As I stared at the house, I saw my dad walking home every day for lunch from his accounting office downtown, his confident gait, taking the porch steps two at a time as he called out that he was home. I saw my mom, standing with hands on hips as she surveyed the row of unruly peony bushes along the property line before setting in to give them all a good haircut. I saw friends, boyfriends, homecoming dates as they ran, walked, inched nervously with corsages in their hands, up the front sidewalk, heard again the call of my mom and dad, telling me that so-and-so was here.

I closed my eyes and tried my pushing-away

technique, so effective in the busyness of New York and so absolutely worthless in Silver Creek. I kept my eyes shut until I felt the car come to a stop less than a minute later, and I knew we'd reached Gigi's house.

"Home," she said, pulling the key from the ignition and turning to me. "Let's get you settled."

Not likely, I thought as I pulled on my door handle and stood. I stretched my legs and the stiffness in my neck while I took in the house before me. Another house with a host of memories. This house had been a harbor from the worst storm I'd endured, and I felt a surge of gratitude for it and for the woman who inhabited it.

I walked to the back of the van, where Gigi was already manhandling my second bulging suitcase from the trunk. I nudged her aside and took over, but I realized I, not she, was panting from the exertion. She chuckled to see me struggling and said, "Well, that is good for an old lady's ego."

I dropped the bag. "Gigi—you're too good to me, even when I haven't visited as often as I should. How long has it been? Two years already?"

She raised one eyebrow. "Three."

I winced.

"If you're counting," she said. "But I'm not. Love doesn't count, as I'm sure you remember from all those mornings in Sunday school." I could hear the teasing in her voice, but I winced for a second time as we each hefted a bag and made for the back door.

"Right," I said, huffing. "I do remember that. Along with the vanilla wafers and David Beloit's habit of eating crayons. He did it well into junior high, as I recall."

Gigi sniffed. "David Beloit sells insurance and is a bit of a weasel. I wouldn't trust him with *my* premiums, that's for sure."

"So it all started with the Crayola tastings," I said, inhaling deeply as we entered Gigi's light-filled kitchen, pleased to find the same mix of lemon cleaner, cinnamon, and coffee greet my nose.

"Oh, it probably started earlier than that," Gigi said. She coaxed the handle out of the top of the suitcase and rolled it toward the bottom of the staircase by the front door. "The Beloits have a long history of weasels. Especially the men."

I laughed and followed Gigi up the stairs. The bags thumped on each step until we reached the top. I started toward the guest room, the room that had been mine since I'd moved into the house during my junior year, but Gigi stopped me.

"Honey, I have you in your mom's old room this time," she said. Her face looked pained when I turned around. "I have a little project going right now, and I just didn't have the time between your text and today to clear out all the mess."

I peeked in the door of the guest room and was greeted with mayhem. The longer I looked, the more I could see some semblance of order to the mayhem, but it was chaos nonetheless. Piles of bright fabric sat on the bed, some sort of fort or something was disassembled and lying on the floor, and empty clothing racks spotted the floor space.

Gigi had slipped past me and was standing next to the brass bed in my mom's room. She smoothed my mother's worn white quilt with her hand. I knew it had been a gift to my mom from Gigi's friends when she'd gotten a scholarship to college. I knew she'd left it at home instead of taking it to the dorm because she loved that quilt and didn't want to risk it getting worn or spilled on or damaged during her college years. I knew this because my mother had told me herself, many times. I could hear her voice as I set my bag and purse carefully by the chair in the corner.

Gigi sat down easily on the bed and patted the space beside her.

I obeyed but sat more gingerly, feeling as if I were trespassing, though I knew that was ridiculous. My mother was not the kind of woman who withheld. She would have wanted me to crawl right under those covers and take a long, good nap, though she might have forced my teenage self into a pillow fight first.

I leaned my head on Gigi's shoulder. "It's still so hard."

She stroked my hair, and I could feel her nod in agreement. I thought she was going to speak, but she just stayed close, her hand on my head. I felt my body relax as we sat, the only sound our breathing and a robin singing a throaty serenade outside the window.

"It's definitely hard," Gigi said after a long silence. Her voice was quiet and sure. "But we can do hard things."

She kissed me on my hair and nodded toward the pillow at the head of the bed. "Take a nap. I'll wake you when something important happens." She fluffed the pillow and pointed to it. I obeyed and let my head sink into its coolness. "Judging by our town's last hundred years or so, I'd guess you'll get a good long sleep in before I need to intervene."

My eyes were drifting shut already, the emotion of the day mixing into a heady and exhausting cocktail of sadness, grief, and nostalgia. I heard Gigi pull the curtains shut, a soft click of the door, and nothing else before falling into a hard, still sleep.

five

When I woke, I blinked into the sunlight streaming along all the borders of the curtains Gigi had pulled. My nap, it appeared, had yawned straight through the night and into the following morning. I tucked my head under the covers, feeling the warmth of Mom's quilt and the softness of Gigi's clean, flowered sheets. Even in my half-awake state, I knew she'd dried them for a half cycle in the dryer and then hung them on her backyard line so they'd smell "like the sun." I inhaled into my pillow. There were some things about this place that would never be matched in New York.

New York. I opened my eyes. Time to get up. Time to make a plan. Time to start making my way back.

Twenty minutes later, I'd successfully located my dark-wash skinnies from the bottom of one suitcase and a silk top that brought out the green in my eyes. I layered with a large knot sweater in the same hue as my jeans, touched up my hair with a flat iron, and put on a fresh face of blush, eyeliner, and gloss. I took stock of my reflection and smirked. Not exactly what I would have worn for a job interview in Midtown, but it would more than pass in Silver Creek.

Gigi sat at the table sipping her coffee, a Bible open before her, when I entered the kitchen.

"Well, this is a change," she said, a smile already forming. "The Grace Kleren who last lived in this house would never have darkened that door a minute before eleven. Unless forced. And I do remember a bit of forcing." She watched me over the lip of her mug.

I crossed the kitchen to the coffeepot. "I thought I'd head over to the Chickadee this morning, try to get a word with Martin before the breakfast rush."

I poured myself a full cup and splashed it with cream. The dining room of the Chickadee was an easy memory to recall, as I'd spent countless hours there over the years. Silver Creek's only restaurant not counting Subway, the Chickadee was the place to eat after church on Sunday, when celebrating a birthday, and when entertaining out-of-town guests. It was also where I had worked as a waitress all through high school. I took a small sip of the hot coffee and tried not to focus on the embarrassment I felt to be retracing such old, outgrown steps.

"Ah," Gigi said, nodding. "Martin will be happy to see you. He always asks about you. Says you were one of his best and all-time favorites."

I smiled at Gigi, sure that she was fabricating the compliment for my courage but grateful for it all the same. "We'll see if those fond memories get me a job."

Gigi rose, her chair stuttering backward on the wood floors. "I have pancake batter all ready in the fridge. Bacon or sausage?" She walked briskly to the sink to dump out the dredges of her coffee.

"Don't worry about me," I said, leaning over to peck her on the cheek. "I'm racing the clock. In fact, I'm probably already behind. I forget that farmers get up before the crack of dawn."

Gigi shook her head. "Honey, it's seven o'clock. Farmers are ready for lunch." She handed me a muffin from a tin on the counter. "At least have this. You'll be more convincing if you don't look so hungry. You slept through dinner last night, Grace. You need your strength."

I took the muffin, smelling apples and cinnamon within. "Thanks," I said. "I guess I won't be able to pick up a bagel and schmear at the little spot on the corner of Ninety-fourth and Lexington."

Gigi looked confused. "I'm sure you won't be able to pick up a bagel and schmear within a hundred miles." She frowned. "The muffin will taste better anyway."

I took a huge bite as I pushed my way out the

back door and into the bracing cold air of early spring.

The muffin was long gone by the time I had the nerve to actually stop and park. I'd circled the outskirts of town three times, well aware that if I pulled that stunt around the town square, I'd be at best suspicious and at worst stopped in the middle of the block by a concerned citizen who wanted to know who was driving Gigi's car. I combed every residential street, feigning interest in local real estate and plastic lawn ornaments. I even drove down a few adjacent back roads lining fields newly broken up and ready for spring planting. Thirty minutes of wandering later, I finally gathered the resolve to park a half block away from the Chickadee's front door, giving myself a few extra steps to square my shoulders and ready myself for what lay ahead.

The bell over the Chickadee's door announced my entrance and I saw that Gigi had been right: I was about an hour too late for an empty dining room. Nearly all the tables were packed, all of the seats along the counter were full, and even though the noise of the bell barely competed with the volume within the room, most of the heads turned toward me. I smiled weakly, glimpsing familiar faces, but I was unable to greet any of them properly because Martin came roaring from behind the counter and scooped me up in a big bear hug.

"I heard it but I didn't believe a word of it," he said as he twirled me around. "Somebody said they saw Grace Kleren sneaking into town with her grandma yesterday afternoon. But I didn't believe it. Chalked it up to small-town gossip." He grinned, his eyes crinkling and his thick salt-and-pepper handlebar mustache arching up to full, ruddy cheeks. There was more salt than pepper in that mustache, and the lines around his eyes had deepened a bit, but Martin still looked like my boss from high school. He wore one of his myriad Sturgis T-shirts under his trademark red-and-white striped apron. "And how's the belle of New York City?"

I forced a laugh. "Oh, you know. Parties all the time, closet full of gowns, lots of Prince Charming sightings." I swallowed, but Martin didn't seem to notice.

He shook his head and put out his fist for a bump. "I'm not one bit surprised. Not one bit. I always tell your grandma you were one of the all-time greats around here. Nobody could handle a stacked station, answer the phone, cover for a wayward hostess, *and* bring in the tips like Grace Kleren."

I looked over the shoulder of Martin and caught the eye of Erin Jackson, a high school classmate who sat in a booth with a man and two toddlers. She waved before she started cutting pancakes for one of the kids. *Erin Jackson,* I thought, stifling a sigh. The girl who had egged my car when I'd been chosen as decorating chair for prom because she'd wanted the job for herself. This is what I'd come to, working up the courage to ask for a job where I'd be serving the syrup-sticky offspring of Erin Jackson.

"I'd better get back to work," Martin was saying as he wiped his clean hands on his apron. "It's real good to see you, Grace. Stop by for a meal before you head back to the big city. We aren't any four-star joint, but I seem to remember you had a fondness for my cinnamon rolls." He started to back away.

"Actually, Martin," I said quickly, both to halt his progress and to hang on to my resolve. "I'm going to be in town for a while, and I, um, wondered if I might pick up a shift or two. Or more than two." I smiled what I hoped was a convincing and confident smile but feared was a pained one.

Martin cocked his head and studied my face for a beat. "Taking a break from parties and princes?" he said, not unkindly.

I nodded, grateful Martin wasn't a person to pry. Most of the people in that room and in the whole of Silver Creek, for that matter, wouldn't be quite so tactful. "Do you have any openings?"

He shook his head sadly. "Grace, I'm so sorry, but I don't. I'd love to have you on board again, I would, but the college kids are headed back in a few weeks, and if anything, I'm overstaffed." The bell on the long counter connecting the dining room to the kitchen sounded three insistent rings, and Martin looked over his shoulder. "I promise to let you know if anything opens up, okay?" He looked genuinely sorry as he gave me one last squeeze. "Nobody works as hard as Grace Kleren. Any business would be lucky to have you."

I nodded, trying not to show on my face the disappointment I felt. "Thanks, Martin. I appreciate it."

"And I'll keep my ear to the ground," he added as he walked, at a volume I would have preferred he kept for his outside voice. "I'll call you if I hear anything, all right?"

I nodded, gave a quick wave, and booked it out the front door before Erin Jackson or anyone else could follow up on Martin's declaration.

No work at the Chickadee, I thought glumly as I walked back to my car. What now? I turned the key in Gigi's car door and sat down heavily behind the wheel. I took a quick inventory of my other options for work in Silver Creek, trying to remember what people around here did for a living and if I was qualified for any of it. I let my head rest on the steering wheel and struggled to keep calm in the face of a rising panic. I babysat before I started at the Chickadee, but I had a feeling nanny services weren't exactly in high demand, not for a working wage anyway. I could detassel corn or walk beans, I thought bitterly as I started the car and backed up out of the parking space onto Main. Detasseling was what many of my high school friends had done every summer, rising well before dawn and taking a school bus to be dumped in the middle of endless cornfields to sweat, get charred by the sun, and be devoured by bugs all day. I whimpered aloud and gunned the gas, wanting more than anything to rewind and take back and start over so I could still be walking through the morning crowds in Manhattan instead of driving through the deserted streets of Silver Creek.

I made a hard right onto Maple, eager to avoid Azalea Street this time, and I jumped when I heard a slap on my hood. I slammed on the brakes, adrenaline coursing. I frantically scanned the area outside the car, not seeing anyone at first and hoping against hope that I'd hit a really big bird and not a human. When I craned my neck farther into the windshield, I saw a man in a weathered blue ball cap looking back at me.

Oh, dear Lord in heaven, have mercy on my soul. I gulped as I put the car into park and got out.

I swallowed hard when I looked into his face. Just the person I did *not* want to run over.

He took a few steps toward the car, eyes fixed on mine. "A little rusty on the brake pedal, Gracie?"

"Please tell me you slapped the hood with your hand. Intentionally. And not with some other limb that I've just broken."

He nodded behind me. "You took that corner at the speed of a drag racer. I had to jump out of the way, but I'm pretty spry. All limbs accounted for."

I bit my lower lip. "Tucker, I'm so sorry." I was going to say more, I certainly owed him more, but instead I opened and shut my mouth, not unlike a fish.

He swallowed, holding my gaze for only a moment. "Grace Kleren, at a loss for words? This morning is full of surprises." His voice was quiet and intense and held a rush of memories. That voice had grown up with mine, first as kids on the playground, then adversaries in junior high, when boys and girls pretended their crushes had cooties, and finally as my first, maybe my only, love. I stared at his face, drinking in the details I'd once known so well and, at one point, loved so well, before I threw it all away, packed a bag, and flew to New York.

I finally found my voice. "How are you?"

He nodded slowly, crossed his arms over his chest. "Good. Things are good. You know"—he shrugged, eyes on my face—"nothing too wild. Things around here tend not to be."

"Oh, I don't know." I cleared my throat, feeling my way through a tangle of nerves to be talking to a man who, until now, had visited me only in memory and reluctant daydreams for the previous ten years. "I seem to remember things getting interesting when two bored teenagers decided to set loose a certain sow from Mr. Thiebalt's farm. Or when armed with a gallon of paint and the blank canvas of the Silver Creek water tower."

He nodded quickly, frowning. "True enough," he said. I felt my heart sink, seeing how the concession, the mere acknowledgment of our past still cost him.

Tucker ran a hand across his face, and in the silence between us, I took my chance to stare. The face was the same, the eyes more guarded, not the easy welcome they used to be, just for me, but the cut jaw, the cheekbones, the mouth— all the same. My hands were shaking, I realized, and though he couldn't possibly have seen their tremors, I shoved them deep inside my jeans pockets.

"You in town long?" he asked. He didn't look at me when he said this, suddenly absorbed with his cap, which he removed and reshaped before putting it on again.

"No, not long," I said without pause. "I'm just back for a visit." I cleared my throat, fumbling for any possible rationale but the truth. "It's Gigi," I blurted. "She's, um, sick. She needs some help while she recovers from . . . feeling sick."

Tucker's eyebrows reached for his hairline. "Gigi's sick? I hadn't heard."

I shook my head. "She doesn't want anyone to know. She's pretty private about stuff like this. I'm stuck here till she feels better." I marveled at how convincing I sounded. Perhaps I should forget the Chickadee and instead look into local politics.

"Stuck, huh?" Tucker was taking in the new buds on the trees above us. He nodded slowly. "This place always felt too small to you, didn't it?" He looked at me then, and I saw wariness there, a wariness I deserved after leaving him with too many questions I couldn't answer and a heart I'd broken with my own restlessness.

"Not always," I said carefully.

We were quiet then, and I could hear birdsong in the rustling trees.

"Well," Tucker said suddenly, giving a sharp rap of his knuckles on the car's hood. "It's good to see you, Grace. You look good. Healthy," he amended quickly. He started to walk away when Martin called my name. We both turned to see him hurrying down the street, apron still on.

"Grace, I thought of something." We were only a block away from the Chickadee, but Martin's forehead was damp with sweat. He stopped to catch his breath and nodded upward at Tucker. "Morning, Tucker. How're things in the construction business? You all are coming into the busy season, right?"

Tucker nodded. "This year has been a nonstop busy season, so I'm grateful."

I was startled to hear him use that word: *grateful*. I listened to their easy banter and remembered how Tucker Van Es was not a man eager to recount his victories. After years meeting, even dating, men who peppered conversations with tales of their success, I wondered just what he meant, how fantastic a year it had to have been for him to describe it as a busy one worthy of gratitude.

"Grace," Martin said, mopping his brow. "You forgot to give me your number so I can call with updates."

Tucker looked at me. There was a coldness that flashed in his eyes when he said, "She does have a history with that."

Martin winced, I squirmed, and Tucker met my gaze, almost daring me to disagree.

Silence stretched between us until Martin cleared his throat. "Also," Martin said, "what about the Anthem? I know it's twenty miles away, but Winston has had a bit of a boom in the last ten years, and the Anthem had to expand their dining room. Maybe Jim is hiring."

Tucker raised one eyebrow. "Oh, Martin, didn't you hear?" His eyes sparkled with mischief. "Grace is only here for a short time. Visiting, you know, because her grandmother is ailing. Isn't that right, Grace?" He seemed to be thoroughly enjoying my obvious discomfort.

"Ailing?" Instead of sounding concerned, like any self-respecting, mind-your-own-business New Yorker would have, Martin sounded skeptical. "I haven't heard anything about Georgina feeling ill. She was in just a few days ago and she looked fine to me."

Tucker tsked. "Scary how fast things can change these days, isn't it, Martin?"

"It really is," Martin answered, shaking his head in concern.

"Yes, well," I said briskly, "I'll call the restaurant and leave my number for you, Martin." Climbing back into Gigi's car, I called through the open window, "I'll give Gigi well wishes from you both."

I started the car and pulled away, not wanting to see the look on Tucker's face as I left.

six

Early dusk was beginning to fall that night when I sat at Gigi's dining room table, pushing around the food on my plate. She'd made me her BLAT, a spin on the classic BLT but with slices of tart feta cheese and a sliver of bright green avocado under homemade sandwich bread. The bacon was thick and salty and local, and for years in New York, I'd tried to replicate the simple sandwich on my own without success. But tonight I stared at the food as it grew cold, not feeling any of the affection I'd had for the dish when I was growing up and Gigi would make it especially for me. My return from New York had brought a different girl to this table, I mused as I picked out a slice of bacon and forced a bite. What had once been the most comforting (and delicious) spot in the world was leaving bitter tastes everywhere I turned.

"Bring your own beverage!" Gigi yelled at the screen, poking her fork into the air for emphasis. "How can you not see that?" She shook her head, disgusted, and took a swig of milk from her glass.

Gigi had a long history of berating the dim-witted contestants on *Wheel of Fortune*, and it was clear that ten years had done nothing to quell her irritation.

"I will never cease to be amazed at the stupidity of people," Gigi said as she muted the television and rose from the couch. She walked toward my spot at the table, her empty plate in hand. "Any room for seconds?" she asked before glancing at my plate. Her eyes widened. "Honey, are you sick? When I used to make this for you when you were in high school, I had to double up just so I'd get some for myself. You'd down the better part of a loaf of bread out of the oven without a backward glance."

"If I did that now, I'd look like Tillie Markers," I said glumly, turning my angst on a woman who worked at Silver Creek's only gas station and who had spent a lifetime in this town trying to live down the moniker Two-Ton Tillie.

Gigi snorted as she continued toward the kitchen. "Actually, Tillie had gastric bypass not long ago. I'm afraid your prophecy would fall short, dear girl." I heard her run a brisk fount of water and soap over her dishes and scrub them briefly before stacking them on the drying rack. I didn't need to see her to know she was wiping down the sink and counter, hurrying to get back to *Wheel* before the end of the commercial break.

"I know you wanted the Chickadee to work out, but don't worry. Something else will," she called from the kitchen.

"Whatever," I sighed under my breath, feeling like a sulky teenager. Gigi rounded the corner just then and heard my dismissal. I looked up, a bit of repentance peeking through my scowl.

"Sorry," I mumbled. "I'm just having a hard time picturing what's next."

Gigi came over to kiss me on my hair. I let my head rest on her waist.

"I saw Tucker," I said quietly.

She murmured assent. "I know, honey."

I snapped my head up, disbelieving.

Gigi made a face. "You were standing on a street corner in the middle of rush hour, sweetheart. Everyone knows."

I groaned. Rush hour? I didn't remember one car passing by, though that might have had more to do with the distraction of the guy in the ball cap than traffic patterns.

"People in this town loved you two together, even if you wreaked havoc at times." Gigi sighed. "They will always talk about what might have been, in part because Tucker is much loved around here."

"Unlike the girl who left town and barely looked back," I said, my frown deepening.

"First of all, do not self-pity. It's unattractive in strong women," Gigi said, annoyance creeping into her voice. "And secondly, people love you too. We just see Tucker all the time, and he's done very well for himself through lots of grit and hard work. He's earned respect, particularly after growing up with such a louse for a father."

Tucker's dad had been unreliable at best and a mean-spirited drunk at worst. I'd heard that he and Tucker's long-suffering mother had moved to another small town sometime right after Tucker had finished high school, and while I knew Tucker maintained a cautious relationship with them from a distance, Gigi and the rest of the town had long ago sided with Tucker in the whole affair.

I had picked up a pen and was doodling on the paper napkin next to my plate. A reflex for as long as I could remember, I tended to fill empty spaces with drawings, most times without thinking.

Gigi gestured to the napkin. I focused on what I'd been drawing: sketches of my Milano winter line. The one that had been summarily dismissed by Nancy Strang.

"You know," Gigi said with a squeeze of my shoulder, "there's a sewing machine in your old room, along with the rest of that tornado. You're welcome to it whenever you'd like." She froze and then shouted, "Diamond in the rough!" She walked quickly toward the television and fumbled with the remote to take it off mute. "These people are *blind!*"

I looked at the sketch of the dress and added some embellishment to the hem before crumpling up the napkin and tossing it onto my uneaten sandwich. Gathering my plate and silverware, I pushed back my chair roughly and walked to the kitchen. After scooping my food into the trash under the sink, I fished my phone from my back pocket and tapped into Instagram with more force than strictly required. I wanted to see a glimpse into the outside world, the one where people were living real, beautiful lives full of stunning clothes and city streets and Lincoln Center and noise. *So much noise,* I thought with longing as I started to scroll through the curated images. It was so quiet here, a quiet that was already making my skin itch every time I stepped into the expansive space outside Gigi's back door.

I jumped when my phone rang loudly in my hand. Isa wanted to FaceTime. Isa, calling from the land of the living! I clicked to accept and grinned when I saw her beautiful face fill the screen.

"Hey, lady," I said. "It's so good to see you!"

"Grace!" she squealed. Then she called beyond the camera, "She's here!" The screen grew blurry and disjointed as she panned to another shot. The view settled on a long table in a crowded restaurant. "Everyone say hi to Grace," she called over the din. "She's in Iowa." She said the last word deliberately, as if speaking a second language.

I waved gamely, forcing a smile on the scene. I

recognized some faces from work, though many of them didn't pause in their conversations to look at Isa. I was particularly happy to see Luca among the revelers. He approached the camera, drink in hand, and kissed the screen. "We miss you terribly," he said, face suddenly mournful. "Please escape flyover country at once and come back to Gotham. You can sleep on my couch. Yolo won't mind sharing."

I smiled and started to thank Luca, but Isa had commandeered the screen once again. "I miss you," she said. Then looking both ways and pulling the phone closer to her mouth, she said in a slightly lowered voice, "Every one of these people, other than Luca of course, is annoying the life right out of me. How did I not notice before that you were the only woman here who could carry on a conversation?"

"Oh, listen," I said, leaning against Gigi's counter, "I could tell you stories. I have seen more unfortunate denim in the last two days than—"

"I can't hear you, hon." She pulled the phone closer to her face, which only made me a little dizzy instead of helping her hear me better. Her voice, of course, rang out clearly in the empty kitchen. Pat Sajak was the only distant sound coming from the closed door to the living room.

"I miss you," Isa said again. "When are you coming back?"

"I'm not sure." I picked at a tiny bit of adhesive on Gigi's Formica. "I'm having trouble finding work."

Isa didn't hear me. Her face had turned and she was holding up a finger to ask someone for a pause.

"Hey, can you wait just a second, Grace?" she said, nodding to the side, finger still up to ask whoever was beyond the frame to give her a minute. "They are asking for our order." She smiled. "I think I'll go with the osso buco. Remember the last time we shared an order at that place in the Village? So ridiculously good?"

I heard every word but I couldn't take it anymore. "What was that?" I said, hoping concern registered on my face. "Isa? Are you there?" I shook my head. "I can't hear you. . . . Must be a bad connection. Bad service out here in the sticks," I added for good measure, even though the service in Silver Creek had been blazingly fast, probably due to the lack of competition. "Can't . . . you aren't . . ." I frowned. "I'll have to call you again some other time—" I clicked off the call before finishing my sentence. The room was suddenly silent again, the only sound the quiet hum of the refrigerator. Even Pat and Vanna had gone dark.

I leaned my forehead against the upper cabinets and closed my eyes. *So, so pathetic,* I mused. Seeing Isa's view of laughter and camaraderie and beautiful clothes everywhere the camera could drink in a new image . . . That entire conversation had been lemon juice in all my still-smarting paper cuts.

"Rough call?" Gigi asked, startling my eyes open. She stood in the doorway to the kitchen with her coffee mug. "Sorry, but there really isn't much privacy in this house, you might recall."

I nodded, grabbing a sponge to wipe the already spotless counters. No privacy. Another log on the bonfire of my adult shame.

Gigi continued, "Unless you count the root cellar, if you remember from the days when you and that Tucker would sneak down there to make out."

I turned back abruptly. Eyes wide. "You knew about that?"

Gigi frowned. "I might be ancient, young lady, but I do notice red lips and flushed cheeks when my granddaughter and her date come through the back door, not the front, and the boy uses way too many 'Yes, ma'ams' to distract me from his own blushing cheeks."

I shook my head and turned back to the counters. "Nothing is sacred. And I thought we were being so covert."

Gigi snorted. "You weren't. And you still aren't." She tucked a strand of hair behind my ear. "You okay?"

I shook my head and stayed put, numb and tired and worn.

"Hey," she said suddenly. She put her hands on my shoulders and nudged me to arm's length. Her eyes were alight with a plan. "I know what will make you feel better."

"An Uber straight to New York and a suitcase with a million dollars in it?" I said, sullen.

Gigi ignored me. "You need to come with me tomorrow morning to the flea market."

I groaned and tried to slide out of her grasp. "No, thank you. I think I've put in my time with you and flea markets, as in every market within a sixty-mile radius, every weekend for the first sixteen years of my life, until I could drive and escape your plan."

Gigi rolled her eyes in a way that recalled the years she herself was a teenager. She was still rather good at it. "Oh, give me a break. You loved it. You got your first pair of high heels that way, missy. And an impressive collection of purses, if I recall."

I frowned but held my tongue. She was right. And I tottered around on those rose-red heels with the chunky soles for years, slowly growing into them until I could buy a pair that wasn't secondhand and had been made for the current decade.

"Then it's settled," Gigi said. "Tomorrow's the first of the outside season. We'll need to be at the county fairgrounds by six to set up, so bring a sweatshirt."

A strangled sound came from my throat. "Be there at six? Set up for what? Did you volunteer for the grounds crew or something? Gigi, can't someone else do that?"

Gigi waved her hand as she walked away. "We can talk tomorrow. We'll have plenty of time," she added as she opened the door to the backyard. "I'm going to check on my lettuce," she said, and I knew she would be lost to her garden until it was too dark to see.

seven

I'd forgotten the size of the sky.

I shivered into the parka Gigi had forced me to wear, no longer caring that it made me look like an Oompa Loompa. The air was still chilled with close memories of a winter just past, and I could see stars on the far western horizon.

But that *sky*. The shivering may well have been a result of the awe such a sky inspired. The sun had risen above the long line of empty fields that bordered the fairgrounds to the east, and with it had brought a symphony of color, made all the more vivid by the clouds reflecting their hues. I stood gripping the Styrofoam cup of coffee Gigi had thrust into my hands as soon as she'd come back from checking in at the registration table.

She sipped her own drink and looked to where I was staring. We stood in silence for a beat and then she spoke. " 'The heavens declare Your handiwork,' " she said, and then she turned to me, fighting a grin. "Come on," she said, gesturing to that sky. "Who else could pull off something like that?"

She had a point. Any retort I could muster felt

out of place under the expanse of that view. It felt wrong to tell Gigi that I'd found God to be cruel in His arbitrary gift giving and taking and that He felt as absent and empty as the millions of miles that separated each and every individual star.

I turned instead and walked through the parted flaps of the tent and toward our last hour's work. Shaking my head for the hundredth time, I said, "Gigi, I can't get over this."

The tornado in my former bedroom, it turned out, was Gigi's dress shop. We'd hauled all of it in the back of her minivan: two clothing racks, a stack of dresses, a folding table and two chairs, a tablecloth for the table, and a cash box, ready to make change for our first customer.

Gigi shrugged. "Keeps me busy."

I laughed. "I don't remember you having any trouble in that regard."

She smiled into her coffee cup. "True enough," she said before pausing for a long pull. "If I'm honest," she said, voice lowered, "I do it more for the social aspect."

I nodded, agreeing instantly this was a good plan. The dresses, after all, were ghastly. Gigi had followed the sewing instructions directly from patterns she'd bought in the seventies, each of the dresses a stitch-by-stitch tribute to the past. Oversize collars and cuffs, high necklines, exposed zippers, silhouettes that brought to mind a recession and all things Travolta—Gigi had been entirely faithful to the original designs. The only pleasant surprise was the fabric. I set down my coffee cup on the table and ran my fingers along a flowy, semi-translucent chiffon, printed in a unique paisley I'd never seen before. I bunched up a bit in my hand and let it fall, watching how it moved.

"Speaking of socializing, we'd better get a move on before the crowds hit." Gigi took my arm and we set out among the other booths. We passed stacks of dishware, a collection of old fans, and a neat line of luggage. A few of the pieces had some character and spoke of destinations reached, but the majority were Samsonite rollers, most of them black and uninspiring.

"And completely unused," I muttered.

We reached a booth that was tricked out in glittery zebra-print wrapping paper. On top of the black-and-white lines was oversize hot pink lettering spelling "Goldie's Emporium." I smiled as the booth's namesake came scurrying toward me, short white hair teased and rhinestone hoops swinging as she walked.

"You're home!" Goldie said as she enveloped me in a hug. "Let me look." She pulled back and gave me a once-over. She frowned at Gigi. "Could we do no better than this? Do you not own a winter coat that has some shape to it? For shame, Georgina Hanson."

Gigi clucked her disapproval and gestured to

95

Goldie's trim frame, covered up almost entirely by a full-length down coat. "And who are you to criticize? When it comes down to it, a girl wants to be warm."

Goldie leaned into me. "You and I both know that these coats hit the floor as soon as the real people start arriving."

I winked at her, filled with the affection of many years. My grandmother's best friend and sidekick might have leaned too heavily on the eye shadow, jewel tones, and her Bedazzler, but I'd always seen her as a kindred spirit.

"It's so good to see you, Miss Goldie," I said, squeezing her hand. "And your booth looks fantastic."

"It does, doesn't it?" she agreed. She swept an arm toward the turning racks of cell phone cases, all different sizes and all decorated in a style befitting Liberace. "I get them from China," she said quietly. "A few rhinestones here, a glitter gun there, and voilà. The Goldie touch with a fifty percent markup." She cackled and I joined her in her conspiracy. Goldie was ready for a spot on Canal Street and she didn't even know it.

"Madge! Bev!" Goldie waved over two women who were walking our way. "She's here!"

With all the clucking and exclamations, Madge and Bev made me feel like a celebrity. Widowed twins, they had the habit of finishing each other's sentences, which made for rapid-fire conversation I had to watch closely in order to keep up.

"We heard you'd gotten in, that your flight wasn't even—"

"Delayed! What a miracle! And was the traffic okay—"

"In Des Moines? We haven't been since—"

"The fair last year. But we took University—"

"Avenue to avoid the interstate. Makes us nervous. Especially when you—" There was a brief pause as Madge turned to Bev, who picked up the thread.

"Oh yes! Got a horrible virus. Hit right after the Ferris wheel. Fever for days and loose stools that lasted for weeks."

"All right then," Gigi said, pulling me along. "Show's over, ladies. We'll be happy to have you for dinner soon so we can all interrogate Grace on her life in the big city. I know Madge and Bev have started a list of questions, isn't that right?"

The women nodded, smiling as Gigi led me back toward our booth. "It's up to three pages! Single-spaced!" Bev called out with a wave.

I chuckled as we made our way back to the bright rainbow spilling out of Gigi's booth. "Do they always talk like that? And have they always had matching perms?"

"Absolutely," Gigi said. "Took me three years just to tell them apart. You can remember that Madge has her ears pierced. Bev does not. The thought makes her squeamish."

We reached the booth and I marveled again at the unique fabrics making up the dresses. I was turning to ask Gigi where she'd found them when she cleared her throat in a way that was everything but subtle. "Customer, nine o'clock," she said. "Follow my lead."

A woman pushing a stroller smiled as she parked it just outside the booth. She glanced at her sleeping baby, a stunner with round, apple cheeks and eyelashes that fanned over them.

"I have at least ten more minutes while she sleeps," she said softly, already scanning the racks. "And then it's go time."

I laughed and waited for Gigi to do the same but she had a fixed smile on her face and began speaking in a halting tone.

"I make all the dresses by hand," she said, sounding a bit like a robot. I stared. "The fabrics are vintage, which means they are original to the time period. The time period is the nineteen seventies."

The woman cocked her head, a quizzical look on her face. "I see," she said slowly.

I cleared my throat. "That print looks beautiful with your skin and hair."

The woman's eyes lit up as she considered the dress in her hand. "Isn't this great? I really love the colors."

I narrowed my eyes and with sudden inspiration said, "Hold on."

I walked around Gigi, still frozen to her spot, and found the toolbox she'd stashed under a folding chair in the back of the booth. I rummaged around in her emergency sewing supplies, past buttons and spools of thread and scissors, until I found a seam ripper. Walking back to our customer, I took the dress from her hands and looked at Gigi. "May I?"

She nodded, eyes glued on the seam ripper.

I carefully removed the oversize collar and set it aside. Pretty, even stitching lay where the collar had been and I smiled. "Do you have a moment to try it on? I can finish the look when you're in the dress."

The woman nodded and with a quick glance at the baby, still sound asleep, she ducked behind a screen, Gigi's makeshift changing room. Gigi caught my eye and I nodded, excited. The woman appeared moments later and walked to the full-length mirror propped up against the side of the booth. She nodded appreciatively, and her face lit up as she took in the view.

"I love the way this dress makes me feel," she said, turning to the side. "I just wish—"

I knew exactly what she wished and I was already on it. I took a cushion ripe with pins and started to work, seeing the dress for what it could be as I worked. I raised the shoulders, fitting the dress to her pretty curves. I cut a long line, making a slit up one side, adding another inch when the woman nodded encouragement.

"You have a great waist," I said through a mouthful of pins, "so let's show it off, shall we?" I pulled up the waistline to where her natural waist fell, and heard her murmur her approval. Taking a step back, I looked at the changes and said, "I can finish them for you this week and have it ready by Wednesday." And then, because it was true, I added, "You look gorgeous."

The woman was smiling, shaking her head a bit. "I can't believe you did that. It's perfect, like it was made just for me."

I shrugged and met her eyes in the mirror. "It kind of was."

She turned to Gigi. "I'll take it. What's your price?"

Gigi had been silent through the impromptu alterations, but now she just looked confused. "My price?"

"Sixty dollars," I said.

"Done," the woman said, and went to change back into her street clothes.

Gigi turned to me and mouthed, "Sixty dollars?"

I cringed. "Is that too low?" I whispered. "You weren't saying anything, so I—"

The woman returned, paid for the dress, got Gigi's address for a Wednesday pickup, and pushed the stroller just as her baby began to fuss. "Victory!" she said over her shoulder, waving as she walked away.

"Gigi," I said, "I'm so sorry. Did I underprice? I should have waited for you to speak. They're your dresses, after all."

Gigi whooped a laugh and then caught herself when people turned to look. "Are you kidding?" She grabbed me by the shoulders and kissed me loudly on each cheek. "I would never have asked for more than ten for its original condition. Sixty dollars! And she seemed happy about it!"

I laughed, glad to have helped sell a dress. "Of course she was. She looks phenomenal in that dress." I fingered the next dress on the rack and said, "How many dresses do you typically sell at these things?"

Gigi waved the thought away with her hand. "Oh, I haven't sold a single dress in months."

I stared and she saw the shock on my face.

Shrugging, she said, "I told you this was more for the social aspect. Plus, I like making the things. Keeps the mind sharp." She smiled at my open mouth. "Silly girl. Don't you remember that life isn't all about money? Though," she said, hands up in defense, "sixty dollars is nothing to sniff at, I'll give you that."

A deep voice interrupted our conversation. "Just when I think I've seen it all, here is Grace Kleren, up and at 'em before noon." Tucker shook his head. "These kinds of changes are too much for a small-town guy like me."

I felt my stomach flop and scowled in response.

"Of course I'm up before noon," I said, noting how easily the feistiness came back into my voice when talking with Tucker. "In New York, I'm up every day by six to make it to work by eight."

Tucker let out a low whistle. "That's some commute."

I gave a tight smile, tipping my chin. "It's not bad once you get used to it."

He kept my gaze and said with a quiet but distinctly sharp edge, "I suppose that can be said for all sorts of things."

My heart was beating wildly and I was grateful when he looked away. "Morning, Gigi," he said, and went to hug her. She could barely fit her arms around his strong frame, but she made a valiant effort before pulling back.

"How are you doing, Tuck? You eating well? You bachelor types aren't always so good at feeding yourselves."

He grinned. "I do all right. Though I'll never pass up the chance to eat something from your kitchen. I'm available every weeknight. And weekends too, come to think of it." He sneaked a glance in my direction. "Of course, I wouldn't want to put you out, especially since you haven't been feeling well."

Gigi frowned. "I'm sure I don't know what you mean." She bristled, stood straighter. "I feel perfectly fine. People think that once you hit seventy, you spend your days dodging one ailment after another. It's rather irritating, if you ask me. And incorrect!" She poked a finger into Tucker's chest.

He chuckled. "Point taken, Ms. Hanson. Unless given copies of your medical report, I will assume such news is only small-town gossip and nothing more."

I watched them laughing together and felt a pang of regret, that I'd hurt both of them with my absence and that I'd missed so many years of their easy friendship.

"Listen," Tucker said, catching my eye. "I know she's on the clock, Gigi, but would you mind if I stole Grace away for a bit? Before the rush? I believe I owe her an apology." He looked at me, and I felt instantly nervous, although I couldn't place why.

"Well"—Gigi drew out the word—"typically I wouldn't allow it, but since Grace just sold one of my first dresses ever, I'm feeling generous." She pushed us out of the booth before I could voice a protest, Tucker one half-step behind.

We made our way through the growing crowd. At one point, we navigated through a mini-throng and Tucker put his hand on the small of my back to guide us through. I tried my best to ignore it, or at least neutralize the rush of adrenaline at his touch. *This is ridiculous,* I thought. *You're not eighteen anymore. Get it together.*

We reached the outside of the large tent, and

Tucker nodded toward a little stand to the side of the entrance. I smiled.

"That's what I thought," he said before walking to the order window. He returned a few minutes later with a white paper bag full of piping-hot, fresh-out-of-the-fryer mini-doughnuts, bathed in a glorious dusting of cinnamon and sugar. I waved to Mr. Jenkins, who had ducked his head through the small window of his portable doughnut stand.

I closed my eyes as I bit into the first doughnut. "Unbelievable," I said, plucking out another for quick consumption. "These are crazy good. The kind of good that can make a girl forget all sorts of things, like being fit and sometimes vegetarian and a lover of ancient grains."

"Think of them as a peace offering." He shoved his hands into his pockets, face serious. "Listen, Grace, I'm sorry for the way I spoke to you in town the other day. It was small of me to make it tough for you during that conversation. It hasn't been sitting well with me since, and I want to apologize before I waste another day wondering about it." He clamped his mouth shut, his expression unreadable. It struck me just then how different he was. The old Tucker was an open book, and the one before me was concentrating on his words, treating them with too much care.

I offered the bag to Tucker, who took two and popped them into his mouth. I swallowed hard.

"Pretty sure a rough welcome back is the least you owe me."

"Nah," he said, taking another doughnut for himself. "Ancient history." His smile seemed forced. He nodded toward the path. "Want to walk?"

I followed him as he continued talking.

"I'm going to ignore the bit you just said about vegetarianism," he said as we settled into a comfortable pace. "You do remember my uncle raises cattle."

I raised my eyebrows at him. "I do. His beef is the principle reason I never order a steak in New York. Even for two hundred dollars, those steaks always disappoint." I ate a doughnut, letting the sugar and cinnamon melt on my tongue.

He nodded, seemingly satisfied. "Smart girl." He caught my eye before continuing. "How about a take two?"

"Take two?"

"My first attempt at seeing you again after a decade didn't go that great, so I'd like to try again." He smiled shyly at me. "How are you, Grace? You look well."

I laughed, relief filling my chest. I could handle small talk. "I am quite well, thank you," I answered, mirroring his formal tone. "And you, Tucker? Catch me up on the last ten years."

He thought a bit before answering. I waited as our footsteps fell quietly on the carpet of spring grass. "Things are good. I build houses, start to finish, and I love it."

"I'll bet you are fantastic at it." I was sincere in my compliment. I remembered well Tucker's willingness to work hard and work well, his bright mind, his eagerness to do something right, whether it was sneaking a key from the janitor and filling my locker with white tulips, my favorite, or helping to paint a friend's barn until the job finally finished at three a.m.

He blushed under my gaze. "I'm grateful to do work I love," he said gruffly, and then turned the question to me. "What about you? I'm assuming you've taken the New York fashion world by storm by now."

I returned his smile with effort. "Oh, yes. Right. The storm is barely able to keep churning in my absence." The words caught in my throat and I turned my head so he couldn't see my face.

We walked without speaking for a while, beyond the hay-covered "parking lot," then along the newly tilled fields that surrounded the fairgrounds. Tucker reached down to gather a handful of soil and I felt a wave of sadness, remembering all the times we walked the perimeter of Silver Creek and how he would do just that, letting the dirt run through his fingers slowly as he formed his thoughts and words. I waited for what he was working on, but he remained silent.

Soon we came to an old footbridge, and I felt my heart pick up speed, remembering. This bridge was the place where Tucker had finally gathered the nerve to kiss me for the first time, a million years and miles ago, when we were still kids in junior high. I felt suddenly awkward and looked at him out of the corner of my eye, trying to gauge if he was thinking of that moment too, or if those memories were long gone, covered in the dust of too many other hurts and broken promises.

He cleared his throat, and winced as he came to lean against the railing. "I know it's old news, but I should probably also apologize for the subpar kissing skills I showed in this spot a few years ago. I was, ahem, a bit inexperienced."

I laughed, relieved I wasn't the only one lost in that memory. "I just remember my legs shaking and hoping you didn't notice."

He raised an eyebrow, then turned his attention back to the ambling creek below. "I definitely did not notice your shaking legs."

We stood still, a healthy distance between us, watching the water. The air was crisp and clear, still alive with the lingering chill of winter, still ringing with the simple honesty of Tucker's admission.

"So here's the thing," I blurted before I lost my courage. I turned and started to walk again, across the bridge and along a neat line of trees bordering the next field. "I'm not here because Gigi is sick. I'm here because I totally blew it in New York and I need to get back on my feet. Turns out I didn't have what it takes. . . ."

Tucker listened as I told him the story of my downfall, how I'd outspent and undersaved, how, after a hopeful beginning at Milano, I'd wasted years of my life with nothing to show for it, not even a houseplant. He listened, just as he'd always done. When I'd finished my full confession, I realized we'd slowed our walk to a stop.

He turned to me. "Gracie, you're really good at what you do." He looked at his handful of dirt and let some slip through the cracks in his fingers before continuing. "I hope you give it some time before throwing it all away."

I plunged into my next words before I could stop myself, my hands gripping the half-empty bag of doughnuts until my fingernails dug into my palms. "Tucker, I'm sorry for how I left."

He shook his head and said, "You don't have to—"

"I do," I said. "I should have apologized years ago, but I was young and dumb and scared."

A half smile formed at the edge of his mouth, and he looked at me. "Scared? I can't see it."

I sighed. "Oh, believe me. I'm a big scaredy-cat when it comes down to it. And I'm sorry I didn't give you what you wanted. What you deserved. Still do, as far as I can tell." I blushed.

He cocked his head, looking confused. Mischief in his eyes, he said, all innocence, "Grace, are you asking me if I'm seeing anyone? Because I feel like you are."

I stopped breathing for a second. "No. I mean, of course not. I have no right to ask." I started back toward the tent, but he stopped me, laughing.

"Gracie, I'm just giving you a hard time." He turned me toward him, leaving his arm around me for a beat before letting it drop. "We have history, and that's perfectly fine. We're grown-ups now, right?" He smiled, and for the first time, I could see, really see, a new sadness in his eyes. "You can ask me if I'm single."

I tried to look friendly, mildly interested, like I'd asked him if he had seen the latest episode of *American Ninja Warrior*.

He leaned over to scoop up another handful of soil but let it run out quickly before he stood up again. With a wicked grin, he said, "Sort of."

Starting toward the tent, he walked five paces before calling over his shoulder, "You coming, Kleren?" He turned to walk backward a bit, his gait easy and strong, the grin on his face pulling me in just as it had when I'd first developed an all-consuming crush that had propelled me straight through junior high and to the day I left on the Amtrak train six years later.

I sighed. "I'm coming," I said, and jogged to where he was waiting for me to catch up.

eight

Gigi was on a tear.

She didn't even want to take the dresses back upstairs to the spare bedroom. As soon as we walked in the front door, arms heavy laden with the colorful fabrics, she barked, "Drop them on the couch, on the chairs, anything soft here in the living room. I've got a lot of work to do."

I laid a pile of dresses on the armchair next to the fireplace. Gigi hustled to the toolbox and retrieved her seam ripper. Without a word, she picked up the nearest dress and started in on the collar. That one done, she moved to the next dress on the pile.

"Gigi," I said, "I didn't mean you had to change all your dresses. That style just worked for that woman. The dresses are very . . . well made."

Gigi made a face as she ripped into dress number three. " 'Well made' hasn't made a whit of difference before this morning. Let's try for 'stylish' and see what happens. Sixty dollars!" Her eyes sparkled as she said the number. "The last time I paid sixty dollars for a piece of clothing it was for the dress I wore to your parents' wedding, and I fretted about it the whole time. But that young woman paid sixty without a second thought!"

I reached for a dress and hoped Gigi couldn't read on my face just how many times in the last few years I'd paid sixty dollars for a *T-shirt*.

We worked in silence for a while, Gigi tackling another collar while I inspected the construction of the dress in my hands. "Good grief, Gigi," I said, admiring the inside of the bodice. "Your sewing is perfect. You would have made some of my classmates at FIT weep in envy."

Gigi snorted and set another collarless dress aside. "That's the easy part. Any monkey can make even stitches and count inches." She shook her head. "No, your mom and I always had a deal: she'd pick the style and I'd read the map. But you, my dear." She winked at me, hands still working. "You're the real talent, Gracie girl. Your mom was right about you." She smiled at me, a hint of sadness in her eyes. "She said from the time you were little, 'Gracie has the hands and the mind of an artist.' "

"She said that?" I searched Gigi's face. My curiosity won over my knee-jerk reaction to push away thoughts of my parents as far and as fast as possible.

"She absolutely did. For years. I'm surprised you don't remember it yourself. She was hardly quiet about her admiration of your creative bent."

I ran my hand over the floral print I was holding. "You know, Gigi," I said slowly, "I really don't let my mind wander to Mom and Dad too much." My words caught in my throat and I stopped talking.

"I understand that," Gigi said, and I knew she did. She had mourned a husband when I was still too little to remember him, and she'd grieved the loss of her only child and a son-in-law she'd fiercely loved. She'd earned a spot at this table.

"Grief is hard. And it doesn't obey any normal rules of time. I still find the funniest things to stop me in my tracks." She glanced up from the dress she was dismantling and looked at me. "Your hair right now is just the color, just the same long waves your mom wore in her hair when she was dating your dad." She smiled. "You look more and more like her."

My heart ached, a tender mix of pain and loss and pride that I looked like a woman I so admired, loved, and missed. "Gigi, I'm sorry. I wish I didn't bring up those memories every time you look at me."

She frowned, her face abruptly stern. "Grace Eliza Kleren. Never, ever apologize for reminding me of the daughter I loved and love to this day. You're giving me a gift. Even if it's a gift that hurts a little, it's a sweet and precious gift." She returned to her work. "You also remind me of her when you pout. That part isn't quite as sweet and precious."

I laughed out loud. My heart still felt heavy, but it wasn't making me double over, the way I used to feel when thinking about Mom and Dad. I touched the waistband of the floral, fingering Gigi's perfect stitching while lost in thought. I wondered why I had pushed Gigi away so much in the year after the accident. She was deep in her own grief too, but she knew things, things about sorrow and loss and heartache and survival. I'd been too young and foolish to realize what a help she could have been as I sorted through all my own pain.

I was so deep in my reverie, I didn't realize I had taken apart the waist and sleeves of the dress and was piecing out a new version on the coffee table before me. Gigi cleared her throat and pointed. Sometime while I'd been lost in thought, she'd brought her sewing machine down from the upstairs bedroom and had placed it next to where I sat. I chuckled.

"Thanks. Did I have the look of a girl who hankered for a sewing machine?"

"You were definitely hankering." Gigi walked to the kitchen and I could hear her open the fridge. She returned with two glasses of lemonade. Handing one to me, she said, "Honey, I want you to know that it's completely understandable that you avoid talking about and thinking too much about your mom and dad."

I held the glass, feeling it start to sweat into my palm. Gigi's brow furrowed before she continued.

"But it's also okay to talk and think about and cry about and laugh about your mom and dad too. All of those things are okay. I don't want you to get stuck forever in the avoidance part." She reached out to brush my hair away from my face. "The loss never leaves entirely, you know. We've been warned. There's a verse that says God has placed eternity in our hearts. We weren't built for this to be the end, so death will never feel quite right. It chafes against the way our souls are wired."

I was still, letting the coolness of the glass seep into my palm while I digested Gigi's words.

"Sorry," she said, pecking me on top of the head. "Bible stuff again. Don't mean to offend the sensibilities of the cosmopolitan among us."

I rolled my eyes, knowing she was not one bit interested in not offending me. Before I could form a reply, she continued.

"Though you might just consider the age and reliability of said Bible. I mean, it has sold a few copies."

I snorted as I returned to work.

"In a few languages, I might add," Gigi said as she ripped through stitches. "Staying power and historical veracity have to mean something, right?"

I arched one eyebrow. "Did you just use the word *veracity?*"

She pursed her lips in annoyance. "I sure did. I watch *Jeopardy!* too, you know. I sure wouldn't get that from the idiots on *Wheel,*" she added. Then, pointing her seam ripper at me, she said, "And one more thing before I let you go back to your spiritual denial."

I was laughing at this point, and the laughter felt good.

"The Bible will sure as shooting outlast all those horrible 'girl' books Goldie keeps yammering on about. Orphan girls, girls on trains, girls in cabins, girls gone and not even *in* the books." She wrinkled her nose. "Give me a good passage from Song of Songs any day of the week."

I choked on my lemonade and came up sputtering. "Oh, dear Lord, have mercy," I muttered, shaking my head.

"Ha! Now I've got you praying!" Gigi crowed. "I am *good.*"

Just then the doorbell rang, startling us both. Gigi had moved to taking out a pair of cuffs and was midrip, so I walked to the foyer and, falling right back into Silver Creek etiquette, didn't even look through the side windows before opening the door. I stepped back a bit when I saw Tucker waiting, freshly shaved, no ball cap, and toolbox in hand.

I swallowed hard. "Hey," I finally said.

"Hey," he said gruffly. "You're blushing," he said, and I thought he looked pleased at the fact.

I put my hands on my cheeks, defensive. "It's not because of you. It's because of the Bible."

Tucker didn't seem to hear me. He shifted and stole a glance at his truck in the driveway behind him. "I can come back, Miss G," he called behind me. "I thought you said this would be a good time to measure that bit of your roof that needs to be reshingled, and these longer days are giving me extra daylight for odds and ends. But I can see you two are busy."

Gigi came to stand next to me, hand on hip. "We most certainly *are* busy." She gestured toward the living room, which looked a little like Chernobyl. "Grace is helping me with my dress business."

I raised my eyebrows to Gigi at the word *business.* One sale made a business?

Tucker kept his eyes on Gigi, serious, but a slight upturn of his mouth betrayed his intent to tease. "I hear congratulations are in order. The town's all worked up about Georgina Hanson selling a dress."

Gigi tsked. "This town has too little to talk about if they're worked up about my business affairs." She frowned. "Besides, the goal was never to make a million dollars. I do it for the social aspect."

"So we've heard," Tucker and I said in unison. Tucker laughed but caught himself and cleared his throat. I added quickly, "Maybe you're not out for a million dollars but sixty would work, right?"

Gigi launched into her story with Tucker, including the bit about her own overpriced mother-of-the-bride dress and tossing in some extra advice to millennials. Before she could move to the mortgage crisis, I interrupted.

"Perhaps you can call Tucker later about the roof?" The poor man didn't come by to rehash 2008. "Or even better, I can call Roger down at the hardware store and he can come take a look. I hate to have you bother with this." I was having a tough time not looking at Tucker, so it was a relief to actually speak to him.

"It's no trouble at all." He looked at me for a beat, his own expression unreadable, before turning to where he'd stacked replacement shingles and a toolbox at the top of the porch stairs. He hefted them and said, "I'll just leave these in your garage and come back another time."

I raised an eyebrow at Gigi but she pursed her lips and stepped past me onto the porch, following Tucker's long strides to the garage.

"When were you going to mention he was

coming over this evening?" I whispered frantically when I caught up to her.

She ignored me, which perfectly answered my question. "Tuck, I know I promised you a homemade dinner for the paint touch-up you did a few weeks ago since you're stubborn as a mule and won't take regular old American dollars as payment."

Tucker propped the shingles against one wall of the garage and turned, brushing his hands on his jeans. "No dollars, Miss Gigi. Dinner sometime is more than enough."

"Well"—Gigi drew out the word, and I could practically hear the wheels clicking as she formed her reply—"tonight won't work so well, I'm afraid. These old bones need a break after the wild day at the market."

"No problem at all, Miss Gigi. I wasn't expecting a dinner tonight anyway, what with your out-of-town company and all." His lips turned up in a small smile, eyes on Gigi. "I hope you'll let me win this round by just calling us even." He nodded at me. "You ladies enjoy your evening."

"Not so fast," Gigi barked, startling me enough to make me jump. "I mean," she said more smoothly, "my daddy always said, 'Fast pay, fast friends.' I don't like to have a debt unpaid. So you're getting that dinner." She turned and started for the house at a clip. "Just wait here," she called.

Tucker looked at me, the question on his face.

I shrugged. "No idea. The woman marches to her own beat."

Tucker sniffed. "Funny. I haven't seen that character trait elsewhere in your gene pool."

I narrowed my eyes and was readying myself for a zinger of a response when Gigi pushed open the back kitchen door with a vengeance. She'd slung her purse over her shoulder and had grabbed my soft yellow cardigan, which she shoved in my direction.

"Now, Tucker Van Es, I don't want to hear one word from you. It doesn't matter a whit to me whether you approve of this transaction or not. Respect your elders, young man."

Tucker's eyes widened. "What's your proposition, Miss Gigi?"

She pushed the money into his palm. "I want tacos. From La Condesa." Gigi nodded at me. "Grace, you're hungry too, right?"

I stammered a response. "Yes. I mean, no, not really—"

"Of course you are. Tucker, you're driving."

She turned and marched for Tucker's truck.

Tucker's eyes flickered to mine and I could see in his face the same nerves that I felt at Gigi's mention of a shared dinner. The conversation at the flea market was one thing, but dinner? Tucker looked just as uneasy with the idea as I was.

After a beat, he cleared his throat. "Seems we have our orders from the general."

"Watch your mouth, Tucker Van Es! My tortillas won't cook themselves. Now come on, you two!" Gigi hollered from the open window of the passenger seat.

He laughed. "Sorry, Miss Gigi," he called, and shook his head at me. "I hope you're in the mood for tacos."

nine

I looked at the clock on my phone. Two minutes had passed since I last checked. "I had no idea it could take so long to mail a letter." I could hear the irritation in my voice even as I tried injecting a lightness to my tone. I glanced to my left.

Tucker sat one chair away from mine in the tiny waiting area of La Condesa. He'd propped his elbows on his knees but didn't look any more comfortable than he had in the myriad other seated positions he'd tried out in the last half hour. "If I didn't know any better, I'd think your grandmother got lost."

I snorted a laugh, then covered my mouth in embarrassment. Tucker raised one eyebrow at me.

"Or we have been ditched."

"Let me call her again," I said, swiping to redial on my phone.

Tucker came to stand in front of me. He took my phone gently out of my hand and pulled me up. I stood before him, too close, but neither one of us backed away. I felt my cheeks start to burn. My stomach growled, betraying me.

"Tacos, then?" Tucker said, stepping aside and opening his arm to the dining room. He nodded at the hostess. "Thanks for waiting, Sofia. We'll take that corner booth now."

I followed Sofia and tried to rein in my scrambled thoughts. First, I was going to kill Gigi. She was the furthest thing from subtle, and I was going to kill her. Second, what on earth would we talk about over an entire dinner? We probably had absolutely nothing in common anymore other than our shared affection for cinnamon doughnuts, I thought as I scooted into my side of the booth.

We took turns thanking Sofia for our glasses of ice water, and then fell to silence. I took an in-depth study of my menu and ordered quickly. Tucker followed suit and then added two tacos for Gigi's carry-out order.

I frowned. "I'm not sure she deserves that kindness."

He chuckled, then ran a hand across his chin while turning playful eyes on me. "You know the mighty have fallen when they need a grandmother to set them up." He cleared his throat then shifted in the booth. "Not that this is a setup."

"Of course not," I agreed quickly.

"Just two old friends," Tucker said, one side of his mouth finding a lopsided grin. "Catching up. Does that sound about right?"

"Yes. Absolutely," I said with a decisive nod.

"We'll have to be the adults in this situation since my grandmother seems to be having trouble with that role."

He smiled, a real, down-to-the-roots Tucker smile. "About time. As I recall, she deserves a break in trying to keep us in line. We can take a turn."

I smiled back, feeling some of the knots in my stomach start to unravel. We started to chat, tentative at first, then falling into the easy and familiar cadence of conversation that we'd perfected so many years before. By the time I was tucking into my second taco, I closed my eyes and murmured, "This is ridiculous."

Tucker chewed thoughtfully and waited for me to have my moment. I'd had a lot of moments since my first bite.

"The tortillas," I said, dabbing the corners of my mouth with my napkin. "I'm having a hard time getting over the tortillas." I reached to the middle of the table. "And the salsa. Give me a break. It's delicious. And bottomless! New York doesn't really do bottomless. I'm so happy." I scooped up a healthy dollop of salsa into a warm, sea-salted house-made tortilla chip and had another moment.

Tucker looked amused. "I'm glad it meets your standards. I haven't been to New York but rumor has it there are a few restaurants. La Condesa could compete, then?"

"Oh my gosh, yes," I said through a mouthful of chips before having the manners to chew and swallow. "This place is the real deal. I had no idea Silver Creek had grown in its culinary tastes."

He shrugged slightly.

"I hope you don't mind me asking," I said carefully. "What keeps you here?"

He finished a bite of a taco *al pastor* that, earlier, had given me one of my more vocal moments. "I love this place. And the people. I love the people here." He spoke simply, his face open. After a pull on his soda, he added, "Sometimes I get sick of the fishbowl and everyone in each other's business. But usually a long drive in the country takes care of that. Preferably as the sun is setting over the fields with a mixtape of eighties music playing on the awesome, tinny speakers in my truck." He smiled, and I noticed a left-side dimple, deep in his cheek, that I'd forgotten.

"You do not still have that tape," I said, disbelieving. "And how in the world are you still even playing a cassette tape?"

"Retrofit, thank you very much." He looked smug as he dunked a chip in salsa. "The car dealer looked at me like I was nuts, but I have a very important cassette collection. The stuff needs to be played, sis."

I shook my head slowly. "There's nobody like you, Tucker Van Es."

His smile faded a bit and he busied himself squeezing lime over another taco. "And New York?" he said with a quick change of subject. "Other than your recent and total failure, how did the city treat you?" He grinned before taking a bite.

I scowled. "It wasn't a total failure," I offered weakly, but with the raise of his eyebrows I conceded. "Okay, it was pretty total."

"Nah, it wasn't; I'm just giving you grief," Tucker said. "You made a home for yourself there. That, in itself, is wild success. I sure couldn't do it."

"Yes, you could," I said. "You'd have it con-quered in a week." I smiled at him, knowing his strength and the way hard work fit naturally on him, and I knew I was right.

He shook his head. "Nope. I tried." He took a swig of Coke and the words hung in the air.

"Wait, what?" I finally said. "What do you mean you tried?" My mind raced to keep up with his words.

"Not New York. Chicago." He popped the final bite of taco into his mouth and chewed, too slowly for my taste, before continuing. "I moved there the year after finishing school. Drove the truck right into downtown with enough money in the glove compartment for two months' rent. 'Boy with broken heart seeks to understand the pull of city life for the girl he loved.' " He winked at me, no trace of anger or hurt on his face. "It was all very poetic."

I shook my head. "What happened? Why didn't you stay?"

An eyebrow arched. "You mean other than the pervasive smell of urine and black gunk that came out in a Kleenex whenever I blew my nose?"

I made a face. "Okay, so it wasn't your thing."

His laugh was easy, his eyes lost in memory. "I found a job easy enough. The money wasn't bad, and my boss was always freaking out about my 'small-town work ethic.' " He made ironic air quotes with his hands. "I just never caught the bug, I guess. I made a few friends, and I liked being near Lake Michigan. But I realized all I wanted to do was head to the lake. Walk past the skyscrapers, past all the crowds and the gray and the stuff, good and bad, that made Chicago a city, and get myself to the wide open of the lake, even when it was frigid outside." He stopped when a plump woman wearing an embroidered magenta top hurried up to our table. Tucker stood, towering over the woman, and enveloped her in an affectionate hug while she clucked about how tall he was. They turned to me.

"Gracie, I'd like you to meet Beatriz Molina, the woman behind all the good food you've inhaled tonight."

I winced at *inhaled* but couldn't deny the truth behind the word. I stuck out my hand to shake. "So great to meet you, Ms. Molina," I gushed, feeling a little like I was meeting a celebrity chef at the newest craze in Tribeca. "Everything was absolutely delicious."

"*Gracias, hija*," Beatriz said, holding my hand with one of hers while her other arm still draped Tucker's waist. "It is an honor to meet you, *nena*. Tucker only brings his favorite girls to La Condesa." She spoke with pride, and I stifled a giggle as Tucker frowned.

"Right, only the favorites," he mumbled, his cheeks reddening. "And so I think we're ready for the check," he said more loudly.

Beatriz smiled knowingly. "Ah, yes." She patted Tucker on the cheek and said, "But this dinner is my treat. Thank you for coming. We all loved how you enjoyed the food." She smiled at me and nodded toward a row of servers who had gathered along the wall. They waved and grinned, and Tucker laughed.

"I guess you've had an audience. You were pretty loud."

I sighed. "I'm still getting used to the idea that people actually care about what you're doing around here." I scooted out of the booth.

"Thank you," Tucker said, kissing Beatriz on the cheek and taking the carry-out container that held Gigi's tacos. Beatriz hugged me before she

128

left, waving the servers back to work since the show was over.

"Let's go," Tucker said as he opened his arm for me to go first. "I want to show you something. And that mixtape is calling my name."

I shook my head at him, at where I was in that moment. He turned to leave but not before tucking a very large bill under his plate, quickly so no one would notice. The amount was far too much for our dinner and then some. He walked ahead to get the door and I looked long at the bill on the table, remembering how one of the guys I dated in New York used to drop big cash tips on tables as we were leaving but how he always seemed to catch the eye of the server before we were out the door, nodding as he or she practically curtsied with gratitude. I walked toward Tucker and through the door he held, but my thoughts lingered on his quiet generosity, struck by how the very same act could be so different.

I inhaled a shaky, cold breath as Tucker opened the passenger door of his truck. Warm air and a heated seat met me as I settled in. I turned to Tucker, who had climbed into the driver's seat.

"Seat warmers and a remote start," I said. "With a cassette deck."

He was already doing a very not-smooth car dance to A-ha. "Just goes to prove money really can buy happiness." He reached for a falsetto "take on me," and he failed.

I turned down the volume on the stereo a bit. "I want the rest of the story. You were standing on the banks of Lake Michigan."

Tucker drove us through the quiet residential streets heading out of town. "Right. So the day I realized I'd organized my entire workday around taking a quick lunch and riding two lines of the L to get to the lake so I could glimpse it before heading back to work for the afternoon, I knew I was done. Handed in my notice and was back in Silver Creek three days later."

We rode in silence, and I watched the town fall away and the still-indigo sky form a perfect dome above us. I knew the restlessness Tucker was talking about, though I didn't tell him about it, about how, throughout my years in New York, I would develop a sudden and urgent need to walk through Central Park, in all kinds of weather. How, on certain days, the crowded sky above me, littered with buildings and steel and windows and glass, felt like it was closing in and I had to stop on the sidewalk and breathe hungrily until the feeling passed. I assumed these impulses were stress, signs of working too hard or too long. Hearing Tucker's account of his time in Chicago made me wonder if they were instead a suppressed longing for the wide-open spaces of home.

"Where are we going?" I asked.

"I'm showing you why I left Chicago," he said

quietly. "So what about you? Tell me about your decade." He took his eyes briefly off the road and glanced at me.

I must have looked pained, because he nudged my arm with his elbow. "Hey," he said softly. "You can say as much or as little as you want. No pressure here. Old friends, right?"

I felt a tightness in my chest, the idea of being friends with Tucker a new and disorienting concept. I sighed and made myself relax into the seat. I looked out the window, seeing a few stars start to appear above the horizon. "I really love New York," I said, "even with all its crazy and nonstop energy and insane rent. It's a great place. And it's the place I've wanted to prove myself since long before I left Iowa."

Tucker nodded. "I do remember something like that." I could hear the smile in his voice. "And your mark out there isn't over yet. I'm pretty sure of that."

It was such a small thing, such a tiny, smooth, precious gem of a gift that he gave me with those words. "Thank you," I said as we rolled to a stop. I turned fully toward him. "Tuck, you're a good man. You know that?"

He unbuckled and put one hand on the door handle. I could see his cheeks getting splotchy even in the dimness of the dashboard lights.

"I mean it," I said, anxious to say words that needed to be said. "I know how you've taken care of Gigi's friends when they've needed it."

He glanced at me, wary. "I've hardly done a thing."

I laughed softly. "Really? Because it sounds to me like you're the on-call maintenance man for the over-seventy set." I watched his face. "They're very grateful."

He rolled his eyes. "It's not charity." His voice was edged with a pride affronted.

"I know," I said quickly. "It's kindness. But it's not just the ladies. I know how you've helped your uncle Sal when he's needed it, how you've made it possible for him to keep his farm when he couldn't do it alone."

"He's my uncle and the only dad I've had for years," Tucker said. He pulled on a ball cap wedged under the center console and busied himself tightening and loosening the back. "And it's not 'helping.' That makes him sound weak."

"Well, he is," I said, not backing down. "And you're a good man to help him in his weakness without making him feel small. And here's another thing: you treat Gigi like gold, and I appreciate it." My voice caught and I clamped my mouth shut.

Tucker gave me a sideways glance. "How do you know about all this? I thought you cut ties."

I rolled my eyes, in part as an effort to keep them from filling. "I know stuff. I'm very much in tune with the goings-on of Silver Creek, Iowa."

"So Gigi had a few things to say during the flea market."

I frowned. "Maybe." Then, smiling, "She told me about Sal years ago, but I didn't know about the handyman work until you showed up today with her latest request."

He looked at me then, long and full. It had been a really long time since I'd felt studied by a man, not just taken in or evaluated or wanted, but studied. I forced myself to stay still.

He slapped the steering wheel with both hands, making me jump. "All right. Things are getting a little stuffy in here, don't you think?"

I sputtered a response but he wasn't listening. He'd opened his door and jumped out, walked away from the truck. After a beat he looked back at me. "Come see."

I followed him, the cool night air was nippy, coaxing a shiver to break through from me. Tucker took off his jacket without a word and helped me shrug into it. I kept my hands cocooned within his long sleeves and followed him as he walked.

"This is my newest project. Watch your step." He offered a hand to help me navigate over a pile of two-by-fours. "We're building a farmhouse, one that looks like the ones our great-grandparents built but tricked out with all-modern everything. Good, clean lines, floors finished with wood from an old barn just torn down east of town, big, soaring windows that will take in sunsets from floor to ceiling." He was talking fast, gesturing to where each room would land. "A spacious farmhouse kitchen here, light-filled, south-facing, with enough room for a big table and lots of family and friends." He stopped, lost in imagining the space as it would be, not the empty acres before us.

I said nothing as he led me around the site, pointing out progress here, a roadblock there. We circled back to the truck and he pulled several blankets from within the cab. He spread them on the bed of his truck and offered me a hand to climb up. He took the lead and sat down on the blankets, back against the cab and face toward the sky. I stood awkwardly, uncertain of where I was to go.

"Good grief, Kleren," he finally said. "You coming down here or what? The stars are a lot easier to see if you're actually looking up." He patted the space beside him. "No funny business. I promise." He grinned and I sank to my knees, still nervous to be so close.

Get a grip, I thought. *It's just Tucker.*

I sat next to him, leaning my side into him slightly for warmth. Trying to keep the mood friendly, I asked again the question I'd tried once before.

"So . . . who's the 'sort of'?"

"Excuse me?" he asked, laughter around his eyes.

"When I asked if you were single you said, 'Sort of.' Old friends should know this about each other."

"Ah," he said, nodding slowly. He let out a long breath before continuing. "It should be such a simple question."

I felt my heart dip, like a buoy getting pulled under a wave. I willed it back up. "What's her name?"

"Natalie," he said softly. "It's still new. We met a few months ago. Set up," he said, giving me a sideways glance. "Not by Gigi."

"Thank goodness. I'd hate for her to start thinking this was some sort of calling," I said, noticing abruptly that I was bouncing my leg and making the truck move. I threw on a smile. "What's she like?"

He paused before answering. "She's smart. Kind. Generous."

"Pretty?" I was trying so hard to sound platonic, it was taking all my concentration. These were new waters for me and Tucker, and I was working like mad to keep him from knowing how choppy they felt.

"Yes." He sounded sure. "She's pretty."

I paused before saying, "She sounds like quite a catch."

He looked at me quickly, then away. "You're right. She does sound that way."

Falling silent, we drank in the hush of the surrounding fields. We watched the stars, more than I'd seen in years, cluttering the sky with an extravagance fit for the showroom of Tiffany's. The blue-black backdrop filled my vision, from horizon to horizon, and we watched, transfixed, as the moon rose. If only New York had this.

"It's so beautiful," I said quietly. "I never would have said that before, but it's true. You live in a beautiful place."

I sneaked a peek at him out of the corner of my eye. This Natalie was a lucky girl. Tucker sat in silence, eyes on the sky. After a long while, he said gruffly, "I'm glad you're here, Gracie."

I said nothing but nodded, assuming, correctly, I thought, that even across years and experience and heartache, he knew I was glad too.

ten

I leaned against the closed front door for a moment, the only light in the house filtering in from the porch light. The quiet darkness of the house contrasted sharply with the sound of Tucker's truck pulling away. I closed my eyes, trying to process the swing of emotions from an unexpected evening. So many things were the same about Tucker: his slow laugh, his wry asides, the way he made me feel as if we were just joining a conversation that had been in progress long before we'd found each other.

I tugged off my shoes and laid them soundlessly on the wood floor of the foyer. A small lamp on the kitchen counter illuminated a path from me to it, and I padded quietly through the living room, doing my best to dodge the disaster Gigi and I had created earlier in the day. I stumbled a bit and dropped hard onto the couch, still thinking about Tuck.

But there were so many ways he was different. For one, he was broader. His hands were hardened from years of working with tools. His jaw was speckled with a stubble that threatened to become a full beard if left ungroomed. But he also spoke like a man who had found his own way, like a person who was entirely sure that life would bring hard things but that he would be able to navigate them. He talked about the bedrock of faith, a subject we used to deftly avoid after my parents died. Tucker made faith sound like something very close, practical, daily, and I envied his assuredness, though the God he described didn't sound like the one I'd known.

And yet I could see hesitation in Tucker's eyes at times, how he looked away abruptly when we inched toward a discussion of his personal life, how he'd said good-bye in his truck as if we were former teammates on the basketball team instead of each other's first hard and breathless crush.

I didn't blame him, I thought as my eyes adjusted to the darkness in Gigi's house. I was in no position to consider anything but polite friendship either. I had one foot dangling in Iowa and the other firmly planted back in New York. There was too much water under too many crumbling bridges with me and Tucker. And anyway, I reminded myself, he was seeing someone else. As he should be. Still, I wondered if there was anything we could do or if our history would always just be something we had to step carefully around when we were in the same room.

We got some good practice tonight, I thought as I settled into the couch. I smiled, thinking of

Gigi's ridiculous plan and how, while it was not what she'd hoped for, it wasn't the disaster I'd feared either.

I closed my eyes, auditioning for sleep, but knew I was nowhere near tired. In fact, I felt the opposite. Wired. Ready to go. Or *do*. My eyes flew open and I reached for the lamp on the end table closest to me.

Picking up the dress I'd just been using as a pillow, I felt the fabric, a heart-stopping orange silk that fell through my hands like liquid. I worked quickly, my hands sure of the design that fabric was meant to have. A much lower V for the neckline, a higher waistband in a narrow, fabric-covered line, long layers for the skirt. I hand stitched the layers into gentle waves of fabric, humming to myself as I envisioned how the dress would move.

Finished, I shimmied out of my jeans and T-shirt, barely glancing to see if the living room curtains were drawn and not caring that they weren't. No one in Silver Creek was up at one thirty in the morning, and if they were, they were about to see a ridiculously beautiful dress.

The fabric fell just as I wanted, and I caught my reflection in a mottled farmhouse mirror propped near the fireplace. The dress was stunning. The color was unique and fresh, and the silk felt like total indulgence against my skin. I removed the dress carefully, laid it out on the one empty chair, and picked up my next victim.

I clicked to publish the last dress and slumped into the couch, now empty of dresses and calling my name for a long, heavy sleep. A full moon suffused silvery light into the living room, and I tossed my phone onto the nearest stack of finished garments.

They were gorgeous, and I was exhausted.

The fabrics had dictated the designs, and I shook my head again, surprised at how inescapable the process had felt. The exuberant, geometric print was screaming to be a minidress, boatneckline here, V-neckline there, this one with embroidered trim, that one finished with a belt to bring the eye to a slender waist. The deep yellow silk, a cousin to the orange, was now a light and airy pantsuit with spaghetti straps and perfectly wide pant legs that would make a woman feel glamorous and comfortable with every step. One of my very favorite reincarnations was a floor-length maxi dress that would be equally at home as a day dress at the farmers' market and dressed up for a summer's night out. I'd posted that dress last on Etsy before falling onto the couch in a heap.

We'll see if anyone else thinks they're as beautiful as I do, I thought as I felt myself hurtling toward sleep. I had nothing to lose. I was blissfully close to oblivion, my aching shoulders and hands so tired that Gigi's living room might as well have been a cave.

I didn't know how long I'd been dozing when I heard a ping from my cell phone. I ignored it. It pinged again, and I knew it wouldn't stop until I silenced it. Sadly, that action would require me to move.

I sighed loudly, eyes still heavy with sleep, and swept my arm along the couch cushions until I found the location of the pinging. I blinked hard, doing my best to focus on the screen. I blinked again, hard, to verify the message and make sure I was, in fact, awake.

"Etsy Alert!" the screen read, right next to a miniature image of the maxi dress. "Your first item has sold! Way to go!"

I laughed out loud, still staring at my phone. One sold. I checked the clock on my phone and saw only a few hours had passed since I'd put the dress up for sale and fallen asleep. One already sold! One dress, at least, given the blessing of a stranger who saw its beauty and said yes. I laughed again, hope filling me in a way I hadn't known in weeks.

"Well, good morning. Finally," Gigi said, coming into the cluttered room from the kitchen. "You didn't even stir when I came through here at seven or so." She looked amused at my rumpled hair and face. "How was dinner?" She grinned. "Sorry I got waylaid at the post office."

"For hours?"

"Sadly, yes."

"After it closed for the night?"

She shrugged, still grinning. "I know people. People who have keys to post offices."

I narrowed my gaze. "You didn't even go to the post office, did you?"

"Nope." She sounded gleeful. "Came straight home and heated up leftovers. I hoped you wouldn't be back with my tacos until long after suppertime, and I was right!" She leaned against the railing and folded her arms. "So?"

"So," I said, drawing out the word, "it was nice. Super weird at first," I said, more sternly. "Very awkward and full of interminable silences during which I plotted my revenge."

Gigi rolled her eyes. "A necessary evil. But it ended all right? Did you talk and smooth things over and act like adults?"

"We did," I said with a gracious nod of the head. I gave her no more details, and I could tell it was killing her.

"Adults who could one day fall back in love, get married, and give me some great-grandchildren?"

I shook my head, unable to stifle a laugh. "Not that kind of adults, no. But ones that still enjoy each other's company, yes."

Gigi pursed her lips. "You sound more elderly than my bridge club." She scanned the room, and her brow furrowed. "Have you been at this all night, you crazy girl?"

I stood, wobbly with fatigue and happy to have a distraction. I picked up the maxi, twirling it slightly as I swayed with it against my frame. "What do you think?"

Gigi's eyes grew wide as she watched the dress move. "How did you do that?" she said, shaking her head. "How did you make my clunky, ho-hum dress look like that?" She pointed, eyes still big.

I laughed. "And it's already sold! I just got the ping from Etsy! Sold, and it's only been up for a few hours!"

Gigi walked toward me, concern registering. "Honey, I think you'd better get some sleep. I don't understand a word of what's coming out of your mouth." She put her hand to my forehead but I intercepted it and forced her to waltz with me around the piles of dresses. By the second time around the room, Gigi was giggling like a schoolgirl and I was whooping in a way that would have been right at home in Times Square when the clock struck midnight on New Year's Eve.

"Now, wait just a minute. You're going to kill an old woman," Gigi said, stopping to catch her breath. "Explain to me in normal-person language what is making you stay up all night and act like a lunatic." She froze, a hopeful smile starting in on her face. She pointed a finger at me. "Tell the truth, now. Did you and Tucker find your way to the root cellar? Is that it?" She tsked, faux disapproval lighting the mischief in her eyes. "You sly dog, you."

I rolled my eyes. "No cellar visits, Gigi. I told you. We are friends. Nothing more."

She raised one eyebrow.

"Promise. Besides," I said, prickly, "can't a woman be this excited about something having nothing to do with romance?"

"Sure," Gigi said. "I can't imagine it's as fun as the cellar, but explain to me the pinging Essie and I'll let you know." She pointed me toward the kitchen. "Coffee?"

I followed her to the kitchen and launched into a brief explanation of the online indie marketplace and how we'd just made twice what we'd made at the flea market, on only one dress. My phone pinged again from the living room and Gigi put a hand over her mouth.

I grinned and took the cup of coffee she'd set on the counter before me.

She waited as I sipped. She worried her bottom lip for a minute before shrugging. "I'm glad you understand the bit about the Etsy. That part sounds like something Goldie would like and I would hate. But I'll tell you this much, kiddo." She clinked her coffee mug on the edge of mine. "You might have just found

144

yourself a way back to that big city you love so much."

I toasted her back, and then again, for good measure.

eleven

I was just about to check out at Henrickson's Market the following Friday, my little red basket burgeoning with requests from Gigi, when my phone buzzed with a new text.

Gigi had added another item to the list, her fourth addition since I'd arrived at the grocery store twenty minutes before. I turned on my heel and headed back to the shelves, screwing up my face as I stared at her message.

It read, *Paste. Thank!*

Pasta? I assumed she didn't need any Elmer's, so I headed for the small selection of noodles. After brief consideration, I tugged a box of penne off the shelf. On my way back to the front again, my phone buzzed. I groaned out loud.

Two more things, Grace. I'm sore sorry! Please pick up a brunch of asparagus and Gaelic. Making paste for dinner tonight!

I rolled my eyes on my way to Henrickson's produce section. A paste of asparagus and Gaelic something-or-other. Sounded perfect.

I neared the produce, thinking about my growling stomach and that I might need to stop at the Chickadee for a midafternoon cinnamon roll, when I stopped short. Tucker stood by a display of raspberries and blackberries, talking with two women who stood with their backs to me. He was turned so that he couldn't quite see me, but I could tell even from my compromised angle that he was blushing as he spoke to the women. When I recognized Erin Jackson, I realized why.

I hadn't seen her since our brief interaction the morning I'd started my job search at the Chickadee, but if my instincts were correct, Tucker was just as unhappy to be cornered by her in a grocery store as I would have been. When Erin's unmistakable, high-pitched laugh rang out and I saw Tucker flinch slightly, I set my jaw and started their way. We might have been new to the whole friendship idea, Tucker and I, but I was sure friends did not let friends agonize through conversations with a frustrated prom decor queen.

I reached them and put on my best faux-surprised expression. "Well, hello," I said, forcing them to widen their little circle as I stepped between Tucker and Erin. I smiled at the three of them, making quick eye contact with Erin, Tuck, and a woman I didn't recognize. "I hope I'm not interrupting anything, but I had to stop over and say hello."

"Hello indeed," Erin said, with more enthusiasm than I'd thought she'd have for seeing me.

"Grace, I don't think you two have met." She turned to the woman at her side and said, "Natalie Connors, this is Grace Kleren."

I put out my hand to shake Natalie's impeccable manicure. Natalie. One glance at Tucker's blush and I knew this was *that* Natalie. I stared at her a beat, unaccustomed to seeing such a polished look in Silver Creek. Natalie had long, glossy chestnut hair and huge brown eyes that were tastefully lined and shadowed. She wore a fitted black dress topped with a cropped black jacket and absolutely covet-worthy black heels. She saw me staring and laughed easily.

"I suppose my attire is a bit out of place," she said. Her smile showed an impressive two rows of straight and white teeth. "I was in court this afternoon, and I stopped by Silver Creek on my way back to Des Moines. I typically don't shop for groceries in heels, but Erin insisted I tag along so we could chat a bit before I went back." She turned to Tucker. "And then we had the happy surprise of running into this guy." She reached out and touched Tucker's arm, and I found myself glaring at her touch and at Tucker's level of comfort with leaving those red nails right where they were.

I swallowed. Hard. Gripping my basket more tightly, I said, "Court appearance, eh? Got caught doing something illegal? Money laundering? Tax evasion? Meth?" I laughed weakly but the three of them just stared. Tucker frowned.

"Grace," Erin said slowly, as if talking with someone who needed extra time to process, "Natalie is an attorney. A very good one, actually. You probably saw her name in the *Register* a lot last year when she won that case that returned millions of dollars to health care fraud victims." She turned to Natalie, admiring. "You helped so many innocent people get justice. Our state is so lucky to have you."

I must not have agreed fast enough because Erin looked at me pointedly.

"Wow," I stuttered. "Right. Great work. It sounds like you're a real world changer."

Natalie, still smiling, tilted her head at me. "Wait. Are you Grace the former New Yorker? The fashion designer?" I could feel her taking in my own ensemble and knew a graphic T-shirt and my oldest pair of jeans were not exactly screaming "Fashion Week."

"Yes." I did my best to stand straight, though I was starting to feel the weight of the basket full of Gigi's requests digging into my palm. "I am a designer."

"Actually"—Erin drew out the word—"Grace here is back home after a long stint in New York City." She shook her head, faux concern in full force. "Didn't quite work out, right, Grace?"

I seethed internally but maintained my smile.

Tucker, who had, until that moment, been silent,

mercifully interrupted my downward spiral. "We're glad to have her back in town," he said with a curt nod in my direction. "And I'm sure she's plenty busy. We won't keep you, Grace." He locked eyes with me, eyebrows raised.

"Of course," I said, now the one to blush. Here I had marched over to save Tucker, maybe even ask him to join me for coffee and a cinnamon roll at the Chickadee, and he was the one who had to rescue me.

"It's lovely to meet you," I said to Natalie, who said a gracious good-bye. Erin wasn't as subtle.

"Say hello to your grandma," she called, a smirk undergirding her words.

I didn't turn back to acknowledge I'd heard her, though I did hear Tucker's quiet reprimand. My cheeks burned as I checked out and threw down a bill to pay for my purchases. "Keep the change," I said to the gleeful teenager, who thanked me for a large tip. I took the bags from the end of the conveyor belt and pushed through the door as if pursued. *Get me out of here,* I thought as my eyes burned with embarrassed tears, and I knew afresh that I wasn't thinking only about Henrickson's. I was thinking about the entire state.

I made it to the minivan and opened the side door, intent on loading the groceries and driving to the refuge of Gigi's house as fast as I could without getting stopped by the sheriff, when I glimpsed a tower of packages in the back of the car. I moaned, letting my forehead rest against the frame of the van door. In my haste to get out of Henrickson's, I'd forgotten the reason I'd come to the town square in the first place. The groceries had been a favor for Gigi. I was really in town to mail a stack of new orders.

The post office was only a block down from Henrickson's. I watched the door to the grocer's for a full minute before filling my arms with the packages as quickly as I could. I gripped my unwieldy load and worked two fingers free to pull the van's roller door shut. It was tricky, but I managed to balance the packages as I walked, finally reaching the post office and carefully backing through the door and going up to the front desk. I sighed with gratitude, both for making it to the counter without having the boxes keel over and for the gift of not having to see Tucker and his new girlfriend on my walk down the block.

Miss Evelyn took one look at me and slapped the counter with both hands.

"Grace Kleren, I do believe I've seen you more in the last week than in the whole of the last fifteen years," she said, reaching out to take my packages and setting the first one on the scale. She placed stickers on each package in turn, and then took my credit card from me without needing to ask my shipping preference. "In fact," she said, looking over her reading glasses so I could catch her eye, "this trip marks your fourteenth time this week."

I felt my eyes widen. "Fourteen? That's even more than I thought." I felt my chest expand with the deep breath I inhaled. Gigi and I had been working like dogs to use every bit of her fabric. We'd settled on three of our favorite designs in order to keep our sanity and to speed up production, but even with that decision, her house had been a whirlwind of activity in an attempt to keep up with the orders that came in steadily from our Etsy shop. Fourteen trips to the post office, with each trip representing at least ten dresses sold—my math was looking awfully promising for a return to New York earlier than I'd hoped.

"I know it's unusual," Miss Evelyn continued as she placed the packages in a waiting canvas bag, "but I've always had that gift."

I pulled myself out of my calculator mode and must have looked confused. "Sorry?" I said.

"The counting gift," Miss Evelyn said, nodding. "I don't even mean to do it. It just happens. I keep track of how many packages I send or receive for a particular person each week, even when I don't really want to know." She lowered her voice and looked around the empty foyer. "And believe you me, sometimes I most assuredly do not want to know. Like Hal Lundstrom's fixation with that Beyoncé woman. He's been a member of her fan club for fifteen years, and may I just say that if he refers to her as 'Queen Bey' in my presence one more time, I fear I might lose what little composure I still maintain." She sighed, lips pressed into a thin line. I bit my cheek, waiting for her to inhale, then exhale. When she'd gathered herself, she smiled at me and patted my hand. "I'd much prefer to be of some help to your dress business. Georgina tells me it's going gangbusters. I'm so happy for you, Grace."

I rushed to change the subject before I heard about anything else the people of this town were ordering by mail. Some things one could never unknow. "That light green box with the tiny polka dots isn't to ship today."

Miss Evelyn paused, one hand above the little box. She looked over her half-moon glasses. "You'd like me to hold on to it, honey? Send it out tomorrow or next week?"

"No," I said, unable to contain my smile. "That box is for you, Miss Evelyn."

Her eyes lit up with pleasure. Not too many years shy of eighty, and Miss Evelyn still looked like a kid at Christmas when presented with a gift. "Grace Kleren, what have you been up to?" she asked, trying to sound stern but failing miserably. She lifted off the lid of the box and slowly extracted a personalized stamp with a beautifully carved wooden handle. She looked at the example imprint on its side and gasped. "This is my name and home address! I've never in my life . . ." She turned to me and reached over the counter to pull me into a hug. "Where on earth did you find such a thing?"

"Online," I said when she pulled back from our embrace. "I know how much you love letters and stationery, and you mentioned a couple of weeks ago that you hated the boring old return address stamp that your husband has used for your personal mail for years."

"Ugly as sin," she declared, still looking at her new treasure.

"I thought a post office matron of all people deserved her own monogrammed stamp. How would it look for Silver Creek if your corre-spondence didn't live up to your position?"

She shook her head. "You are too kind, dearie. I'm so glad you're back in town." She paused and then said with a knowing look, "I do hope your business continues to thrive. It's so refreshing to see someone doing well."

"I'm definitely not out of the woods yet," I warned. "We're just starting out, feeling our way."

"Well, I'm certainly rooting for you." She placed the gift box to the side and continued weighing and postmarking the remaining packages of dresses. "I'm sure you've noticed all the empty storefronts on Main." She shook her head sadly. "It's a tough time to be a small business around here, online or otherwise. First Marv's Hardware, then that little clothes shop that Cassie Velton tried to make a go of, then the bookshop that was in the Harding family for three generations—all gone within the last few years." She patted the top of the stack of packages and looked me in the eye. "I'm cheering you on, Grace. It's not easy to do what you're trying to do."

I nodded slowly, lost in thought and feeling a healthy dollop of guilt that I too was making my plan to leave Silver Creek and take my business with me.

"Well, I should get back to that company I'm building," I said, feeling in my coat pocket for the keys to Gigi's van. "There are two stamp pads in that box, so I hope you go crazy tonight and stamp everything in sight."

Her delighted laugh pealed like bells. "Oh, Grace, you are too much. I'm just pleased as punch you thought of me." She covered my hand with her own cool palm. "Godspeed to you, sweetheart. I hope those dreams you're growing take you exactly where you want to be." She winked. "And that you send me a postcard when you get there."

I smiled as I pushed open the glass door, the bell above it announcing my exit. I turned toward the town square, taking a silent inventory of all the shuttered businesses, all the empty real estate. I walked slowly to my car, lost in thought. As I turned the key to open the driver's side door, knowing Gigi would have thought me a crazy woman to lock the door in the first place, I saw movement out of the corner of my eye. I turned and saw Tucker working in Goldie's yard, loading bundles of dead branches into the back of his truck. He didn't see me and I stood a moment, watching him leverage his strong arms and back to stack the wood in the truck bed. Goldie talked with him from a spot on her front walk, and I smiled when he paused in his work and laughed, tipping his head back as he did so.

I folded into the driver's seat, my mind full and processing all the ways Silver Creek had changed and, I noticed as I drove past Goldie's house and Tuck lifted his ball cap at me, all the ways it remained the same.

twelve

I turned the knob, pushing the back porch door open with my hip, and heard Gigi's squeal from the dining room. I dropped the groceries with a thud onto the kitchen countertop and rushed to make sure it was a squeal of joy, not pain. One look at her face and I had my answer.

"I'm on the Etsy," she said excitedly. She jabbed her finger at the screen and I winced at the fingerprints she left. "We are sold out! Not one dress is left! Boom shakalaka!" She jumped up from her chair and roped me into a mix of the boogie and the twist. I laughed and danced with her until we were both breathless. Gigi looked at me, eyes shining.

"You did good, kid," she said, panting. "I'm so proud of you." She kissed me on the cheek and then started in again with the boogie. "All those dresses, all over the country! Girls are wearing our dresses, and now girls can't even *get* our dresses because we're all out. We are limited editions!" She giggled.

I clapped giddily. "Let's make more! Where do you get your fabric? I can put in an order tomorrow." I was already walking to the laptop to Google Gigi's fabric source and write down the phone number.

Gigi laughed. "Do you have a time machine, kiddo?" She shook her head and picked up an empty teacup next to the computer. "I bought that stuff from a fabric store in Des Moines in 1979. Betty Lou's Window Shop, I remember. It closed not long after, but I loved that store." She kept talking, reminiscing about Betty Lou while I stared at the screen.

Nineteen seventy-nine? I stopped, my hands poised over the keyboard. No name, no serial number, not even the store where it was purchased. I stared at the screen, feeling my breathing become shallow. Google would be no help to me now. No fabric would bring our little enterprise to a grinding halt. No fabric meant New York was still dangling far out of my reach.

I'd earned enough to pay off my credit cards, give some to Gigi despite her protests, and save a bit for sewing supplies. I was operating in the black, but just barely. To grow at all, I knew, would mean an investment, but I'd been hoping Gigi's fabric supply would be local and cheap. I could only imagine what vintage bolts might cost if I had to start sourcing them bit by bit from individual vendors across the country.

It was just before I let myself fall asleep that evening, my breathing finally becoming steady after my mind took a long and rambling replay of the day's events, when it came to me. My eyes flew wide open. I knew someone better than Google. I knew Luca.

"The fabulous and gifted Grace Kleren!" Luca's Italian accent exclaimed into his work line. I winced, hoping no one else within earshot of him knew my name and the likely legendary story of my Nancy freak-out and bathroom breakdown.

"Hey, Luca," I said more softly, as if trying to encourage him to turn down his own volume. "How are you?" I was calling from a perch on Gigi's front porch swing. An old Buick puttered by on an otherwise empty street. A squirrel scolded me from the crook of an oak. "Wait. I have to ask. What can you see right now?" I hated the longing in my voice, but there it was.

"What am I seeing?" He paused, taking it in before answering. "I'm standing in my office, so I see a stack of back issues I need to comb today, looking for an inspiration for a spring plaid. I see the detritus of my morning, which includes the remains of a pastry from Bubby's and a mostly empty coffee cup from Sid's."

I whimpered. I couldn't help it.

"And," he finished, "I see a view of Midtown, sunny and full of all sorts of people who should be dressing better. It's a tiny view, as my window size is commensurate with where I stand on this corporate ladder, but it is, in fact, a window. And you, sweetheart? What is your view of Iowa?" He drew out the word as if trying it on for the first time.

I sighed. "A squirrel." I stopped there. The squirrel was enough.

Luca laughed. "Oh, honey. Time to get yourself back to New York."

I sat up a bit in the porch swing, stopping its momentum with the toe of my sneaker. "That's the plan," I said. "In fact, it might come earlier than I'd thought, but I need your help with a little detective work."

Forty-five minutes later, I was helping Gigi weed unwanted rogues in her backyard garden when my cell phone buzzed in my pocket. I straightened, feeling back muscles I hadn't remembered for years, and swiped to answer.

"I found it."

I let out a whoop. "Luca, you are a marvel. You found the source with only photos of the dresses? I am in awe of you."

"As is only natural," he purred. "The fabrics are all from the same warehouse, still in business, and just outside Omaha, Nebraska."

Why was it that whenever Luca said the name of a Midwestern city, it sounded like he was consulting a phonetic dictionary? Gigi was watching my face and I said, phone away from my mouth, "Luca found our fabric at a warehouse in Omaha."

"Hello, Granny!" Luca called through my phone. "Lovely to meet you, darling!"

"Luca says hello," I passed along to Gigi, who smiled.

"Tell Luca he's welcome here anytime. I owe him a home-cooked meal for his trouble," she said before turning back to the first row of butter lettuce.

"Oooh." Luca was cooing after hearing his invitation. "I'd love that. I have the perfect pair of trousers that would serve that occasion. A gorgeous linen, exquisite hand, magenta. To. Die. For. I got them in Firenze with my *mammina*. I could get Yolo a matching collar. We would *stun*."

I bit the inside of my cheek to prevent my laugh-snort from escaping. How I would love to see Luca striding the streets of Silver Creek in his magenta linen pants. This town could use a little shake-up, and I thought Luca in magenta was a great place to start. Erin Jackson might have to take to her bed to recover, but I was all in.

"Bring the pants and come anytime," I said, wishing he'd take me up on it. "And thank you so much for your sleuth work, Luca. I owe you big-time."

He gave me the name and contact info for the warehouse in Omaha and we were just about to hang up when he stopped me. "Grace, honey, I almost forgot. The woman on the phone said she had more than enough fabric for you, about two hundred bolts."

"Wow," I said. "Yes, that should do it and then some. I won't need nearly that much."

"Well, that's the thing," Luca said. "She said you can have the fabric but you must take it all."

My eyes widened and I felt a knot settle in my stomach. "All of it? Luca, I can't possibly afford all that." The business was going well but not well enough for what two hundred bolts of vintage fabric would cost outright.

"Oh, I think you can," he said breezily. "If you can pick it up, she said, it's all yours."

I hung up with Luca, thoughts spinning. Gigi stood, hands on the small of her back, and wiped the sweat from her neck. "What's the trouble?"

I started to pace. "The good news is that we have the opportunity to acquire a whole lot of beautiful fabric for free."

"Good gravy." Gigi opened her mouth slightly, mirroring my shock at our good fortune. "What could possibly be the bad news?"

I turned on my heel and started up the walk. "The bad news is that there is no way two hundred bolts of fabric will fit in the back of your minivan."

Gigi waved away that concern with one soil-caked gardening glove. "Well, that's not bad news at all. There are plenty of people with trucks around here."

"Right," I said, stopping now to open the contacts in my phone. I frowned with my fingers over the screen. "Gigi, you're going to need to give me names. I don't know anyone well enough to call with a request like this."

She nodded, serious. "True. It is a big ask. Taking a day off work, driving all the way to Omaha and back, lots of time on the road when you could be spring planting." She shook her head quickly. "Never mind. You were right. This is bad news." She turned back to her gardening but was humming. Loudly and with too much happiness than befitted the situation.

I crossed the distance between us and stood, watching her work. I narrowed my eyes at the top of her gardening hat. "Gigi."

"Hm?" She didn't stop her work breaking up the soil in the flower bed under her feet.

"Why do I get the feeling you are not worried about this truck issue?"

"Oh, honey, because I'm not."

"Want to clue me in?"

Gigi stood and faced me. Her eyes got unnaturally large and unnaturally innocent. "Why, Grace, you do know just the right person for this job. He's not a farmer, he's as kind as they come, and as Providence would allow it, he has a very nice truck." She passed me her phone with a grin. "Look under 'Favorites.' Right below your name."

I stood motionless, staring at Gigi's phone in my hand, well after she went back to work and well after I admitted to myself that she was right. I needed help and I knew the only one able and willing to do what I needed was the guy I least wanted to trouble.

I hung up three times before taking a deep breath and letting the call go through.

"Miss Gigi," Tucker answered, "I think there's something wrong with your phone. You called me three times before we got a good connection."

I swallowed hard. "Tuck?" I said, and I could see Gigi's shoulders shake a bit as she started to laugh. "I need a favor."

thirteen

Tucker pulled slowly into the sprawling parking lot of Triad Fabrics and Textiles and found an empty spot in front of what looked like administrative offices. He tugged the keys from the ignition and turned to me. "We made it."

I had to stifle a sigh of relief, and not because we'd covered the last mile between Silver Creek and Omaha. We'd made it through almost three hours of polite conversation, a feat I didn't know I could repeat on the return trip. It turned out that being friends with this man required an attention to detail I hadn't known I possessed. Turning to him, I forced eye contact and said, "I'm really grateful for this kindness, Tucker. I know you had to rearrange all sorts of stuff to make this happen today. So thank you."

He broke our gaze but not before I saw a smile form. "I know it's hard to believe, but spending time with you is a step up from drywall repair. Even if it's going to Nebraska."

I laughed, rolling my eyes. "You Midwesterners are so elitist." I pulled open my door before Tucker could point out the hypocrisy in those words coming from a recent New Yorker. We covered the distance to the front door, my pulse starting to quicken as I got closer to the next step in building my nascent business.

A woman with a pinched expression sat behind an oversize computer monitor. "May I help you?" she said. Her hair was impressive in its height. I must have stared too long because Tucker cleared his throat.

"Yes, we're here for some, um, fabric." Definitely the first time he'd uttered those words in his life, and I stepped in to rescue him.

"Yes," I said. "I believe my friend Luca Beneventi from Milano called? We're here to pick up the entire Ibiza collection."

The receptionist was smiling at Tucker, who had taken off his ball cap and was combing his fingers through a messy mop of hair. The effect seemed to mesmerize her.

"All of it," I said, too loudly, in an effort to make the woman look at me and not the hunk of burning love next to me. "Two hundred bolts, if I'm not mistaken."

The large number had the effect I wanted. She tipped her face to me, her expression skeptical. "The Ibiza? Are you sure you have the right name?"

"I'm sure," I said, smiling. "I know you've had it awhile, but I'm happy to take it off your hands."

"That's a whole lot of fabric for an elementary teacher or a 4-H project or whatever you're thinking." She pursed her lips and clacked a bunch of keys on her keyboard. She shook her head. "I'm going to need you to submit a written request for such a large comp order. My guess is your Luca person talked with my sub, Lorraine, who had no authority to make this decision." She raised her eyebrows and stared me down, willing me to defy her. I opened my mouth but Tucker intervened.

"Ma'am, I appreciate that you're doing your job. I own my own company and I know how important it is to have someone I can trust, particularly in your position. The face of the company, that is."

The face of the company looked up at him and batted every one of her mascara-heavy lashes.

An hour later, we were back on the road, all two hundred bolts snug and protected under the tarps in the back of Tucker's truck.

I shook my head again. "You were shameless with that woman." I took another lick of my ice cream. We'd stopped at Ted and Wally's, and I was happy to report the breathless hyperbole we heard from locals at a nearby gas station was based in truth not hype. My balsamic caramel blackberry was changing how I felt about the world, and Tucker's scoop of smoked salted bourbon Ho Hos (yes, Ho Hos) was making even a broad-shouldered construction king swoon.

Tucker swiped a spoonful of blackberry and swallowed thoughtfully. "Nah, not shameless. Just polite. People appreciate good manners these days."

My laugh wasn't dainty but it made my point. "Manners and eye candy. A deadly combo." I grinned at him. "Thanks for using your chiseled jaw to help me avoid paperwork. It was very gallant of you."

He scratched his head and looked pained. "You're welcome? Is that what I say to that? Good grief, Kleren. You can make a man blush."

I was enjoying watching him squirm. "I believe you have a forever fan in Blanche of Triad Fabrics." I returned to my ice cream and tried for a cavalier tone of voice. "The list of women who've fallen for Tucker Van Es gets longer by the day."

He polished off the end of his ice cream. "*My* list is actually pretty short." He stole a glance at me before shifting his gaze back to the road. "And stubborn."

I saw the half smile on his face and felt my stomach flip. "Well, I'm grateful that you didn't let our sordid past keep you from doing me a solid today. Thank—"

"Grace," he said firmly, taking his eyes off the road to seek out mine. "If you thank me one more time, I might have to toss my cookies. And

I don't want to do that, Grace. I just ate some incomprehensibly good ice cream, and I'd rather not ruin it."

I laughed at his intensity, which only made him scowl. "All right. I get it," I said. "As long as you know I'm grateful. I mean, you don't exactly owe me anymore. Now that we aren't a thing. Or not *that* thing, anyway. Now that I'm off the list." I cringed as soon as the last word was out of my mouth. I stared straight ahead, wishing my old tendency to ramble was one I'd left in New York.

A few moments into my self-berating, I realized Tucker's shoulders were shaking with laughter.

"What?" I demanded, still stinging with my utter failure to keep the conversational plates spinning.

"I just can't get over this new Grace. The one who is so careful with her words and worried she'll say the wrong thing." His eyes brimmed with mischief when he stole a glance in my direction. "It's a little odd, I must say."

I crossed my arms over my chest. "This is not the new me," I said, defensive. "This is the new Grace-with-Tucker-but-not-dating-Tucker me. I'm trying it out."

"How's it working?" He didn't even try to hide his grin.

I pursed my lips. "It's exhausting." I slumped in my seat while he laughed. I just let him have his moment. My dignity was in shards anyway.

After a minute or so, I said, "At least I have one consolation."

"What's that?" he asked through a smile that hadn't faded.

"At least I know my name was stubborn on that list of yours." I shrugged. "It feels pretty good to be a legend."

"Oh, I didn't say you were a legend necessarily," he said breezily as he changed lanes. "Just stubborn." He didn't turn to witness my frown but I was pretty sure he knew it was there. "Crazy stubborn. And I tried all sorts of things, I'll have you know."

"Like what?" I turned to watch Nebraska fly by my window, my heart picking up a bit of speed. I thought of Natalie the grocery goddess and her perfect figure and glossy hair and wondered where Tucker placed her on this list of his. I tilted my head and waited for his response, my body language conveying more bravado than I felt.

"Oh, let's see." Tucker sighed. "I went through a long angry-country-song phase, trying my best to replace any remaining hope that Stubborn Girl would find her way back to me with the more realistic emotion of anger. No dice. She stayed on the list."

I turned back to my window, watching the bright green of spring fields rush by in a wash of color.

"I tried hypnosis—"

I snapped my gaze back to his profile. "You did not."

He laughed. "You're right. I didn't. But I did pray a lot."

"You really did?" I said, curious.

"Sure, I did," he said easily. "I pray about most things, so stubborn women definitely make the list."

"Why?" I said, a little roughly. I tried more gently. "That is, why do you pray? What do you get out of it?"

He raised one eyebrow when he looked at me. "We're going there, then?"

I shrugged. "We have about three hours left in the car. Might as well tackle God while we're at it."

He chuckled. "Three hours might not do it, but we can take a stab at it." He stretched out a bit in his seat. "I pray to continue a conversation."

"A one-way conversation?" I said, not liking the bitterness that crept into my voice but deciding if we were doing this, I might as well be honest. "The last time I tried to pray in earnest, it felt distinctly one-way." A snapshot of myself curled up on my pink bedspread, my teenage self racked with grief, settled in my thoughts, and I felt anew how lonely one could feel when waiting for a distant God to break His silence.

He nodded slowly. "Sometimes it feels one-way. Often it doesn't." He paused. "Gracie, when was the last time you went to church?"

I looked out the window, rethinking my decision to be honest. The last time I had been inside a church was for my parents' funeral. The idea of walking through those doors again still made me feel sick. A God that would let the best people I'd ever known die was a God I wanted nothing to do with. I decided to dodge the question. "You don't have to go to church to believe in God, you know."

"Oh, I do know," he replied. "But church helps. It's just tough to do all this alone." Tuck let a long breath out through his nose, like he was trying to decide what else to say.

"What do you talk about?" I said more quietly. "When you pray, that is."

He considered before answering. "Whatever's on my mind. I'm better about bringing up problems, stuff with the business, things with my family, stubborn women." He looked at me out of the corner of his eye. "But I try to remember to be grateful too. I tend to be a spoiled brat, so I'm constantly trying to change that."

I shook my head. "Tucker, you are the farthest thing from a spoiled brat."

He sniffed. "That is called revisionist history. You're not remembering the whole story. Like the boy who waited in his run-down Chevy pickup on the street outside your house until you came home at midnight just so he could get one more kiss before sleep."

"Pretty much the kind of romance every girl dreams of."

He waved it away. "Needy and annoying. I know because my needy self sat all alone in that truck listening to Hank Williams and feeling sorry for myself that you had ditched me for your friends that night."

I giggled. "You sound angry."

"I still am. What a dork. And what about the time I picked a fight with you because you talked with Dan DePhillips during study hall and you knew Dan DePhillips had liked you since seventh grade?"

I was laughing. "I just saw Dan DePhillips last week. He's struggling with a receding hairline and a conversion van full of kids. You win."

"Not the point. I should have been the bigger man."

"You were sixteen!" I exclaimed. "Your spoiled brat evidence is pathetic. Rest your case."

"And what about," he said slowly, "when I let the girl of my dreams walk away and I was so busy nursing my pride, I did nothing to stop her?"

We sat in silence, the only sound coming from the truck as it hurtled us forward, the road slipping away in a long, uninterrupted line behind us.

I turned toward him. "That girl was unstoppable, I'm afraid. The whole stubborn thing was already an issue." I watched his profile, the flex of his jaw.

He shook his head. "I should have tried. I mean, I did try. Just in the wrong city. Chicago is a few miles from New York. Even a farm kid knows that." His grin was shaky and we looked at each other for a long time. So long, in fact, that he turned back to the road with a nervous laugh. "Better keep my eyes on the road if I'm going to get you and your fancy fabric back home safely."

I returned my gaze to the view outside my window, though reluctantly, and we made our way to Silver Creek. Gradually, the tenderness of our conversation faded and we eased into more safe and shallow waters. We listened to Tucker's beloved eighties mix, even after I made an apparently unconvincing demonstration of the superiority of Spotify in his fully loaded truck. He shook his head when I scrolled through the myriad station options and just reached over to turn up Bon Jovi, who was belting out "Livin' on a Prayer," a moment Tucker insisted was serendipity. Culture Club was on when we pulled off the interstate and onto the two-lane highway that would eventually lead us into the town square. We passed three abandoned farmhouses in a row and I reached over to turn down the music. I asked Tucker why there was so much emptiness in the acres we were passing.

"Large corporate farms have been swallowing up these smaller family farms for years," he said. "Lots of the smaller operations, like the one my uncle owns, need supplementing with other streams of income in order to stay afloat. Or they depend heavily on family to help keep things running." He pointed to a large long building that had a commercial real estate sign out front. "When the Atlantis factory moved operations overseas, that was another blow. Lots of jobs lost, lots of hurt people who'd worked there for decades, suddenly unemployed. This area hasn't recovered."

I stared at the empty building, lonely and vacant, long parking lot empty.

"Makes me sad to see things so lifeless. Silver Creek seems downhearted. I hear it in conversations all over town, and Gigi has talked about it too. The spunk is gone."

Tucker slowed as we entered town and turned onto Gigi's street. "We're not the only ones, either. The same story plays out over and over around here."

Gigi scurried out to the driveway when she heard the truck. "Did it work? Did you actually get it?"

"Thanks to some charm from Tucker Van Es here, we sure did," I said.

"Not true," Tucker mumbled, but Gigi wasn't

listening anyway. She was ogling the fabric under the tarp.

"Holy catfish, that's a lot of bolts," she said, suddenly somber. "We'll be sewing until I'm two steps from the grave."

I looked at her, hit with a thought. "Gigi," I said carefully, as if wary of frightening a barn swallow, "how long does it take you to sew a dress—not the kinds of alterations we've been doing, but from start to finish?"

Gigi thought, her breath coming out in a forceful exhale when she decided on an answer. "I'd say . . . a month?" She winced. "I never really kept track. I was mostly in it for the social aspect."

Tucker caught my eye but I ignored his smirk.

"A month?" I felt a blanket of dread descending. "One month per dress won't work." I ran my hand over the top bolt of fabric, wondering if we'd just made a long trip in vain. No business could survive making one product a month, no matter how unique the product, how vintage the material.

"Now, I must say," Gigi added, "I wasn't exactly moving at top speed. I would mostly work during Sewing Club."

"Sewing Club?" I asked, hand paused on the fabric. "You mean the ladies from church?"

"Every Tuesday night in the fellowship hall for years, until we decided to take a break last fall after a bad snowstorm. Just never started up again after the holidays." She looked at Tucker. "We rotated who brings snack."

Tucker nodded as if this were the most pertinent information. "Sounds fair. Just between you and me, Gigi"—he lowered his voice and looked around the neighborhood—"whose snack night did you do your best to avoid?"

Gigi didn't hesitate. "Myrna Hopkins. She took whatever was in her pantry and threw it on a plate." Gigi shuddered. "Any woman who thinks stale Wheat Thins and spray cheese can be dignified as a snack for a group of hungry women is deluding herself."

I tried to rein in the conversation from spray cheese. "Gigi," I said, impatient. "We need to troubleshoot here. One dress a month is about fifty dresses too few. Maybe worse." I held back for a beat, hoping this wasn't a nail in any sort of coffin to ask Gigi the question that might be too risky. "Gigi. Do those Sewing Club ladies still sew?"

"Of course," she said immediately. "It's like riding a bike. Only not as dangerous as one ages."

I was still processing when I saw Tucker standing with his arms crossed, his smile wide. "Gracie, it sounds like you've just found yourself a workforce."

Gigi's eyes got wide as the plan dawned on her.

"Moses," she said, the closest she came to cussing.

"It's a lot to ask," I admitted, worry already creasing my forehead. "Do you think they'll do it?"

"Of course they will," Gigi snapped, her sternness revealing just how sure she was. "You keep forgetting where you are, city girl. Around here, we help each other when help is needed." She started for the front porch, already feeling in her pocket for her cell phone. "Of course, we also gossip about you and shame you for your spray cheese, but you take the good with the bad, right, Tuck?"

"That we do, Miss Gigi," Tucker said, laughing.

I bit my lower lip as I watched Gigi let the screen door slam shut. "Oh man," I muttered. "I hope this works."

Tucker leaned against his truck and crossed long legs in front of him. I felt a spike of adrenaline watching him, his chin tipped up in thought, one hand running across his day-old beard. "It will work," he said finally. "Though the fellowship hall isn't going to be big enough."

I felt my forehead crease at this new worry. "It's not? What will we do? Where will—"

Tucker stopped my words with a wide, beautiful grin, a technique I found to be both disconcerting and rather effective. "I've got it," he said. He jogged around to the driver's side door and turned the key in the ignition. I could hear

Bonnie Tyler belting "Total Eclipse of the Heart" as he started to pull away.

"Wait," I called. I walked toward his moving vehicle. "What about the fabric?"

"Don't you trust me?" A roguish grin spread across his face.

"Totally," I said without reservation, then blushed at my ready response. I smiled tightly, glad he couldn't see the color of my cheeks in the gathering twilight.

"All right, then," he called back.

"Tucker," I said over Bonnie. "Listen, thank—"

"Don't do it, Kleren," he said in a warning voice before stepping on the gas and driving away.

fourteen

Five days later, Tucker and I walked through the grass, our shoes quickly covered in dew. The sun had just arched over the eastern fields. Shimmering light caught the droplets on the ground and on the leaves of a sprawling bur oak that reached for wispy clouds overhead. We passed the farmhouse in progress, and I glimpsed a finished porch floor, new since the time Tucker showed me the site a few weeks before. He nodded at a path ahead of us and led me farther onto the property.

Tucker reached the barn first and heaved open the two mammoth doors. When the creaking stopped, we stood side by side, watching the sunlight cut into the darkness. Tucker walked to one side and flipped a switch, causing the room to flood with light, and I inhaled sharply.

"Tuck," I said, my eyes greedily taking in the scene. "This is perfect."

The Sewing Club ladies were set to arrive within the hour for our first day of work, and a beautiful work space would be here to greet them. Tucker had told me not to worry, advice

I had completely ignored, but he turned out to be utterly trustworthy. Over the weekend he'd tweaked the space inside this barn to be a perfect spot for dressmaking. Long tables stood in rows, each already set up with the sewing machines I'd gathered from the ladies over the last few days. Each workstation had ample overhead and desk light, rolling drawers for supplies, and clean, weathered plank flooring underneath comfortable office chairs. A lump formed in my throat when I saw each station had a Ball jar filled with a small bouquet of farm flowers.

Without pausing to think, I reached for him and buried my face in his chest. The good, clean smell of him was familiar and warm and I felt a lump form in my throat. "You got them flowers," I said.

I could feel him shrug slightly as he hugged me back. "Girls like pretty stuff," he said, sounding embarrassed.

"Thank you," I said, my face still in his chest. "I am in your debt. Huge. Really big. Scary big."

He laughed softly. "Well, if all it takes is a few extension cords and picking some flowers for you to feel like that, I think I'm the winner here."

Gigi knocked on the big white door leading into the room and we moved away from each other quickly, dropping our arms to our sides and jumping back a step as if burned. But Gigi only had eyes for the barn and its facelift.

"Tucker Van Es, you have outdone yourself." She shook her head as she entered the room, her eyes traveling upward to the high beams of the ceiling. She seemed lost in a memory, and after a moment she smiled at Tuck. "Your uncle ever tell you what used to happen in this barn?"

He nodded. I was likely the only one who would ever notice, but his cheeks were a bit pinker than normal. His face was somber, and he studiously avoided looking in my direction, training his eyes instead on the room. "Miss Gigi, he certainly did. Those stories were a big part of why I took on this property in the first place."

"What stories?" I asked. I walked to one of the tables and set down my bag and a folder of design instructions. "I want the stories."

Gigi walked slowly to the perimeter of the room, her hand running lightly on the white-washed walls. "This is the old Morrison barn. The Morrisons were a lively family, six kids and all the happy chaos that suggests. When I was a girl, they were famous for hosting dances and parties in this barn."

I'm sure my eyes lit up with this information, because Gigi frowned at me. "Now, don't start asking about the level of scandal. There wasn't any."

Tucker raised his eyebrows, a grin playing on his lips.

"Okay, fine," she conceded. "There was a little

scandal. But mostly dancing and laughing and more dancing till the wee hours." She pointed at me. "Your grandfather and I had some lovely times in this barn."

"In or out of the hayloft?" Tucker asked, and she swatted him as she walked by, her gait back to business and firmly off memory lane.

"I will not be dignifying that with a response," she said, chin up.

"So in the loft," he said, loudly enough that I could hear. I giggled and we glanced at each other. I let my gaze linger and swallowed hard when he did the same.

We heard the chatter before we could see them.

"They're here," Gigi said, and led us to the source of the noise. Walking three astride to the entrance of the barn, we saw The Ladies. They made their way toward us, arms linked.

"Morning," Tucker called out as he strode toward them. "I know none of you needs a hand, but a gentleman always offers."

I smiled as they clucked over him, clearly charmed with a boy they'd known who was now a handsome man. They stopped in front of the barn, facing me with open faces and warm smiles. I started at the right and went down the line, hugging each of them in turn.

Goldie was first, and she finished our embrace with a slap on my tush. The twins were there, wearing matching embroidered sweatshirts, one that rooted for the Iowa Hawkeyes and one for the Iowa State Cyclones. Myrna Hopkins was next, and I recognized her as a front door greeter from church, every Sunday growing up. She held out the hand I'd shaken many times before but pulled me into a quick, efficient embrace right away. "You look just like your sweet mom," she whispered into my ear before letting me go. Edna Kuiken had worked as an English teacher in our high school for years, even while raising five children on a farm. I remembered her as a ruthless grader, but she took both my hands in hers and said, "I'm so glad to be here, honey. Sometimes a crossword puzzle just doesn't do it for me." She stepped back and shook her head, gathering a full image of me, head to toe. "I helped potty train you in the church nursery, Grace Kleren. And now look! A fancy New York designer!"

Tucker bit a cheek to halt a grin but the orneriness in his expression was firmly planted in seventh grade. "That Grace Kleren," he said with appreciation. "She always was a quick study."

The women were tsking in disapproval of his uncouth talk, with the exception of Goldie, who was egging him on.

"To that end, ladies," he continued, still working the smile downward. He pointed to a door in a corner of the room. "We do have a rest-room and it's not even a porta potty."

The women murmured in appreciation and

184

Myrna Hopkins called out, "Tucker Van Es, a restroom is the least you owe us. Several of the women here were the ones who held you down while your aunt Jane, God rest her, pulled three wasp stingers out of your rear end when you were a little, screaming terror. So, yes. I'd say you owe us a beautiful, clean restroom." She winked at me. "Grace, honey, don't you worry. There are lots more stories where that one came from."

The ladies nodded, and several started in on their favorite Tucker Van Es stories. He clapped his hands before raising them in defense. "Right. So that's my cue to leave here, probably for good." He turned to go, tipping his ball cap at the ladies and smiling sheepishly at me, but Goldie stopped him with a rhinestone-heavy hand. She looked up at him, tugged him closer to her.

"Before you go, Tucker, I think I speak for all of us when we say thank you to you both." She reached for my hand and stood between us, patting our arms affectionately. "Tucker, you made this place so pretty, just the kind of spot where we want to come and work. And, Grace." She paused, her dark blue eyes shining. "Thank you for involving us in this dream of yours. We're honored to be here, and we will give you our best." She squeezed my arm and said, quietly enough that only Tucker and I heard, "It feels good for us old ladies to be called into action. You see us, Gracie."

I felt my eyes sting, and when I glanced up at Tucker's face, I saw him looking at me in a way that made my heart jump.

"To the youngsters!" Goldie said, and though we held nothing to toast, no other moment in my life had held such a resounding ring of celebration.

The women took turns hugging me and giving me a peck on the cheek. I laughed and allowed myself to be kissed and hugged but stopped, suddenly thrown together with Tucker in the center of the circle. He cleared his throat, eyes on mine, and said, "To work, then."

I nodded, trying to find my voice but discovering the way he was looking at me a distinct impediment to productivity. "To work."

"Where do you want us, Grace?" Myrna sounded like she was ready to be unleashed.

Tucker smiled a small smile, the spell broken, and he turned toward the open barn doors and soft light of morning.

I shook my head and smoothed my hair as Tucker walked away, the look on his face still with me and a complete and total distraction to the huge day that lay before me, before all of us. Not exactly the most professional way to begin a business venture, but I had to admit it was a lot more interesting than my cubicle at Milano.

"All right, brave women of Silver Creek," I said, standing straight and steeling myself to the real task at hand. I turned toward them, finding their eager smiles contagious. "Shall we begin?"

Two hours later, I took a break. Leaning against a support beam, a cold bottle of water just plucked from a stocked cooler Tucker had left at the back of the room, I took it all in and shook my head, not for the first time. The women had scooted all the tables closer to each other, meeting at the center in a beehive of activity. They knew each other well, including individual strengths and weaknesses, so they'd quickly determined who would be best at which tasks. By unanimous vote, Myrna was given the job of cutter. She was the most particular, the most organized, the most experienced, and irrespective of her fondness for spray cheese, the ladies all agreed she would be the best person for the most high-stakes of the jobs. Edna would be the serger, finishing all the edges, Bev would be setting in sleeves, her twin would be next to her doing side seams, and Goldie would be putting in zippers. Gigi, also unanimously elected, would be the director of operations and would keep the entire production line working under her watchful and exacting supervision. I'd known Gigi as the director of operations for many years, so I felt giddy at the idea of her manning this part of the ship.

The women quickly settled into a rhythm of their own, and I largely stayed out of the way after giving a tutorial on three garments. Myrna clucked regularly about the inappropriately low neckline on two of the three designs, and Goldie responded every time with her feelings that the neckline should be lower. Gigi had to interrupt every now and then with a bark to stop yapping and get back to business, but in general, I'd never seen a production line hum along with such efficiency.

I listened to their chatter as Goldie finished a humdinger of a story about her husband, Frank, and his ongoing trouble with a particular tele-marketer. The twins hunched over their sewing machines at exactly the same angle, their shoulders shaking in the same way as they laughed at Goldie's theatrics. Myrna frowned, absorbed in her cutting, but Edna had to stop sewing for a minute to dab her eyes, the laughter getting to be too much.

Gigi saw me staring and she put down a spool of thread and came to stand next to me. After a beat she nudged me.

"This just might work."

I shook my head again. "It really might. Who knew?"

Myrna looked up and frowned at us. "I'm assuming you two are on your way back here to help us out? Lunch break isn't until noon, as I recall."

Gigi sniffed and I grinned. "Sorry, Miss

Myrna," I said as I walked back to my table, practically bouncing as I stepped. "I was just taking in the view."

Myrna snorted. "I can't imagine a bunch of old ladies sitting in a barn is anything compared to where you've been living."

I threaded a new spool into my machine. "Don't underestimate just how stunning you are, Miss Myrna," I said, and out of my periphery I saw her lift her head and look around, trying to see what I saw.

fifteen

I pulled Gigi's minivan into a parking spot in front of the Silver Creek post office and turned down the radio when old Mr. McNeely glared as he tottered by. I tried for my most winsome smile, but that man had never liked me after Tucker snipped a handful of his peonies for an impromptu bouquet for me on a walk toward Azalea Street. That this offense had occurred three presidential administrations ago did not make my smile any more winning to Mr. McNeely, who, as I remember, had required Tuck to do all his spring mulching that year as payback, standing over him the entire time and grousing about how he wasn't doing it right.

I chuckled at the memory and retrieved the two shipping boxes from the passenger seat. When I pushed through the door to the post office, hustling to make it before it closed promptly at five o'clock, a bell chimed to announce my arrival. Miss Evelyn took the boxes from me without a word and weighed and stamped the package. She ran my credit card and I signed for it, all in less than a minute.

We grinned at each other across the counter. "That might just be a personal best," Miss Evelyn said, and I returned her high five.

"We're pretty much professionals at this," I agreed, and waved her to a good evening as I turned the sign on her door to "Closed." I hadn't stepped both feet onto the sidewalk when I saw a familiar ball cap from behind a windshield. The truck came to a stop, double-parked in front of the post office, and Tucker swung out of it. He grinned at me as he weaved his way through a line of parked cars.

He stopped in front of me, eyes lit up with, if I wasn't mistaken, a familiar mix of mischief and hope.

"Good evening, Grace."

I raised an eyebrow. "Good evening, Tucker." I waited, saying nothing to the half smile that appeared.

"Listen." He bit his lower lip as he considered his next words. "Are you busy right now? You're not, are you?"

I must have looked surprised because he barreled on.

"Let me try that again." He stepped a bit closer, eyes fully on mine. I felt a sudden chill run down my spine. I'd forgotten what it felt like to have Tucker Van Es's full attention. There was, I remembered in a rush, nothing else quite like it.

"Grace," he said, voice low. "I would really

like it if you would go out with me tonight. On a date," he added for clarity, eyes on me.

My heart was beating in the exact same rhythm it had fifteen years before, when, standing by my locker, Tucker asked me out for the very first time. I answered the same way I had then.

"Are you sure you can handle me?" I searched his eyes, looking for a hint of hesitation. I found none. I decided to ask the question I was burning to know. "What about Natalie?"

"What about her?"

"I take it she's in Des Moines tonight?"

Tucker looked hard at me, a frown quickly pulling at his mouth. "I'm not sure where Natalie is tonight," he said in a measured tone. "But I can see the old Gracie is back. Not a lot of beating around the bush, then?"

I could feel heat in my cheeks. I shrugged, feigning nonchalance. "I know I'm late to the party, that's all. I don't want to get in the way of your other relationships."

He snorted. "That sounds very New York and very not–Grace Kleren." He paused. "You're serious?"

"I saw the way she looked at you next to the brussels sprouts. She might be in love with you."

He sniffed. "Not likely." When he saw the look on my face, he conceded. "Okay, fine. She might be a little in love. But she also has a hard time listening, that's for sure."

Satisfied with his answer, I asked, "So again, are you sure you can handle me?"

His eyes showed a mix of relief and amusement. He offered me his hand. I took it and noticed it was warm and strong. "Pretty darn sure." We walked hand in hand to his truck, and he opened the door for me.

I took in a deep breath and let it out slowly in the few seconds I had alone in the cab while he walked around the truck. *This is happening,* I thought, my heart still pounding. He was grinning, even waved to a passing car that had to pull into the opposite lane to get around Tucker's illegally parked truck.

When he swung up into the driver's seat, I turned to him and tried to act like the answer to my question didn't matter as much as it did.

"So are you sure it's over with Natalie?" I said, wanting to hear him say it.

"Very sure."

He was making a series of turns but I was too keyed into what he was saying to care where we were going.

"Explain, please."

We pulled onto a side street and he drove more slowly, both hands gripping the steering wheel. "Erin's the one who set us up, a few months ago. This place is not like the city," he said, a little rough. "The pool of dating partners is a fixed number around here. Natalie and I both knew

Erin well enough to have her set us up and I guess I weakened. I broke it off the moment I knew I'd rather be on my man couch than go on another date with her."

I burst out laughing. "Tucker, you have nothing to explain to me." I noticed it pained me a bit to say these words, but when the images of my own dating life passed through my thoughts, I had no self-righteousness left. "I don't blame you a bit. Natalie's a beautiful girl. A beautiful, smart girl who is friends with our class valedictorian. She's clearly taken with you, Tuck. And she is, notably, here."

"What about you?" He glanced at me out of the corner of his eye. "It's going to be tough to compete with the epic romances I've experienced during the last ten years, but you can do your best." The somber expression in his eyes didn't match his attempt at humor.

I sighed. "Oh, you know. I dated. Here and there." I paused, long enough for Tucker to start drumming his fingers on the steering wheel.

"Anyone recent?" he asked, an unnatural lilt to his tone.

"Not really. Except maybe James." I said his name, and it sounded foreign to me after what felt like such a long time since I'd last seen him in the offices at Milano. "James was a maybe, but nothing much more than that. He was, um, kind of my boss."

Tucker winced. "Dang."

"Right," I said. I picked at the threads on my shirt, trying out the words in my head before they made it to my mouth. "Nothing happened, really. A lot of flirting and a lot of wondering, but nothing we really acted on. We were just starting to think about the possibility of us, actually, but then things fell apart at Milano." I turned to him, hoping I sounded brave and confident. "He's the one who packed up my desk and did the official firing. So we haven't exactly kept in touch."

Tucker frowned. "What a total idiot."

I smiled. "I appreciate your loyalty."

He slowed to a stop on a residential street, parking under a cherry tree in full bloom. A breeze lifted the branches and dropped a shower of pink petals onto the windshield. Tucker turned to face me, his brows knitted together. He started to speak but then closed his mouth. A small smile formed. "Erin wasn't our valedictorian. Hunter Olsen was. But she gave the graduation speech because Hunter had a massive anxiety attack in the locker room beforehand and Principal Matthews had warned Erin to be ready."

"Seriously?" I shook my head in disbelief. "I don't remember any of that."

He opened his door and stepped out. "That's because we left the ceremony early to go hill jumping."

I winced as he came to open my door. "I can't

believe we did that. It is so dangerous. Driving like lunatics on gravel roads, just to get some air on the hills? We were totally reckless. We could have killed someone."

He shook his head. "Nah. Everyone else was at graduation."

I laughed and let him take both of my hands and gently pull me to stand before him. His touch felt like electricity.

"Everything does tend to feel a little reckless with you around, Kleren. That's true." His smile was sly, and I was having a hard time remembering to breathe, standing this close to him. "I seem to remember things starting out that way from the beginning." He nodded behind me, and when I followed his gaze, I realized where we were.

I smiled. Below us, set into the hill on the edge of town, lay the Silver Creek High School Stadium. When the town was still flush with railroad cash years before, the council had done generations beyond a favor by building what was the prettiest football field and track within a hundred miles. The seating curved into the hill, bordered by red brick and what, by fall, was a riot of ivy crawling up its old walls. I took in the view, the beautiful old structure, immaculately cared for and still standing proud guard on the edge of a town that would never be able to afford such an indulgence now.

Tucker handed me a blanket before hefting a wicker basket from the back of his truck. He nodded toward the field, sheepish.

"Thought we might try again. I know the guy who's in charge of the sprinkler system, so we won't have that surprise this time."

I shook my head, totally charmed by his gesture. "I don't remember minding getting soaked. It added to the adventure."

He took my hand as we walked down the hill toward the stadium. "You're rewriting history, sis. It was the end of November and that water was *cold*."

I laughed at the memory. "We were kids. Cold didn't even touch us."

Tucker produced a key from his jeans pocket and opened the lock on the tall wrought-iron gates leading into the stadium. We walked silently onto the perfectly trimmed grass, its Technicolor green heralding the hard-won warmth of an Iowa spring. We set up on the fifty-yard line as the sun dipped behind the mountain of bleachers.

"Well, now, this spread is a few steps upward from our first date." My mouth watered as I dropped to my knees on the plaid blanket. "I mean, the PBJs and cans of Mr. Pibb were wonderful. But, Tuck, when did you learn how to do this?"

Tucker retrieved two paper plates and started

filling them with pulled pork sandwiches. He added a bright green salad topped with Granny Smith apples, wedges of white cheddar, and sugared almonds before pointing to bowls of strawberries and grapes. "We have some of Mac Svendahl's garage-fried kettle chips too, if that suits your fancy."

I took my first bite of the sandwich and made a noise that would have been deemed inappropriate by every one of our high school teachers. "Seriously. When did you learn how to cook like this?"

Tucker's laugh was low, his face unable to hide how pleased he was with my compliment. "Like I said: lots of time alone with the man couch. At a certain point, a person needs to eat."

We covered all sorts of history, both the ancient and shared, as well as the new and still smarting. Tucker told me about his work, how he reveled in seeing a project take shape, how he loved dreaming and creating and working hard and falling into bed at night, satisfied with a job done well. He loved seeing his ideas come to life and making his clients happy. I heard all sorts of echoes from my own design experience, and I told him about my daily life in New York, the work that inspired me, the work that sapped me. We talked about the dresses Gigi and I were making and shipping, and I laughed as Tucker dreamed bigger than I'd dared, how he started running numbers and making projections about how Gigi and I could expand and grow something that was still just the size of a seed.

We talked about my parents. How I ached for them still, how he'd mourned too, quietly and in a teenage, inarticulate way. I didn't stop the tears from their paths down my cheeks, not feeling the need to censor or change the sadness. Tucker said nothing as I cried, just moved our dirty plates out of the way so he could sit closer. And when the tears stopped and I took a deep breath in, then out, he made me laugh hard with a story about Erin Jackson's husband, Les, who had recently had an unfortunate incident involving a tractor wheel and his brand-new Harley.

The stars were out in full force when Tucker stood to stretch. He pulled me to my feet and we stood together, the star-littered sky our only light but more than enough to see each other's faces. Tuck turned suddenly serious as he gathered me into a hug.

"Are you cold?" he said softly, sending a ripple down my spine.

I shook my head, eyes on his. "No complaints. Thanks for turning off the sprinklers. This is a better ending."

A half smile flickered before disappearing again. His arms held me and I relaxed into them, noticing he was stronger, taller even than when

I'd fallen into these arms so many times years before. I swallowed hard, feeling his gaze pull me closer.

"Gracie," he said, his voice gruff. "It wasn't just the man couch."

I shook my head slightly, momentarily disoriented. "There's something wrong with your couch?"

"The couch is awesome," he said, "but not so awesome that it made me break up with Natalie." He looked a little at war with himself before speaking again. "It's you. That's what made me break up with Natalie."

I shook my head, forming a protest, but Tucker interrupted me.

"I don't blame you for going to New York, Grace. You needed to move away. You needed more than this place, and I know that." He shrugged, arms still wrapped around me. "I just wanted you to know the truth. It's you. Nobody has come close, so I stick with the couch." His grin was lopsided and completely, utterly him. "Full disclosure."

I leaned in and laid my cheek on his chest, my heart racing, but unable to return the favor with my whole, unfettered truth: no one had come close to Tuck either. Out of a city of millions, even with a thousand miles between us, Tucker Van Es was the only one whose face kept me up at night, who visited me in dreams, who made my heart stop when thoughts of him, unbidden, interrupted my days.

I took a moment before turning again to face him.

"Partial disclosure," I said, and he laughed.

"I'll take that."

I swallowed, gathering my courage. My relationships in New York hadn't required much of me, I realized. I was sorely out of practice with this kind of conversation. "You still make my heart flip and my stomach tremble and all the things that can make a girl miserable when she thinks about a boy she likes."

He grinned. "Perfect. I like this disclosure. Physical sickness is a great sign."

I shook my head, not finished. "You know me really well. And you still like me," I said.

Tucker pulled me closer. "Is it that obvious?" he said, and then kissed me, sweetly, perfectly, with a heady cocktail of tenderness and longing. I kissed him back, long and full, underneath a blanket of stars. He held me close and I felt happier than I'd felt in such a long time. I looked at him, watched his eyes light with mischief and affection, and then closed my eyes as he kissed me again, and I wondered just how much of my partial disclosure was being made crazily, recklessly full.

sixteen

Two weeks later, Gigi and I sat in her driveway, depleted after a long day at the barn. We listened without speaking as the minivan cooled down from our ride home. With the windows down, I heard the engine tick and eventually lose the sound battle with a noisy cricket who was giving a performance near the front porch.

"That breeze feels nice," Gigi said, and I murmured my agreement.

"Summer is so pretty here," I said. "It's amazing how much better sun can feel when it's not baking acres of concrete."

Gigi narrowed her eyes at me. "You're starting to sound like a crusty old Midwesterner."

I laughed. "Pretty soon I'll start complaining about the Chickadee's outlandish price hikes and that Martin should know anything over a dollar for a cup of coffee is straight-up robbery."

Gigi opened her door. "I thought I was going to throttle Myrna today if she said one more word on the subject."

I joined Gigi outside the car as she walked to the mailbox, stretching my tired arm and shoulder muscles as I moved. Gigi talked a big talk, and Myrna had admittedly gotten stuck on a loop of coffee inflation, but I knew we had a special thing going. I'd felt plenty of exhaustion in the last decade, but this was a different kind of tired. This tired had the craziest effect of energizing me after a long day of work. The women in Tucker's barn were making me more excited, not less excited, to be doing what we were doing together. I rolled a kink out of my neck as Gigi sifted through the stack of envelopes, and I was struck again at how good it could feel to have every bone in my body in need of rest.

Gigi looked up at the sound of her name and she groaned softly. "Moses," she said, and I followed her gaze.

Miss Evelyn was scurrying toward us, one hand waving while the other clutched a sheet of white paper.

"That woman covers ground like a person half her age," I said through my smile.

"True enough," Gigi said, arms crossed with the stack of mail pinned to her chest. "To our peril."

"Evening, you two entrepreneurs," Miss Evelyn called when she was still three houses away. "I'm so glad I ran into you."

Gigi grunted. "How are you, Evelyn?" I marveled at her ability to make small talk, when

I was certain she was ready for a good porch sit and a glass of iced tea.

"I'm just fine, Georgina, but who really cares about that?" Miss Evelyn's eyes shone as she pushed the piece of paper she was holding into the space between us. "I want the celebrities to sign my copy."

I recognized the banner at the top of the printout and felt a flutter in my pulse. I took the paper and gasped. "They actually did it," I said softly, already scanning the article.

"Who did what?" Gigi asked. She peeked over my shoulder. "What's *Catwalk*?"

"It's an online fashion magazine that's all the rage right now." I was speaking quickly but my brain was still racing ahead of my words. "*Catwalk* is like a real-time account of what's on trend in the fashion world. Everyone follows them. Our publicist at Milano used to fall all over herself just to get a lunch with the *Catwalk* staff. Their blessing can skyrocket a product or a line or a single garment to success." My eyes shone as I pointed to the article. "And they did a story about us."

Miss Evelyn recited the headline. " 'Your Favorite Summer Dress Ever . . . Made in Iowa?' You're putting our town on the map, Grace Kleren! Our state!" Evelyn's hands were flapping as she gestured down the street. "We should have a parade!"

"Have mercy, Evelyn," Gigi said, but she was smiling. "That's a bit much."

I stared at the article, still stunned. "A writer emailed me with some questions, and she asked for a photo, but I never thought she'd actually write it up. I didn't think we'd make the cut. There's so much competition for coverage."

Gigi had taken the paper and was scrutinizing the photo. After a moment, she gave it back to me. "Not a bad photo," she decided. "We look happy."

Miss Evelyn and I looked at the pic together. We really *did* look happy. I'd snapped a selfie with my phone a few days before the writer had emailed, and, assuming it would never find its way into the magazine anyway and far too busy to consider making a more formal attempt at a photo, I'd sent it onward. I laughed to myself, thinking of the thousands and thousands of dollars typically spent on a fashion photo shoot, and how my freebie, taken during a coffee break, was the one that made *Catwalk*.

I hugged both women to me, which was a feat considering I was also jumping up and down. "I can't believe we are in *Catwalk*!" I said into Evelyn's perm.

Evelyn squealed. "I can't wait to spread the word!"

Gigi slipped out of my hug. "All right, all

right." She rearranged her mail and started for the porch. "I'm starting dinner. You two can keep jumping on the sidewalk."

"I'll help," I called, giving Miss Evelyn a last celebratory side hug before walking up to the house.

"Good night, you two," Evelyn called. "I can't stay. I have a lot of phone calls to make."

Gigi rolled her eyes at me. She tugged on the front porch door and held it while I stepped through. "That woman just might do what she threatens and organize a parade."

I giggled, light-headed with the news. "We're already having a hard time keeping up with orders. This is going to make it even more of a challenge. I should check my phone and see what's happening on Etsy."

"No phones," she said suddenly. She turned my shoulders toward the stairs. "You talked all the way home about how badly you wanted to sit in the claw-foot and take a long, hot bath. So go do it."

I protested. "You're tired too. I can help with dinner and take a bath afterward."

She shook her head quickly. "Not an option. I'm getting bossy tonight. Go." With a little more prodding, she had me on the stairs.

"But—"

She put up one hand as she walked away from me. "Go. Don't argue with a famous person."

● ● ●

When I descended the stairs an hour later, I felt the delicious contentment that comes after a good soak with too many bubbles. I'd slipped into a long sundress, an early mock-up of a new design I'd been tinkering with at the barn. The fabric fell like water and moved with the same effortlessness. I had a feeling the deep blue was a good pairing with my skin and the tumble of hair I no longer attempted to straighten in the growing humidity of an Iowa summer. Curls and waves won the battle starting about this time in June and would be the victors until September, if memory served. I caught a glimpse of my reflection in the mirror at the bottom of the stairs and I saw myself smiling. I was right about the dress. I made a mental note to start on the pattern later that night.

When I rounded the corner into the kitchen, I took a long and indulgent inhale. "Gigi, it smells heavenly in here." I walked to the stove, where she was stirring. "You made your Bolognese?" I sighed happily. "You really love me."

"I really do," she said, then took a sip off the end of her wooden spoon. "I loved you all the way to last weekend, when I let this simmer for about six hours before freezing it, all ready to break out on a night when we wanted to celebrate but were too tired to cook. I think tonight fits the bill." She wiped her hands on a dish towel and turned to appraise me. She nodded and said, "Good work. You look nice."

"Do you like it?" I turned, showing her the side profile. "I'm thinking we could use that sapphire silk for—"

"No work talk." She handed me a candle and matches and nudged me toward the back door. "We're eating outside. Light this for me, will you?"

She was so intent on hurrying me outside, I didn't have a chance to answer. The light was beginning to take on the buttery yellow of dusk, and when my eyes adjusted, I took a sharp breath. Tucker was standing under the branches of Gigi's maple, one hand holding a drink and the other shoved in his pocket.

"Wow," he breathed, taking me in. "Gracie, you look, um, really beautiful."

I crossed the distance between us giddily and joined him under the strings of lights Gigi had draped in the branches of the tree. "And you look rather beautiful too," I said before kissing him on the cheek. Tucking my nose into his neck, I murmured my approval. He smelled of cedarwood and fresh-cut grass. "And you smell delicious." I pulled back and looked at his face, one that I was daydreaming about more often than not. "Is this our new thing, then? You show up for dinner looking all spiffy, complicit with my grandma but not letting me know beforehand?"

His smile said I'd nailed it. "What fool would turn down a dinner invitation from the two most beautiful women in town? If I have to keep secrets with your grandma, so be it."

I shook my head. "Outnumbered again. I have no power in this small but mighty town." He stopped my grumbling with a soft kiss.

After a moment, he pulled away. His eyes were bright. "How was your day?"

"Unbelievable," I said, and launched into a breathless account of our *Catwalk* coup. Gigi soon joined us and placed steaming plates of pasta on the patio table. She handed each of us a glass and announced that we were celebrating the success of Flyover.

"Flyover?" Tucker said, his eyes already twinkling.

Gigi grinned. "Do you like it?"

I raised my glass. "To Flyover. Taking back the name and putting Silver Creek in the spotlight it deserves."

We toasted, and Tucker caught my eye as the drink cooled my throat. I smiled at him, taking in his face, the way he looked at me, the way he made me feel lovely and smart and like the only person in every room we shared.

He cleared his throat, suddenly serious. "I'm so proud of you," he said, first to me, and then, remembering himself, turning to Gigi. "Of both of you."

Gigi's laugh rang over us, a musical duo with the rush of the breeze in the leaves above. "Tucker, you are sweet to involve an old woman in your compliments, but you and I both know I am not the main attraction here tonight." She raised her eyebrows at him, and he grinned.

"Miss Gigi, nothing happens around here without your blessing, and you know it. No need to wonder."

They bantered back and forth, and I soaked it all in, fully satisfied with the day, the night, the company, the food. Not around the tables of the most exotic and sought-after restaurants in New York, I was sure, was there this satiating mix of joy and happy weariness of life lived well and in community. I closed my eyes, listening to the lively conversation enveloping me, and found myself trying out the thought that God was real, and that He was capable of giving really good gifts. *Not* only *taking those good gifts away,* I added quickly, sure from wrenching experience that the taking away was His to claim too. But perhaps there was more to it, more to Him than I'd allowed myself to wonder in a long while. I felt a small smile form. *Surprise, surprise,* I thought, opening my eyes and looking at Gigi. *You'd never know it, but the girl who talks tough is also thinking about God, right under your nose.*

I was turning around my own surprise at my

covert musings when my phone rang within the house.

"Good gracious," Gigi said, pushing back her chair with annoyance. "That thing never shuts off. It's the third time it's rung since we got out here."

"I'll get it," I said, rising to my feet. The last time I'd asked Gigi to turn off my phone, she'd ended up punching a series of numbers that caused effects I was still puzzling over. I bounded up the steps to the kitchen and grabbed the phone off the counter. I'd turned and was walking back to the table when I stopped, midstride, the porch door slapping shut behind me.

My eyes widened and I felt a rush of adrenaline course through me. I held up the phone, which had gone quiet for a bit but then began to ring again. Offering it as if evidence, I said, disbelief in my voice, "It's James."

seventeen

I swiped to answer the call. "James?" After our rather public good-bye, I hadn't heard one word from him, and I couldn't imagine what would possess him to call now.

"Grace! Hello!" He sounded triumphant. "I'm so glad to finally reach you. I've been trying for the last two hours, nonstop. Cell service a little rough in the great beyond, eh?" He laughed, but it sounded forced.

I looked at Tucker, who was watching me from his seat at the table, candlelight flickering on his face. Gigi caught my eye and narrowed hers. I'd made rough sketches of James to Tucker, but Gigi had a fuller picture of those last few weeks in New York, including James's notable silence after the Milano debacle. I could see the skepticism fall over her expression.

"How can I help you?" I said, hoping the cold reception would remind him of a helpful Target associate, not a former eager flirting partner and employee.

"Well," he said, drawing out the word, "I have some news. And a proposal."

I broke my gaze with Tucker and walked a bit into the backyard. Tucker within reach and James's voice in my ear was a pairing that was freaking me out. "I'm listening," I said when James didn't continue.

"Great. That's great." I could hear relief in his voice. "I just want you to listen. I've left Milano."

"You left?" I sputtered, trying to imagine a Milano without James and a James without Milano. They were so connected in my mind and in my experience, I could barely comprehend what he was saying. "When? Why?"

"The day after you left, actually," he said. "I'd been trying to get up my nerve for months. I'd been working on a side project in off-hours, really loving what I was doing, and Milano had become a place where I was paid well but not thriving at all. Let's just say Nancy and I had creative differences. Perhaps you can identify."

I paused, waiting for him to continue.

"So," he said when I said nothing, "when I saw how Nancy treated you and how crazy she was to let you go, I realized I was done there. It was time to jump ship."

"Wow," I said, mind reeling. "Sounds terrifying."

He laughed. "It was. But it was definitely the right decision. I know that more every day."

"That's wonderful," I said. "I'm happy for you, James." I said it slowly, wondering what on earth his Oprah lightbulb moment had to do with me.

"Actually," James said, as if reading my thoughts, "this whole story is the reason for my call. Grace, I'm starting my own line, and I want you to be a part of it."

I could hear Tucker and Gigi talking quietly, but with the roar in my ears I didn't register a word they were saying. "I don't understand."

"I've leased a space in the Garment District. I have a full team of people, many from Milano who followed me and my vision. We are creating a full line of women's everyday and evening. I'm calling it Saffron, and I want your new company—your new *genius* company—to be a part of it."

"Wait," I said. I was pacing, my free hand on my forehead. "You want my dresses? Our dresses?"

"Absolutely," he said without hesitation. "You're on to something phenomenal. The fabrics, the silhouettes, the easy elegance, the grannies, everything. I love it all. And I'm not alone, as you know. Congrats on the *Catwalk* piece, by the way." His laugh was a low rumble in my ear. "Iowa girl makes good, Miss Kleren. The whole story is, well, seductive."

I felt my pulse quicken, his words seeping into my parched NYC pride, still injured and smarting months after our last conversation. "I've found a great team here," I said. "We've hit on something really fantastic. And I love it."

"That's wonderful. Grace." His words were coming fast, urgent. "Come back. I'll give Flyover full financial backing, and I'm in the position to do what you need to grow this company. I have a seat on United on hold for you right now. Just say the word and get on the plane tomorrow. I'll do everything else."

I realized I needed to blink. My eyes had widened so big and for so long, I had forgotten to blink. *Get it together, Kleren,* I thought, eyes on the blue-black grass under my sandals. The lights strung in Gigi's tree were far behind me now. "Will it still be my company?"

"Yes." He spoke decisively. "Totally yours, just under the larger paradigm of Saffron."

"What about my design authority? My vision?"

"That's what I love most. Your ideas, your vision, your designs—we want it all. You have the final word on everything."

I looked up then, my view filled with a sky full of summer starlight. "What about my team? The grandmas are a deal breaker. They stay or I'm out." My heart was hammering in my chest, knowing this was a big ask, one that could topple the whole deal before I set one foot in New York.

"The grannies stay," James said firmly. "They are the heart of the company and of the whole narrative. They're a huge part of why this works."

My throat constricted and I struggled to speak.

"Everyone is going to love the grannies." He laughed.

"Thanks for seeing that, James."

He waited a beat, and when he spoke again, he sounded like he was fighting some emotion. "Grace, I need you here. Please come and make this so much better than what it could ever be without you."

When I returned to the table I bypassed my seat completely and sat instead on Tucker's lap. I took his face in my hands and kissed him loudly. "Guess what?" I said, beaming. "James wants us."

Tucker raised one eyebrow. "If this is the James you've mentioned before, I'm afraid I don't want him. Thanks, but no thanks."

I laughed, feeling a lightness that made an already perfect night blossom into something for the history books. "It is the same James, but I mean he wants Flyover. He wants to invest in the company but let me retain all design and staffing authority." I felt my cheeks starting to ache, so wide was my smile.

"Honey, that's wonderful," Gigi said, coming to kiss me on the top of my head. "I'm so proud of you." She tucked a strand of hair behind my ear and looked at me, her expression unreadable. "You've worked so hard, and you deserve to take this dream wherever you want it to land."

"We've all worked hard," I said, jumping up to help Gigi clear the dishes. "That's the best part. He wants the whole team. Says it's all part of the charm of the brand."

Tucker held the door for our little party as we stepped into the dark kitchen. Gigi hit the light switch with her elbow and continued to the kitchen sink, her back to me. "That's unbelievable," she said over the spill of the faucet. "I'm so happy for you, Grace. Really." She offered her cheek to me and I kissed it. "Now leave me alone. I want dish duty on my own tonight. No offense to either of you, but an old lady needs some peace and quiet every now and then." Her smile seemed sad and I furrowed my brow.

"Are you sure you don't want company?"

"Not at all. Just let me be. I'm about to turn on my Garth, and I know how you feel about that." She nodded at my eye roll. Garth Brooks knew how to write a song, I supposed, but when Gigi got her Garth on, she sang along with a wide vibrato that could rival the mating calls of wildlife. "You two sit out under those lights I nearly killed myself stringing. It's a beautiful night, and it sounds like Gracie might be gone for a while. Best to enjoy the evening while you can."

Tucker held my hand as we walked out to the patio again, a cascade of stars and tree lights falling around us. He stopped at a spot out of view of Gigi's kitchen window and pulled me to himself. I could hear his heart beating.

"I'm so proud of you."

"Thanks," I said, relishing the warmth of him. "It's been a really good day." We could hear the strains of music filtering through Gigi's windows and, without saying a word, started to dance, a slow sway under the night sky.

"When do you leave?" he said after a long time.

"Tomorrow," I said, still stunned by the suddenness of it all. I pulled back to meet his eyes. "But this is different. You know that, right?"

I saw his jaw tense before he answered. "Absolutely. We are much older and much wiser. And we have our own cell plans." He smiled, but I saw a hesitation in his eyes that made me frown.

"We won't even need those phones that much." I stopped swaying. "I'll be home on Friday. This is different." I searched his face, willing him to understand.

He leaned down and kissed me, a soft, lingering kiss that made my scalp tingle, it was so good. When he pulled away, a small smile played on his lips and in his eyes. "So far, our adult version of us is even more fantastic than our kid version. So different is good, right?"

"Right," I said, full of confidence in the truth of the word. "Home on Friday."

"Home on Friday." He kissed me again, this

time traveling toward my jawline, my neck. "But don't bring the doof, okay? I want you on Friday, but James can stay in New York in his fancy Italian loafers."

I giggled. "How did you know he loves Italian loafers?"

"Just a wild guess." Kiss on the tender spot under my ear.

I sighed happily. "Friday it is. Just five days away." Though, when he kissed me like that, looked at me like that, the distance between me and Friday felt like five days too many.

eighteen

I wanted to purr. In fact, I must have made some sort of purr-like noise because the man in the seat beside me looked over his reading glasses, amused. "First time in business class?"

I nodded and felt gloriously small in the wide leather seat. "Am I that obvious?"

He shrugged, shoulders lifting within his suit jacket. "You looked like you were getting misty when the flight attendant brought champagne before takeoff."

I made a face. "I have allergies," I said, but he was already returning to his noise-canceling headphones and open laptop. *Just as well,* I thought. He clearly was not going to understand the intoxicating beauty of this moment, jaded business class–er that he was.

I sighed happily and turned toward my window. We'd risen far above the clouds and were soon to make our descent to New York. I thought of Gigi's advice when she dropped me off at the airport in Des Moines.

"Be smart. And enjoy the ride," she'd said before giving me a quick hug and pulling away in the minivan. Still within earshot, she'd yelled out the window, "Don't forget to send Goldie some self shots!"

I sipped my chilled cucumber water and giggled, remembering Goldie taking me by the shoulders and issuing her command. A selfie a day, she'd said. It was the least I could do for the rest of the team. They didn't seem quite as interested in shots of Manhattan, but I readily obliged. I took out my phone and snapped a photo of myself surrounded by the deep blue leather, a view from the window, and a toast of my chilled drink. "Suffering for the brand!" I typed and sent the picture to Goldie and Gigi, awed again that rich people could have Wi-Fi even at thirty-five thousand feet.

I felt the plane begin its descent and I leaned into the window, taking in as much of the emerging view as possible. The city soon spread before me, and I remembered with a pang the way I'd felt when I'd last seen its skyline drifting out of sight below. The defeat, the embarrassment, the discouragement—it all felt close and real, even months removed. I ran my hand along the armrest of my seat and shook my head slightly. I was returning to New York not as one exiled but as one sought after, one courted, one with something to offer that was valuable enough to come with preflight champagne and free Wi-Fi.

What a difference some grit, some inspiration, and the Etsy could make.

By the time I found my way out of the terminal, I was remembering with caffeinated alertness how to navigate the crowds of New York, and that those crowds were absolutely everywhere. As I stepped onto the escalator leading to baggage claim, I caught a glimpse of myself in a shop mirror and saw that a deep furrow had forged a path between my eyebrows. I immediately forced the muscles in my face to relax, determined to remember my well-rehearsed, no-nonsense "city face" that projected confidence, not worry. I was out of practice, I realized, particularly when I'd said hello to about fifteen people before realizing no one was returning my greeting. Silver Creek was getting farther away by the minute.

I scanned the throngs below me, looking on the ever-changing screen for the carousel that listed my Des Moines flight. A man with a smart driver's cap and pressed suit caught my eye and tipped his chin to me. My name, neatly lettered, lifted slightly when he pointed to the placard he was holding. I opened my mouth slightly before shutting it and nodding. *Yes,* I thought, *I am Grace Kleren. And I have a driver.* I swallowed hard, sure the businessman from the flight would have been rolling his eyes to the back of his head if he could have seen me then.

"Ms. Kleren?" the driver said in a deep, smooth voice when I approached.

I nodded, not trusting my Dorothy from Kansas voice to do anything but squeak in that moment.

He gestured for me to follow him through the sliding doors. "I'll show you to the car, where you can wait more comfortably while I get your bags." He opened the door of a sleek black Escalade waiting along the curb. He offered me his hand and I stepped into the car. The door closed definitively behind me and James smiled.

"Welcome home, Grace." He leaned toward me and kissed me on the cheek. "You look phenomenal. Sun-kissed. The plains must have been good to you."

I shook my head, still stunned at the emotional whiplash since the last time I'd been in New York. "James, you didn't have to go to all this trouble. I could have taken the train. Or really lived it up and sprung for a cab. But a private driver?"

He pushed my frugality away. "Standard protocol. Saffron does this for all our big new talent." He offered me a bottle of sparkling water. "How was the flight?"

I took it and sipped, suddenly sheepish. "Perfect. Luxurious. I could get used to it."

James grinned. "That's the hope anyway," he

said, leaning toward me as he raised his glass. "Let the adventure begin."

James let the door click quietly behind him as he left, and I stood a moment with my hand on the handle, taking a deep breath before I turned to face my hotel room. *Room* was such an insufficient word, really, when it came to where the valet had brought my bags and James had carried a bouquet of hydrangeas to place on my bedside table. The "room" was actually a series of rooms in a spacious suite in the Gansevoort, a hotel I had only drooled over when I'd lived in New York. The Gansevoort represented swank and style and a room rate that would have made Gigi spit out her coffee. I walked slowly into the living room, kicking off my flats as I went. My travel-weary feet sank into the plush carpet. I went straight to the sliding double doors and pulled the handle to move it soundlessly on its smooth track. Stepping onto the balcony, I felt warm summer air fall over my skin.

It was nearly nine in the evening, but plenty of light still washed over the city. The sun was just starting to set, and my suite-worthy view allowed me to see a swath of the Hudson glittering below. I stood, transfixed as the light changed by the moment, and I remembered the excitement in James's voice during the ride from the airport as he described his vision for our partnership. Saffron was the perfect place for Flyover, he'd said, because of our shared history and our similar design styles. The vision of my company fit beautifully with his for Saffron, and working together would have none of the drama or the frustration I'd felt at Milano. I'd come into my own as a designer, James said. It was written all over the dresses we were making in Silver Creek. It was time to take the company to the next level, and this was the place and avenue through which to do it.

A particularly headstrong star was pushing through the lights of the city, shining brightly far above the setting sun. A smattering of clouds caught the purple, magenta, rose, and coral of the sunset, and I scanned the western horizon, knowing that a lot of the people I loved were beyond my ability to see them but that I was grateful they were there, waiting, hoping I would do well.

I started, remembering suddenly a note Tucker had slipped into my bag and, after getting caught, had asked me not to read until I'd made it to New York.

I left the balcony and retrieved the note. Under the soft light of a bedside lamp, I read the words, his handwriting a familiar script I knew well from notes smuggled during classes for years.

Gracie,
Remember these New York people are lucky to have you, not the other way around.

> *See you Friday.*
> *XO,*
> *T*

P.S. Leave the loafers.

I looked up and saw the sun had dipped below the horizon. The aftereffect was stunning, and I heard Gigi reminding me of God's fingerprints all over the beauty I was seeing.

"Nice work, then," I said aloud, and then smiled at the thought of Gigi having to wrestle with the idea that pagan Gotham had inspired the first almost-prayer her granddaughter had attempted in years. My worlds collided in that moment, and I waited, letting them mix, letting Iowa meet New York and letting the thought come without censorship: *Maybe I really can have it all.*

The room fell to the velvety black of nightfall before I turned from the window and started to unpack, Tucker's note still open beneath a hydrangea fully in bloom.

nineteen

I clutched my coffee and hoped the warmth from the cup would trigger some sort of relaxation response for my wired nerves. Earlier that morning, I'd arrived at the address James had texted after declining his offer to send a car and saying I would walk the five blocks instead. Hiring a car to drive five blocks? I could hear the sewing ladies cackle at such ridiculousness, and all of them were septuagenarians. Plus, a walk afforded me some time to take a few deep breaths and reorient myself to the city and its rhythm, the symphony of sound already in full voice before eight in the morning. I'd reached the address early and had walked right on by, not quite ready to face the moment without a little caffeine. I ducked into a café on the next block and had taken a few overzealous gulps of coffee on my way to the elevator. I sipped the last of my single-origin pour-over, relishing every drop, and waited to ascend to the fifth floor, one floor below the Saffron headquarters and the space James had allocated to Flyover.

The bell above the elevator door chimed, and the doors slid open to a light-filled loft. I stepped over the threshold and froze, taking it in. Soaring windows on three sides made the room feel like it was a sheer heartbeat away from the energy of the streets outside. Through one break in the buildings, I glimpsed a view of the triangular Flatiron Building, a mark that I was in the heart of the Garment District. I took one step into the room, and James looked up from a worktable to grin at me. He covered the space between us, and I could feel the room go quiet. James took my hands and kissed me on the cheek.

"Welcome to the international headquarters of Flyover, fashion's newest coup and hottest place to work."

A group of people behind James laughed appreciatively at his hype and I smiled at them. "Quite the vote of confidence," I said to James. "But I do like the way you're thinking."

James gestured to the space. "What do you think? Will it do?"

I turned my head slowly, taking in the tall ceilings, the crisp, clean light, the long wall of exposed brick that displayed an outsize framed photo of the Manhattan skyline. "It's fantastic," I said.

"A far cry from the barn," James said, met again with laughter. My smile remained, though the thought of Tucker and how hard he'd worked to get the barn ready for my work made the smile uneasy.

"The barn has its merits," I offered weakly, but James had walked away from me and toward the group. They parted with knowing looks. Behind them stood a mannequin, the center focal point of the room, wearing a Flyover maxi dress. I felt a slow smile spread across my face as I crossed the room. I reached out to touch the fabric, let it fall between my fingers, seeing the perfectly even stitching along the bodice by Myrna, the beading along the waist the handiwork of one of the twins. I looked up at James, my eyes shining.

"It fits here," I said, and he turned me around by the shoulders to greet the group of people standing in a loose semicircle around us.

"Grace Kleren, meet your team."

I shook hands with Moira, my new assistant, who was so excited to meet me, I feared she would curtsy. Chase and Eleanor were next, my assistant designers hired, in Chase's words, "to further the promise and vision" of my designs. Eleanor nodded in agreement, her pixie cut bobbing up and down above impressively wide shoulder pads.

"And these are the people behind the ledgers," James said, gesturing with a flourish to the remaining three people in the room. "Max Grund-wald, Suzanne Billings, and Michelle Epstein, I present Grace Kleren. You all should just group hug, because you're about to make each other all sorts of money."

Suzanne's laugh was higher in pitch than her tall, willowy frame would have suggested. "To borrow a phrase, James, dear, you might be counting chickens before they hatch."

All three investors looked at me with expectant faces, as if I must have felt most comfortable when farming metaphors were used. My smile was forced. "Yes, James, let's talk chickens."

He shrugged. "Oh, this crew is always the worry contingency. Don't pay any attention to them."

Max Grundwald crossed his arms on his chest and looked like he was weighing his words before he spoke. "I'm sure you're a very capable designer, Miss Kleren. In fact, I'm positive of this because I showed your Etsy site to my wife, and she went hysterical. Hysterical, Miss Kleren. As in, she has worn one of your dresses to every one of our social events this spring."

Michelle put a manicured hand on my arm and said confidentially, "The Grundwalds *are* the social event of every spring. So your dresses have been seen by everyone who is anyone in this city, Grace."

Max mopped his brow with a polka-dot pocket square, though the room was cool. "So I know you can make pretty clothes and I see some huge growth potential with Saffron. However—"

"Max, honestly," Suzanne interrupted with a roll of her eyes. "You're going to scare the girl. Grace." She looked at me squarely. "We are thrilled to partner with you. And we know you can do this. You've worked at Milano, which can be a veritable pressure cooker. I went to school with Nancy Strang. The woman is a *beast*."

I was starting to get concerned. What was with all the concern, the preamble, the way Max couldn't stop mopping his receding hairline?

"James?" I said by way of asking all my questions with one word. I searched his face.

"We need an entire line. Fast."

I narrowed my eyes. "How fast?"

He winced. "We present to buyers two weeks from today?"

I inhaled sharply, one step away from shrieking. Two weeks?! I'd worked on my line for Milano for four months, and that had felt lightning fast. Two weeks was insane.

I could feel the eyes of the investors on me. From where they stood around the mannequin, Chase and Eleanor stopped and stared. Moira looked up from a spacious white desk near a window. I could feel my heart beating in my temples.

Two weeks. A full line. Insane.

"No problem," I heard myself say with a confidence I was only beginning to feel. "This is our chance to go big fast, and we can't afford to wait. We can do it."

James was beaming at me as if I'd just gotten a gold star. "You see?" he said to all onlookers as he crushed me in a side hug. "Did I not tell you? This woman is fearless!"

I smiled as another round of handshaking commenced. Max produced a short document for me to sign in order to get on the payroll, and I barely registered his explanations of each paragraph, his overview of the non-compete clause, his assurances that a more complete (and lucrative, he added) contract would follow. I handed the form and his engraved pen back to Max, noting that my signature looked a bit wobbly. Fearlessness, I couldn't help but notice, felt a very close cousin to wild-eyed panic.

As it turned out, Max Grundwald's wife, Julia, *was* hysterical about my dresses.

"You. Have. A. Gift," she was saying, her eyebrows wagging with meaning. "I'm *telling* you, Grace. You understand a woman's body. And I'm talking women of all ages, not just the young chippies who can wear anything. Am I right?" Her laugh was nasal, and she turned to the two women completing our little conversation circle. The jazz combo was nearby, so I couldn't catch the murmurs of agreement by Sophie and Joyce. Or was it Sophia and Joy? Or were those the last two people Julia had introduced and these two were Maria and Janice? I just kept smiling and hoped I wouldn't be quizzed later on.

"Like this dress, for example." Julia turned, giving us a close-range view of her tanned back. "I wore this in the Hamptons over Memorial Day. And I'll have you know," she said, eyebrows telegraphing more important messages, "Gwyneth even commented on it. She loved the detailing on the bodice."

I did my best surprised face, but it was becoming a struggle after hearing this part of the story three times before. Julia had little need for me by that time in her pitch, and Sophie/Sophia and Joyce/Joy listened with rapt attention as Julia detailed her conversation with Gwyneth over chocolate balsamic red beets (Gwyneth was vegan) and avocado gazpacho at a party in Montauk (way less stuffy than Bridgehampton these days). When Julia launched into another telling of her recent allergic reaction to stevia, I took my leave, excusing myself to the restroom without actually following through. As I walked over to a waiter holding a tray of hors d'oeuvre, James stepped in front of me to block my way. We had spent much of the day together, already at work on the new line, before he'd startled at the clock and pronounced quitting time. A party in my honor was set to begin in an hour, and he escorted me up one floor to the Saffron headquarters. Leading me to my very happiest of happy places, he'd shown me a room burgeoning with samples from designers we loved. The Brainstorm, that was his moniker for the room, and he said any dress was mine for the picking, but to do it fast because the car was soon leaving for the rooftop party and it would be a serious gaffe to be late.

He stood before me now and took me in, holding me out by one hand to gather my look from top to toe. A wolfish grin spread across his face. "Stunning," he said, leaning in so I could hear him above the noise. I could smell his cologne, and I felt a rush of memories as he kissed my cheek. "How does it feel to be the guest of honor?" he said into my ear before pulling away to see my face.

I shook my head, still stunned at the day's events. The lights of the city sparkled around and below us. The combo was settling into "Night and Day," and I was wearing a shimmery champagne-hued dress that hugged me in every spot I liked and gave in every spot I didn't. The world was waiting for me, and James was a huge part of that offering, but I couldn't shake a feeling that I was playing dress-up again, that I was an unlikely guest at someone else's party.

"It's unbelievable," I ventured slowly, hoping James would understand my honesty. "I feel like

I'm living a fairy tale but can barely grasp that the tale is my own."

James grinned and waved to a man in a perfectly cut suit and Prada wing tips. "This is all for you, Grace, so enjoy it." He squeezed my arm before starting away. "Gianni from *GQ*. Old friend of my mother's. I need to schmooze. I'll bring him over so you can meet him too."

I nodded, trying to smile away the feeling that I was standing on the outside of something breathtaking but just not able to open the door. The feeling became acute when Julia silenced the combo and insisted on a toast. She did manage to mention Gwyneth but Max was able to rein her in when he looped his arm through hers and raised his glass.

"Ahem, yes. A toast. To the ones who made this evening possible." He smiled, but the effect was more of a grimace, perhaps due to underuse. "To the grannies!"

"To the grannies!" the crowd echoed with a smattering of laughter and clinking glasses.

I could feel eyes on me, including those of James and Gianni, and I raised my glass before I sipped. The faces of the Sewing Club ladies filtered into my thoughts and the champagne wasn't smooth going down, despite its impressive pedigree. I set down my champagne flute a little too hard on a waiter's tray and squared my shoulders, suddenly irritated with myself.

You belong here, I reminded myself before finally snagging one of the elusive hors d'oeuvre, some sort of tartlet with fig and smoky bacon, likely an ironic nod toward my hometown. It was delicious, I admitted freely, and I plucked a second tart from the passing tray. I set my jaw, giving sharp stand-down orders to my nerves and second-guessing. I lifted my gaze to see James and Gianni headed in my direction. *This is all for you,* I said to myself, repeating James's words. *Now start acting like it.* I flashed a smile, took a step forward, and extended my hand to the powers that be.

twenty

By the time James offered to take me home, after the last guests had left, their well wishes still echoing on the rooftop, I was feeling the deep-seated, exhausted satisfaction of a remarkable twenty-four hours. We bid the serving staff our thanks and good night, and we made our way down to street level. I slipped off my heels while we were still in the lobby, already back in the New York–native habit of tucking a pair of ballet flats into my bag for longer walks. James laughed as he held my heels for me.

"We have a car waiting, you freak," he said. "You don't have to walk anywhere anymore if you don't want to." He had loosened his necktie. Above it, I glimpsed the shadow of a beard that would be clean shaven again in a matter of hours.

I sighed happily and took the crook of his offered arm. He looped the straps of my heels in his fingers, using his free hand to open the back door of the waiting Escalade. I climbed in and sank down deep into the black leather seats. The sumptuous silk of my dress pooled at my feet. "So this is what it feels like to live in New York and not be a pauper." I closed my eyes. "It's like visiting a foreign country."

James laughed softly as the car pulled away smoothly from the curb. "You are now a passport-carrying member of the waiting-car club. It suits you."

I could feel him watching me. I opened my eyes and met his gaze.

He laced his fingers with mine. "I've missed you, Grace," he said, eyes on me. "This city has plenty to offer, but even with all that, it just isn't the same without you in it."

I shifted a bit in my seat. "I can hardly believe that's true," I said, tone light. "Though after tonight, I might just believe anything."

He smiled and raised my hand to his lips, leaving a feather-light kiss on my palm. "Believe it," he said just before I pulled my hand away. He turned to look out his window. We traveled the remaining blocks in companionable silence, lost in our own thoughts and in the late-night New York that streamed past our windows. When we pulled up to the Gansevoort, James got out of the car to open my door. I stepped onto the pavement, my feet reminding me that they deserved some time off.

James pulled me into a hug. He spoke into my hair. "You were luminous tonight. All day, really."

"Thank you," I said, stifling a yawn into his

shoulder. "It was certainly a day for the history books."

He pulled away and waited for me to meet his gaze. Then he leaned in, eyes closed, for a kiss. I ducked away, my hands pushing gently on his chest. "James."

He stared at me, hands still around my waist.

"I don't know if this is a good idea," I said, instantly hating myself for sounding so apologetic. Tucker and I hadn't exactly defined what we were, but I knew without consulting him that it didn't feel right kissing someone else.

James forced a wry smile, but it didn't cover the wounded look in his eyes. "You mean mixing business with pleasure? That never bothered you before."

I spoke quietly but I knew he could hear me, even with the sound of a passing cab. "We never got that far. You know that." An image of James holding a box with all the contents of my desk flashed through my mind, but by the look on his face, I could see he was thinking something else entirely.

"How about a nightcap then?" he said, his eyes searching my face, traveling to my neck. "I won't stay." Two fingers up. "Scout's honor."

I smiled but took a step back. "I'm going to go on a limb and assume you were never a Boy Scout."

He put both hands up in surrender before

running them through his thick hair. "Busted. Never a Boy Scout. Though I did help a local troop with a lemonade stand one year. Quadrupled their profits, I might add." He shrugged in mock humility.

"Good night, James," I said, taking a step backward toward the gleaming front doors of the hotel. "I'll see you bright and early tomorrow."

"Sounds good," James said, bowing slightly, the picture of a gentleman. "I'll look forward to it." He turned to the waiting car and called over his shoulder, one hand on the polished chrome handle, "Did I mention how stunning you look this evening?"

I shook my head slightly but smiled as I entered the spacious lobby. *This can work,* I reassured myself. *We can be friends and business partners. This is the twenty-first century and we are both adults.* I crossed the lobby to the elevators and entered a quiet cocoon when the doors parted. The elevator lifted me soundlessly and deposited me onto lush carpet leading to my suite door. I opened the door, dropped the key card on a glass-topped coffee table, kicked off my flats, and collapsed heavily onto the king bed. I stared at the ceiling, dimly lit by streetlight, and a wave of missing washed over me. The day had been a remarkable one, but I couldn't put it to sleep. Not yet. I turned the switch on a bedside lamp and reached for my phone, sensing the day's events would feel real only after I'd talked with him.

Tucker answered on the fourth ring, his voice heavy with sleep.

"Gracie?" he said. "Are you okay?"

"Yes," I said hurriedly. "Totally okay. I'm sorry." I worried my bottom lip with my teeth. "I know it's super late."

"Or early," he said, his voice thick. "Depends on how you look at a clock."

I smiled. "It's so good to hear your voice. I miss you."

"I miss you too," he said. "Even at the ungodly hour of one in the morning, I miss you."

I sighed heavily. "I wish you could have seen today. I was, um, kind of a celebrity."

"Is that right?" He stifled a yawn but I could hear it in his voice anyway. "Sounds about right to me."

"I saw my new offices. They're beautiful. Huge windows, plenty of work space, all sorts of electricity without power cords." I was trying for a joke, but I felt my words fall flat.

"Sounds very modern," Tucker offered after a beat. I rushed on.

"I have a full-time assistant. And two design assistants. And investors who are falling all over themselves to help me expand Flyover."

"They *should* be falling all over themselves," Tucker said, his voice so low and soft I had to turn up the volume on my phone. "You're what makes this all work, Grace. They know that."

"They threw me a party. On a rooftop. It was beautiful. And romantic." I meant to call to mind my wish that he'd been there with me, but Tucker landed elsewhere.

He cleared his throat. "How's James, then?" I could hear the effort he was making to keep the words light and self-assured.

"Oh, fine," I said, one hand instinctively going to my lips, remembering his attempt at a kiss. "He thinks Flyover will be a soaring success. I think so too, but the next week is going to be bruising." I picked at a corner of the hotel stationery. "We have to put together an entire line by a week from Friday. Buyers are coming for potential orders."

"So this Friday will have to wait?" Again with the forced ease, but I could hear a note of disappointment in the question.

"I'm sorry," I said, startled that I hadn't even considered this change of plans before that moment. "I'll need the weekend to work here. But next Friday, I'm all yours."

"I can pick you up in Des Moines," Tucker said, all business. "If Gigi doesn't mind me taking a turn."

I closed my eyes, frustrated with our awkward rhythm. Why was this so much more difficult across miles? "I'm sure she won't mind." I waited a moment before letting us both off the hook. "We can talk later. I'm sorry to wake you."

"Not a problem," he said, and I pushed away the thought that he used that same tone to sign off with his accountant. "I love hearing your voice, no matter the hour."

"Night, Tuck," I said quietly.

"Sleep well, Gracie," he said.

We hung up. I let my head fall onto one of the voluminous pillows on the bed and tried to sort out what went awry in my conversation with Tucker. I didn't get far before I felt my eyelids get heavy and the room start to fade, even with the bedside lamp still illuminated. It took a Herculean effort to stand and unzip my dress, letting it fall to the floor in a soft heap that would have to keep for a few hours until my alarm roused me to a long workday. I turned off the lamp, slipped between the sheets, and surrendered fully to what little was left of the night.

twenty-one

It took me a while to realize it, but Joan Jett had been on repeat for some time. As in, I'd probably been listening to her iconic screech during "I Love Rock 'n Roll" for at least an hour. Maybe more. I hadn't been paying attention to Joan. I was puzzling over the design of a Flyover-worthy evening gown, and even Joan hadn't broken through. The loft was empty but for me and the in-house stereo, synced with my phone and apparently unbothered by a long tribute to "putting another dime in the jukebox, baby." The rest of the staff had left long ago, after clocking in yet another long, full day in our effort to create a line that would be buyer ready in the remaining two days before our meeting.

We were crushing it.

I glanced at the finished pieces that stood in an obedient line along the back wall. The mannequins wore a variety of looks, from day wear to evening, and the winners were exquisite. I studied them as I stood to stretch, newly impressed with what we had accomplished and how well we'd merged as a team, both in terms of workload and design inspiration. Chase was funny, *really* funny, and Eleanor and I were already getting to the point where we finished each other's thoughts and sentences. Moira was a dream assistant, watchful with her wide-set brown eyes, ready with my phone, the latest spreadsheet, the number for the best button supplier in Manhattan. I had, on more than one occasion, professed my undying love for her and a blessing for a long and healthy life. She'd smiled non-committally and handed me another dose of caffeine.

I blinked a few times and rolled my shoulders forward and backward, feeling every vertebra protest realignment from hunched to vertical. The oversize train clock above the elevator doors read three in the morning. I groaned aloud. Time would need to slow down a bit if I were to keep both sleep *and* work in my daily schedule. At least until the buyers' meeting, I thought, my eyes on the sketches before me but my body reminding me that all work and no play made for things like sinus infections and unsightly drool stains on fabrics.

The elevator doors opened and I felt my heart skip a beat. A woman alone in an empty building at three in the morning? Not a recipe for safety or smarts. I reached for the scissors on my desk and was pulling them up to strike position when James stepped from the elevator.

I let out a breath I hadn't realized I'd been holding. "James," I said, unnerved. "You scared me to death." My hands were shaking as I returned the scissors to the desk. "I'm so glad you're not a serial killer."

He walked toward me, his shirt uncharacteristically rumpled to match a wild coif of hair. "You're safe with me, babe. First, that sounds messy. And second, I don't have that kind of time." He walked toward me, his heels marking a crisp rhythm on the floor. "I've been working on an investment proposal upstairs and I thought I heard music." He cocked his head in the silence. "Please tell me I'm not losing it."

I laughed. "You're not. Joan Jett was keeping me company. I just turned her off."

He stopped in front of me and swept a hand at my cluttered desk. "How's it going?"

I shrugged. "I'm stuck on this gown. It will come, but it's not coming easily."

He studied the sketch and, after a pause, nodded. "I think you're close. And you're right. It will come." He lifted his chin at the back wall. "Like everything else. You've knocked those out of the park."

I followed his gaze and let my exhale leave in an exhausted but satisfied rush. "Thanks. I think we're on to something."

James's mouth lifted in a half smile when he turned to me. "Hey. We're both too blitzed to be of any more use tonight. Let me buy you breakfast."

"Oh, I don't know," I said, running a hand over my face. "I would probably do better to go home and sleep for a while."

"You can sleep afterward. Come in late," he said, already turning my shoulders toward the elevator doors. "I'm sure Chase and Eleanor have plenty to do without you here, and Moira can continue organizing the universe until you arrive at noon. Case closed. Time for waffles."

I protested again, but weakly. My stomach had growled at the thought of buttermilk and syrup.

A block and a half later, James held the door open for me at Lou's and I stepped through to the smells of coffee, butter, and bacon. Only in New York, I thought as I scooted into an open booth, could a girl find a full breakfast and a fresh pot of coffee at an hour that most of the time zone was hard at sleep.

We were one of only three couples in the room, so our server came quickly and took two orders for waffles, one with strawberries and whipped cream, one with powdered sugar and blueberries, and both with sides of bacon and decaf coffee.

"So tell me," James said after a dainty sip of ice water. "How is your team working out?"

"Beautifully," I said. "Honestly. I can't believe how seamlessly we work, how little drama there is among us. A bit different from Milano," I added with a wry smile. We hadn't revisited much of our shared work history, James and I, and I was a bit wary of opening that door.

James sniffed a laugh. "That place was like a careening *Titanic*. Always one iceberg away from total destruction."

I laughed, pushing away the knowledge that I was too far down the payroll ladder to have seen anything from the helm of the ship. We had never been close to colleagues, James and I, and I was still getting used to sharing more equal footing with him. I sat up straighter on the red vinyl seat and cleared my throat.

"How are things at Saffron as a whole? Have you been working a lot of nights like this?"

James shrugged. "This is the way it goes, particularly for the first five years or so. We are expanding at a speed that feels just shy of lunacy, but expansion is a good thing. And the late nights, well." He grinned. "Allows me time to share waffles with beautiful women."

I took a careful sip of my hot coffee before responding. "Three a.m. isn't my best beauty hour, but the waffles are welcome." The server arrived with a full tray then, and we took a few moments to start in on the food. I couldn't remember the last time I'd eaten something hot, much less a full meal. Dinner and lunch that day (the previous day?) had been Thai and Ethiopian takeout, both cooled to room temperature by the time I broke long enough to eat. Even cold, they were both delicious, but there was something about waffles that felt like home.

"These are so good," I said between bites. "Almost as good as my grandmother's, though I wouldn't advise mentioning that to her. Recipe pride is a serious thing in my family."

"Wait. Stubborn, fierce pride in one's work? Hm," he said, head to one side and a playful grin on his face. "Weird."

I frowned. "One of the many very positive traits I have picked up from my hometown," I said, filled anew with a longing to see Gigi and Tucker and the sewing girls. "I can't wait to go back." I chewed thoughtfully. "We finish everything up today and tomorrow, present on Friday morning, and I'll be on the first flight out Friday afternoon." I took a long swig of ice water and caught the concern on James's face. "What is it?" I returned the water glass to the table, watching his face as he answered.

"Grace," he said, then stopped to pat the edges of his mouth with a paper napkin. He started again. "Grace, this is a huge commitment, this partnership."

"I know," I said, a bit prickly.

"This week has been intense, to be sure," he went on. "But it won't be the only week like this. Weeks, weekends . . . this is going to get big quickly. You understand?"

I nodded, but I needed him to clarify. "I want this to get big too, James. You know that." I put down my fork, heavy with a big, syrupy bite of waffle that wasn't tasting as good as it had a few moments ago. "What are you trying to say?"

James put his hands up for defense. His tone lighter, he said, "Nothing you probably haven't already thought about. Just that this isn't going to be a back-and-forth thing. You need to be here. In New York. Pretty much all the time until we are fully launched and things are running like clockwork. Which, as you know, can take years." He shoveled an oversize bite into his mouth and set to chewing while he watched my reaction.

I sat, sifting through a jumble of thoughts. I knew the hours would be long and I'd need to be in New York, of course. But I had to go back to Iowa, didn't I? At the very least, I had to visit our production hub there. The sewing ladies weren't just the heart of the company; they were also gold for publicity. Surely James would agree. I was about to mention that particular when he interrupted my thoughts.

"Of course, we aren't necessarily a conventional company."

"Exactly," I said readily. "I was just going to say that."

"Our growth might be manageable enough to allow for the occasional trip to Ohio."

"Iowa," I corrected.

"Right. Sorry," he said with a smile. "Iowa. I just don't want you to expect to be able to hop on a plane every weekend. You'll be needed here."

"I see," I said slowly. "I have to be honest. This is a change from how I was picturing all this."

James flagged down our server and pantomimed being ready for the check. "I understand. I do," he said, returning his focus to my furrowed brow. "It's good we're talking about it at this stage. Think about it." He slapped his hands on the table with an air of assuredness. He knew my drive, he knew my dreams, and he knew they were all within reach, just a block and a half away. "Think about it and we can talk again after the buyers' meeting. Everything out in the open, right? That's the best way to go about this."

I nodded. "Definitely," I said. I pushed my plate away, noting I had lost my appetite.

twenty-two

I stood a minute outside of Lou's. James had left, and I could no longer see his back as he made his way along nearly empty sidewalks, back to Saffron to catch some sleep on the couch in his office before beginning again. Despite his own brutal schedule, he'd insisted again that I head back to the Gansevoort to rest until noon. It wasn't yet six, and the thought of the 1,000-thread count Egyptian cotton sheets waiting for me made me light-headed with longing. But I found myself walking in the opposite direction, down streets just starting to wake, toward the Hudson.

James's words filled my thoughts as I walked. *This isn't a back-and-forth thing,* I heard him say over and over, knowing he was right and wanting him to be wrong. Of course this first push was going to be intense. I knew that was true, and I'd thought I was prepared for it. After all, the last few months in Iowa hadn't exactly been full of beach chairs and mai tais. I'd been working my tail off there too. I frowned with those thoughts, defensive for myself and for all the people in

Silver Creek who had nurtured the beginning stages of this business.

I stepped off a curb and startled at the brash honk of a horn. I clutched my heart and mouthed an apology to the cabdriver who had needed to brake to save my life. The driver lifted his hands in annoyance before continuing down the street, and I paused, leaning up against the crosswalk sign I'd completely ignored. I could see the river walk along the Hudson from where I stood. Looking three times back and forth this time, I crossed the street, beelining for the river and the wide path where I would have a much harder time endangering my life.

I walked along the path for a while, no longer alone. Joggers and bikers, eager to sweat before the start of another workday, passed on both sides of me. The sun had not yet risen, but darkness was losing its battle and the light falling around us was soft, delicate, the pale gray-blue of an early summer morning.

I sat on a bench facing the river. Remnants of old pier pilings dotted the water, dark spots on a deep gray surface that would soon be suffused with light. I watched the water and thought about James's advice. *Not advice,* I thought ruefully, *as much as an ultimatum.* Be here, be available, be all in, or . . . what? Expect to fail? Leave? Go back to the barn and hope another offer comes along?

I reached into my pocket for my phone and made a few taps on the screen.

Tucker answered right away. "Good morning!" He sounded like he'd been awake for hours. "What is with you, woman? I mean, this time works for me. In fact, I've already had my second cup of coffee. But don't you ever have time to call when it's not dark outside?"

I smiled, letting my spine curve into the bench, relaxing at the sound of his voice. "Not exactly," I said. "City that never sleeps and all that."

His laugh was low. "So it's true what they say? I thought that was just a good slogan for a T-shirt."

"Tuck, I miss you," I said, feeling those words to the very center of me.

"I miss you too," he said. "It's embarrassing, really. Apparently I am showing how much I miss you on my face. Pete at work has taken to calling me Hangdog."

I laughed. "That's awesome."

"No," he corrected, "that's emasculating. But when I try to change things up and smile, Pete says that's worse and that I look like I've just swallowed something rancid."

I was fully laughing by now. "Surely it's not that noticeable."

"Myrna brought me a casserole," he said. "It's noticeable."

The sun broke over the horizon, just a sliver,

but the change in the view was remarkable. I watched as the pale yellow, vibrant orange, and notes of fuchsia shimmered across the water to where I sat.

"Other than your obvious depression," I said, enjoying our ease and not wanting to tiptoe into choppier waters, "how are things in Silver Creek?"

"Oh, you know," he said. "Raucous and unpredictable, just like always. I ran into Natalie and Erin in town last night."

"Oh boy," I said, smiling.

"I thought it wise to leave when Erin started in on the benefits of essential oils. She also seemed concerned about the Hangdog issue. Natalie seemed less concerned. A little miffed, now that I think about it."

I giggled.

I could hear his porch door creak as he continued. "I helped the twins with their air conditioner yesterday. It was switching to heat without rhyme or reason, and apparently they let it go for a week before calling me. Didn't want to bother, Madge said. Ninety degrees inside felt a lot like ninety outside, according to Bev." He laughed. "I'd bet they slept a lot better last night."

I said nothing, preoccupied with the thought that I hadn't slept at all yet and that I might have more repeat performances of that schedule in the weeks ahead. After a few beats, Tucker spoke carefully into the silence.

"Gracie, what's going on? You're awful quiet. Is there something on your mind?"

"I had a talk with James."

Tucker was silent.

I sighed. "I guess he didn't say anything earth-shattering. I suppose I knew all of it on some level already."

"Knew what?"

"He says I need to be here. In New York. Pretty much all of the time."

Tucker waited for me to continue and when I didn't, he said, "So no Friday flights?"

"Not now," I said, then rushed onward. "I hate to think of it like that. It sounds so permanent. But it's not. It's just for a while. Just until things are really up and running and I'm not needed on emergency status all the time."

"Are we talking for the rest of this month? The rest of the summer?"

I swallowed hard. "Longer than that, I think. I mean, I can visit. Just not every weekend." I was starting to scramble, both in word and in my thoughts.

"Gracie, what are you saying?" There was a quiet urgency in his voice.

"I don't know." My heart was starting to race. A couple biked by and came close enough to nearly clip the tips of my shoes. I inhaled sharply, another rush of adrenaline propelling my words. "Tuck, I have loved our time together the last couple of months. As in, I've loved it more than any other thing I've loved in a long time."

I was greeted with more silence on the other end of the line. After what felt like an eternity, I said, "What are you thinking? Talk to me, Tucker."

Tucker groaned a bit. "What a fool," he said, almost to himself. "I can't believe how stupid I am."

"What do you mean?" I straightened. The hairs on the back of my neck prickled.

"I mean," he said slowly, and then stopped with a sigh. "I mean I should have been more careful, that's all."

"Just a minute." I stood up and walked along the row of benches. "It's not like we are breaking things off or stopping or whatever. That's not at all what I'm saying. I'm just trying to be honest here. Just being clear that we won't be able to see each other as much as we were thinking, in the short term."

"The short term of a year or more." He sounded resigned.

"Tucker, come on." I was walking faster now. "This shouldn't be a huge deal, right? I mean, we're just starting out. It's only been a couple of months, right?"

"A couple of months plus ten years." I didn't

need to see him to know he was taking off his ball cap and running a hand through his hair, exasperated. "Gracie, maybe time moves differently for you, but for me, this has not been just a couple of months, some fling or some cozy reminder of the good old days."

"That's not what I'm saying." I heard irritation creeping into my voice. Didn't he realize this wasn't my first choice either? That I wasn't getting what I wanted either?

"The night before you left?" Tucker said in a rush. "When we were eating at Gigi's and you got the call from James? Remember?"

"Of course I do," I sputtered, not knowing where he was headed with this.

"That night. I'd been thinking and that night—" He stopped abruptly and was silent. When he spoke again he sounded tired. "I was so distracted by how good everything was, I forgot to watch out for the inevitable."

"That's not fair," I said, feeling my pulse quicken as I walked. "You make it sound like I never planned on staying."

"Stay, go, that's not really the point, is it?" I could hear the anguish in his voice. "I want you to love who you are and where you are. I thought you'd found that place when you were here, but I was wrong. You were wrong. It was so good, Gracie." He stopped. I could hear myself breathing hard while I waited. "The kind of good that made me forget all sorts of red flags and worries and past mistakes. That good. But it wasn't real."

"I can visit," I said again, grasping. "We can call and text every day."

"This isn't summer camp, Grace."

"You're not even going to give it a chance?" My eyes were blurring with tears. I stopped, leaned heavily against the railing separating the path from the river.

"We're not kids anymore," he said, brusque. "We can't see each other once a month, once every other month, and build anything worth keeping. It's been great, right?" I heard the hurt in his voice. I closed my eyes, pushing a wash of tears over the surface and down my cheeks.

"I'm ridiculously proud of you and of your success," he said more gently, and I believed him. "You're going to conquer the world, Gracie. And I'm not interested in being the one to hold you back."

"Tuck—"

"Good-bye, Kleren. Take good care of yourself."

He hung up before I could say any more.

I watched the water, now taking on the same deep blue that was filling the sky. Tears streamed down my face. The light over the water became more insistent. The brightness hurt my eyes, mocking me with the start of a new day that was already marred with an ache deep in my chest. I still clutched my phone in my hand. I looked at it for a long moment while hovering my finger over his number to call him back. We could work through this. We could figure out a way to make it click, make what we'd started in Iowa continue across the miles and the days.

My hand still poised to dial, I looked to my left, toward the city. Manhattan gleamed, resplendent in the early morning. Myriad windows reflected the orange light of the sunrise, and the top of the Freedom Tower rose in triumph, spine straight and determined. I pushed my shoulders back as a reflex, then put both hands on my cheeks to wipe away the tears.

He's right, I thought. It wasn't going to work and the sooner we faced that fact, the kinder we were being to ourselves. I filled my lungs with a slow, ragged breath and let that reality slip into the tattered edges of my thoughts.

It couldn't work.

A couple sweet months of heady nostalgia couldn't compete with The Dream. The dream my mom had had for me and the dream I'd nurtured for over a decade. I tucked my phone into my pocket and began a slow walk back in the direction I'd come. This dream was an old and weathered one, and it weighed heavily. I'd been caught up in the moment in Silver Creek, looking around corners I'd rounded long ago, reveling in something that wasn't even practical anymore.

Tucker was a beautiful person. But he wasn't *my* person. I owed him that much at least, the recognition that I wasn't able to give him what he deserved.

We were adults, he'd said. I felt exhaustion seep into me as I turned away from the water and toward a spot where I could hail a cab. Adults with real lives, real jobs, real responsibilities. Adults who could suck it up and do hard things, including putting away the hopes and fantasies of teenage kids. I took one look back at the river before turning fully toward the city. It was waiting for me.

twenty-three

The silence in our loft space was so pronounced, we could hear each individual tick of the second hand on the big train clock. I had stopped pacing, finally, when Eleanor had rolled a design chair over the floor, its casters bumping with her speed, and had pointed to it. "Stop. Please," she'd said, and I had stopped. And sat.

The room was sparkling. We'd finished final production the day before, and we'd stayed late into the evening sweeping, wiping, fussing, polishing, and perfecting until the room was worthy of the clothes displayed on a long line of mannequins in the center of the room. We waited as the clock pushed onward. Already-hot morning sun poured through the windows as we watched the elevator doors for the arrival of James and the buyers from Solomon's, one of New York's oldest, most venerated, and most fashionable department store chains.

Chase was biting his nails and kept nervously pushing up his oversize black frames. Eleanor stood to the side of the mannequins, every now and then reaching out to trim a minuscule thread or brush off nonexistent lint. Moira sat with perfect posture next to a table loaded with pastries, bagels, spreads, muffins, and fruit. She had stacked vintage cake plates, all variations of white, and cascades of summer flowers spilled down the sides. A bevy of glistening champagne flutes was waiting for her to fill with mango mimosas, and two pots of hot liquid, one tea and one coffee, stood sentry with her at the end of the table. The table was a marvel, and I'd told Moira so when I'd arrived at seven and she was putting on the finishing touches. I did not mention that she'd gathered enough food for eighty people.

Better to have too much rather than too little, Gigi always said, and my heart skipped to think of her. I'd promised to call when I knew the outcome of today's meeting. Acting on reflex, I pulled my phone from the deep pocket of my skirt, a just-finished midi that flared at the perfect length and showcased a new pair of ankle-strap heels I'd found on the way back to the Gansevoort the day before. My phone showed just one new message, from Gigi. It read:

Break a log! I am so proud of you and can't wart to heal about the meat today! You're going to knock their songs off, honey!

I smiled and reminded myself (again) not to feel anything but fine that Tucker hadn't texted.

Tucker was not going to text. I was not going to text Tucker. We were done, just as it needed to be, and today I had no room for extra distractions. I slipped my phone out of sight into the new Saffron handbag James had brought down for me during our cleaning frenzy the day before. I ran my hand across the smooth leather, loving the way it felt on my fingertips, and made a mental note to thank James again when the chaos of the day died down.

The light above the elevator door lit up and I heard Chase take a sharp breath. Before the doors could open I spoke quickly to my team. "You three are outstanding. Be confident. You deserve to be." Eleanor nodded, Chase looked like he was going to pass out, and Moira looked like she was ready to call 911 and drive the ambulance if Chase passed out.

The doors opened slowly and the first leg out was clad in the most exquisite, perfectly tailored pair of trousers I'd seen on a real human. I was pretty sure they were Valentino, I was pretty sure I'd salivated over them in the last *Vogue*, and I was pretty sure they weren't even available to the general public yet. The woman wearing those pants, I realized with a gulp, knew beautiful clothes. She was not going to get distracted by a story about a few sweet grandmas and a converted barn. I would need to know my stuff.

I crossed the room to her, James, and the two

other people in their group. One appeared to be the woman's Moira, only this assistant was so busy studying the phone in her hand, she barely looked up. The final member of the party was a man with a bow tie, shaved head, and smart seersucker suit. His oversize tortoiseshell glasses were so prominent on his face, I had to concentrate to get past them to his eyes.

James made the introductions as I held out my hand, first to the woman in Valentino.

"Grace Kleren, meet Hedda Lind." James's eyebrows were doing a lambada, and I ignored them the best I could while shaking Hedda's hand. It took me a beat to realize this was *Hedda Lind,* as in the daughter of Lionel Lind, the owner of Solomon's and patriarch of one of the wealthiest families in the city. James had told us that Solomon's senior fashion buyer, Aaron De Castro, would be the one we were sweating to impress today. De Castro had a fierce reputation as having a searingly accurate view of how fashion moved and what inventory to acquire. He was enough of a force to have James popping Tums like candy for the last three days. If he'd known Hedda Lind herself was going to stop by instead, he might have needed a quick trip to urgent care, just to get a grip.

"Ms. Lind," I said, more confidently than I felt. "It's an honor to meet you."

She dipped her chin gracefully, as if to acknowledge that yes, it *was* an honor to meet her. She let my hand drop almost as quickly as she grasped it, already looking behind me to the mannequins. I could feel her quiet impatience as I met her assistant, Agnes, and the seersucker man, Claude, who was Solomon's accounting guru. He brandished a sleek, monogrammed calculator while we were still introducing our team and was so absorbed in cleaning off its screen with a microfiber cloth that he didn't acknowledge the profound crack in Chase's voice when he spoke.

James cleared his throat, still wagging his eyebrows at me whenever Hedda was looking the other way, and offered Moira's magnificent table of refreshments to the party.

Hedda waved one slender, manicured hand in the direction of a rhubarb muffin. She shook her head. "Cleansing," she explained.

I caught Moira's eye and tried to convey to her my deep appreciation for the rhubarb and every-thing else on that table. She kept her face neutral, a reminder of why Moira was going to do very well in her life. James's eyebrows could have taken a page from Moira's poise.

"Shall we, then?" he said, leading us to the line. I walked in step with the group, eyes narrowed on the clothes. Hedda Lind, I knew, would not suffer mistakes of any kind. I glanced at James and saw tension radiating in his posture and face.

Hedda led the way, soon striding ahead, her eyes on the clothes. Hands on each bony hip, she came to a stop in front of the first piece, a dress with a fitted skirt that followed a woman's natural curves down to just below the knee, a curved slit making its way prettily up to the lower part of the thigh. Hedda gathered a handful of the skirt fabric, let it fall. She touched the bodice fabric, a coquettish eyelet, and cocked her head as she took in the entire look. After a long beat, she moved on. She walked slowly from left to right, giving each piece her full and focused attention. When, halfway down the line, James asked if she had any questions or wanted to hear more about the story behind the brand, she shook her head slightly, saying only, "No words, please."

James clamped his mouth shut, eager to please. I glimpsed Chase out of the corner of my eye. His head was in his hands. Eleanor was close enough to Hedda to be dissecting with her gaze the way Hedda's own haute couture blouse was moving as she walked. I stifled a smile, feeling the same giddiness underneath my nerves. Normal people, even people within the fashion industry, didn't often get the chance to see clothes like Hedda's up close and personal. I knew Eleanor was thinking what I was thinking, that we would have loved to hold the blouse, the pants, the shoes, the belt, in our hands and read the stitching and con-struction like a map of buried treasure. Of course, asking Hedda Lind to remove her clothing would likely not help us close the deal for Flyover. I swallowed hard as she finished her progression down the row that represented a decade of dreaming and an insane number of hours over the last two weeks.

Hedda finished her perusal of the clothes and kept walking at a measured pace toward the window. She stood there, looking out at the busy street below, for what felt like an entire lifetime. I stole a glance at Claude, seeking clues of how normal this behavior was, but he had co-opted a nearby desk chair and was sitting, seersucker pant legs crossed, eyes closed, and head tipped back slightly. Claude appeared to be either meditating or napping, I wasn't sure which. Agnes the assistant had followed a few steps behind Hedda as she'd inspected the garments, but she had not followed Hedda to the window and was instead standing next to the blown-up photo of New York, hands behind her back as if she were in a museum on a lazy Saturday afternoon.

I shifted in my shoes, feeling my toes slip toward the front of the heels. I heard my stomach growl, finally waking up after so many nerves that morning and so many meals at odd hours that it was never quite sure anymore when average people ate. Hedda had been standing in silence for so long, I was seriously considering tiptoeing to Moira's table and snagging a bagel when Hedda finally turned on one very expensive Blahnik.

"USP." She said the three letters and waited, eyes on me.

I paused and opened my mouth to speak, but James beat me to it.

"Flyover's unique selling point? I really think—"

Hedda silenced James with a hand and the look on her face. "I ask this question of Grace." She returned her gaze to me. "Tell me what makes these clothes worthy of my customers' hard-earned money."

"These clothes," I began, and then cleared my throat, starting over and forcing the timidity out of my voice. "These clothes are about feeling beautiful effortlessly. The fabrics, the lines, the silhouettes, the movement—everything points to ease and elegance without trying too hard. My team and I have worked hard to create garments that make sense on a woman's body. The curve of that skirt, the gentle arc on the back of that blouse, the pretty dip in the neckline of that dress . . ." I pointed as I talked, feeling a fresh wave of pride in what we—what I—had built from scratch. "Those are not just design details meant to look great on a mannequin. Those are details meant to make a woman feel gorgeous. These clothes fit today's woman, and not just because the measurements are sound.

They are inspired by women in my hometown. Hardworking, smart, funny women who love to look pretty and don't take themselves too seriously." I could feel my eyes stinging. "This company is all about joy. I want joy to come out in the designs, in the wearing of the garments, even in the moment in the dressing room when a girl sees herself for real and likes what she sees. That's the unique selling point. Clothes from the full, boisterous hearts of real women. Women who know the value of true joy."

Hedda watched my face, still taking in my expression even when the words had stopped. I met her gaze, completely sure that no matter her decision, no matter if she decided to take on Flyover for her stores, I had spoken the truth. So much truth, in fact, that I knew Gigi and the girls would be applauding if they had borne witness.

Hedda frowned, her deep red lipstick pulling down the porcelain skin around her mouth. "Thank you for your time." She held out her hand for me to shake, which I did, despite her uninterrupted forward motion, eyes on the elevator. Agnes scurried ahead to press the down button.

My shoulders sank. Chase made a soft whimpering sound.

James looked panicked. He walked quickly to catch up with Hedda. "Let's talk later this week—does that sound all right? We can get into market position, some price points, maybe think about cross merch opportunities." His voice was getting unnaturally loud. When he got to Claude, still steps away from Hedda, Claude stopped him with a firm hand on the shoulder.

"No need to get ahead of ourselves, Mr. Campbell. Our office will be in touch." Claude held the door for the women and waited as they stepped over the threshold.

"Right," James said, not even hiding the defeat on his face. "Definitely stay in touch."

Hedda furrowed her brow. "What is the matter with you?" She sounded like a prickly school-teacher correcting her student. She shook her head at James. "Such a face."

I stepped within view of the party, just as Claude entered the elevator and pressed the button to close the door. The doors began to slide shut as Hedda called, eyes on me, "We are taking it all. You should be happy!"

The face she got, I realized after the door closed completely, was one of shock: eyes big, mouth slack, hands paused in midair. I turned to James and saw he wasn't much better.

"All of it?" I finally said, barely daring to utter the words in case I'd misunderstood.

James whooped, ran over to me, and picked me up. He spun in a crazy circle, and I could hear the laughter from Moira, Chase, and Eleanor, tentative at first and then giddy. James spun me until I pounded on his back to put me down, breathless from giggling.

"All of it," I said, shaking my head, disbelief merging deliciously with victory. "I can't believe it."

"I can," James said, all traces of panic fully erased as he strode to Moira's buffet table. He scooped up empty champagne glasses and began filling them sloppily with bubbly and a splash of mango juice. He passed them around our little circle and toasted to our success.

"To flyover country. And to Hedda. And to Grace, the fearless." His eyes shone as we took turns clinking glasses. He tipped his toward me before his first swig. "I knew you could do it. I knew I'd called the right girl."

I smiled, basking in the moment. I stopped short of sipping and set down my glass in a hurry. "Wait," I said, going to retrieve my phone. "We need to capture this."

We posed with glasses raised, each with at least one bagel or muffin in our mouths, grins barely able to convey the relief and thrill of the conquest. I sent the photo to Goldie, asking her to spread the news that we'd won.

Flyover, I typed, *is going big.*

twenty-four

Two weeks later, I skipped down the stoop leading out of Flyover headquarters and into the street. A sense of freedom bloomed in my chest, quickening my step. I had broken loose of the workroom, and it was only seven o'clock. I stretched my stride as I made my way toward Central Park. I wiggled my toes within my running shoes, a pair of lovely, supportive delights I had totally neglected since coming back to New York. I'd warned my team hours before that I would be changing into my workout gear and my feet would hit the floor at exactly seven. And true to my word, even though Chase followed me out the door and into the elevator with a zipper in one hand, a design board in the other, I simply smiled and waited until the elevator doors deposited me on the ground floor and sent Chase back upstairs with the zipper and his question. A girl could take only so much, and I needed a prison break.

The loft office had become my second home. First home, really, in comparison to the time I'd spent in my little temporary pied-à-terre, still mostly empty and littered with sparse furniture and open suitcases. Only days after the meeting with Hedda, and Flyover was a *thing*. As in, *the* thing. Apparently *Hedda* was the magic word, and James had been dropping it with wild abandon in calls to other stores and buyers. He'd been flying down to our floor with increasing regularity, quickly abandoning the wait for the elevator and beating a path on the stairs instead. He would come in, more breathless and wild-eyed with each new proclamation of who was interested in carrying Flyover. I'd been stunned by Nordstrom's interest in a trial run of the maxi dress, then I was bowled over by a tease from Barneys, and then I quickly lost track as the names added up with the number of garments ordered. First hundreds and now thousands of dresses were on order and my head was still spinning at the pace of growth.

The heat of New York in July was stifling as I crossed Fifty-ninth Street and entered the park, and I felt it bear down as I passed a playground bursting with children and their parents. A hot breeze tugged on the leaves of the trees overhead, and I could feel sweat already trickling between my shoulder blades. I gathered my hair up off my neck and pulled it into a ponytail, instantly grateful for the cooler air on my skin. I passed a gaggle of teenagers, jostling one another as they walked, none of them willing to miss any of the conversation going on in the center of the group. I smiled when I passed a family sitting on a bench, all five of them serious as the grave, tongues out and trying to keep up with the ice cream that was melting and running down cones and wrists.

I breathed in deeply, feeling my shoulders relax to be in a large expanse of space again. It was odd how claustrophobic I'd felt during these last few weeks in the city. I used to love how small New York made me feel, like the city was physically limitless and I was delightfully tiny in such a huge, pulsing machine of humanity and ideas and creativity and motion. This time around, I'd caught myself trying to see more sky, looking down streets and craning my neck to see glimpses of the park or the river or a wide view of anything. I needed to spend more time here, I thought as I rounded a corner and came upon a little clearing, the lake and boathouse just beyond. The park was a sure cure for work-induced restlessness.

A crowd had gathered at a spacious spot in the path to watch a street performer. The woman had to be in her late sixties, early seventies, but she had the lithe and muscular body of a woman much younger. She wore a gold lamé scrunchie to fasten a neat bun of white hair, and the hair tie was a perfect match to her gold-and-black sequined leotard. Black-and-gold-striped leg warmers covered the tops of her roller skates. She twirled and spun as she moved to the disco music coming from a portable CD player she'd set on the ground nearby. I stopped and watched, transfixed by her movement, marveling that a woman in her age group was flexible enough to do the splits on skates (or solid ground, for that matter) and reveling in this very New York moment. A circle of strangers, some sipping lemonade, some old and in bemused awe, some young and trying unsuccessfully to act unimpressed, all gathered and watched this woman, who was utterly lost in her performance and appeared to be uninterested in her audience.

"I hope I'm that sassy when I'm old," a young man to my left muttered, and I nodded as he turned and walked away.

I unzipped the pocket at the back of my shorts and retrieved my phone. I took about thirty seconds of video, particularly pleased when the woman held up one leg in side splits, all while spinning. I sent the video to Goldie with a text: *Found your soul sister in New York.*

I was only fifteen steps away, still tucking my phone back into the small pocket, when it rang. I smiled when I saw the name. I accepted the FaceTime.

Goldie looked peeved. I laughed.

"Miss Goldie, it's so good to see you! You look beautiful." And she did, of course. Face perfectly made up, hair highlighted and lightly teased, eyes bright.

"Well, of course, that's the point, Grace Kleren. What are you thinking comparing me to that woman in that horrible leotard and no lipstick?"

I laughed as I found an empty patch of grass to collapse onto while we chatted. "Oh, Miss Goldie, I meant it as a huge compliment. I was thinking of how spry and young you were. I didn't even notice the lack of lipstick, I promise."

Goldie's frown remained but softened a little. "Well, I should say not. That woman looks ridiculous. You must be getting a little too city for us if you think showing one's groceries to all passersby is a good idea." She sniffed, but I saw a twinkle in her eye.

"Now, wait just a minute," I said. "This coming from the woman who first introduced me to the idea of thongs to hide panty lines?"

"Shhh," she said, turning and scanning the room behind her. "I'm at the barn with the girls. Your grandmother is still highly irritated with me for that conversation, even though it happened when you were seventeen and definitely of age to be learning about alternative undergarments."

I heard Gigi calling in the background. Goldie answered, her voice all honey and sweetness. I laughed again, knowing Gigi was on to her. Within seconds, Gigi had taken the phone from Goldie, who was hollering a cheerful good-bye.

"Bye, Gracie honey! Hurry and visit soon. Your grandma is getting crankier by the day."

Gigi was holding the phone far too close to her face, but I could still make out the disapproval there.

"I suppose she brought up those G-strings again," she said with a huff. "The woman is going to careen into her grave without a shred of dignity left."

I grinned. "It's so good to see you and hear you. Though I can't actually see you." I stifled a giggle, knowing this was thin ice. "Would you maybe pull back a bit on the phone? You're coming in hot over here."

"Is this better?" She moved it all right, but to the left, so now all I could see was one eye and one ear and a tuft of hair.

"Much better," I said, knowing when I was beat. "How's it going, Gigi? Everyone doing all right there?"

She nodded. "We're great. Myrna's a little high-strung about all those orders that keep coming to the Googlemail you set up for us, but we're doing our best to keep up. I just hope folks don't mind waiting a bit." An offscreen Goldie hollered back to Gigi, "You tell Grace that Myrna has no right to be high-strung. She just paid off her house with her new fancy job at Flyover!" Gigi turned away from the phone to tell Goldie to hush and took stock of the group behind her.

"I hope it's all right with you, sweetie, but I've taken the liberty to hire some more seamstresses. Irma and Gert are from First Methodist, and I nabbed Shirley from Silver Creek Reformed. They're all hard workers and are picking things up quick. That will help with the lag time."

My mind was racing and I felt the skin at the back of my neck shiver with a new, potentially fantastic idea. First Methodist, Silver Creek Reformed. "Gigi," I said slowly while the puzzle pieces started to fit, "you might very well be a genius."

"Oh, give me a break," she said, before adding, "it's about time you noticed. What'd I do?"

"You might have just solved the problem that I've been turning over and over in my head for days." I stood up, brushed grass hurriedly off my tush and legs, and began to pace the little clearing. "Our orders are actually going to get even more insane within the next few weeks," I said, head down as I walked, knowing that Gigi wasn't watching anyway. FaceTime was beyond our capabilities for the moment. "Lots of orders, and by that I mean thousands, Gigi."

"Thousands? Good gracious," she said, surprise and pride in her voice. "You must be the toast of the town out there, Grace. I'm so happy for you."

"Thank you," I said, mind still reeling. "I'm happy for *us,* Gigi, and I have been racking my brain, trying to figure out how to keep up with

279

the demand. If we don't keep up, if we can't show that we can handle such rapid growth, all our work might be for nothing. Everything can tank just as fast as it rises around here."

"Well, I do have those three new women," Gigi said, and I could hear her wheels clicking. "But that won't be enough to help with such a huge increase."

"Exactly," I said, starting to hop a little as I walked. "That's why you're a genius. You already did what we need to do again, just on a larger scale." I stopped talking and looked at the phone. I could see most of her face. "First Methodist is just the beginning, Gigi. What we need is a whole network of First Methodists and Silver Creek Reformeds—a network of ladies across Iowa who know their stuff and are ready to help this thing take off."

Gigi's face lit up. "A network of sewing clubs."

"Yes. And I think we should start with churches."

She nodded, convinced. "Absolutely. Every small town around here has three or four groups just like ours, women who have been sewing for their families and communities for decades. They're very experienced and very good."

"And they will be well paid for their experience," I said firmly. "I want them to know that from the first. This is not just about Flyover. This is about breathing new life into communities that need a lift. I really believe in this, Gigi." I found my throat constricting with sudden emotion, surprising me.

"I can see you do," she said softly.

"No, you can't," I said, light laughter filling my chest. "You can't see me at all when you hold the phone that close."

"I sure as heck can," she said, all bristly. "And I'm going to finish saying what I started, even though you're being difficult." She paused and pulled the phone back, too far this time, but I could still hear her. "Thank you for thinking this way, Gracie. Your mom and dad would say it if they were here, but since they're not, I will. I'm awfully proud of who you are."

I swallowed hard. "Thank you, Gigi."

She waited and it looked like she was weighing whether or not to say what was on her mind. After a beat, she said, "When's the last time you spoke to Tucker, honey?"

I took a deep breath and let it out in a rush, not ready to give up the heady victory of a problem solved and exchange it with feelings still bruised and tender. I shook my head. "It's been a while," I said, wishing now we were not using FaceTime and that she couldn't see my expression. It was easier to fake cheeriness when it only involved my voice. "How's he doing?"

"He's all right, I suppose," Gigi said, her voice sounding pinched.

"What's that face for?"

"He may have been seen skulking around town with that Natalie girl last weekend," Gigi said, apologetic.

My heart stopped for a moment.

"Oh."

The screen panned sharply upward and I heard Gigi calling across the room. "I have to go, sweetheart. Bev has a bobbin issue." She lowered her voice. "Again. The woman attracts calamity, I swear."

Our good-bye was cut short as Gigi pushed to end the call abruptly. I stood in the clearing, feeling the breeze cool the sweat on my skin and raise a crop of goose bumps on my arms.

I'd wanted to know, I realized with a heavy weight settling in my chest. I'd really wanted to know how he was doing. I walked slowly back to the path and heard a sigh escape my lips as I moved onward, head down, no particular route in mind. I missed him. The sky here was wide enough, I'd stopped long enough, it was quiet enough, and I couldn't escape what was true. I missed Tucker. And Tucker, I realized anew, my feet hitting the pavement with increased speed as I pushed away the thoughts with a stubbornness I was remembering better with each step, Tucker wasn't anywhere close to me. In fact, Tucker Van Es was worlds away.

twenty-five

I sat at the worktable, bare feet tucked under me, and stared at the spreadsheets littered across the desktop, the only sound the hum of the air-conditioning that cycled on and off, dispelling the muggy heat of outside.

Saturday night meant a quiet office, which was just what I needed. I'd tried figuring out the problem at hand while sitting at the makeshift desk in my pied-à-terre, but to no avail. All I wanted to do in that cozy space was sleep the week away, and that wouldn't solve the issues I was facing on the papers in front of me.

The day before, I'd been quick to encourage Chase and Eleanor to enjoy their weekend. They'd put in plenty of overtime throughout the last days and weeks, and I was determined not to have Flyover become Milano, Part Two. That I myself was never more than a breath away from the office was a separate issue. This time, the company was mine, the direction was mine, the work was mine. I needed to be there. The other designers, however, needed a break, a long breakfast at a sidewalk café, a walk along the Hudson, a movie or play or show. I would not repeat the way I'd been required to sacrifice my life at Milano. Flyover would be a more humane place to work, even if it killed me.

I chuckled at the irony as I ran my fingers through my unwashed hair and reflected that it just might do that, kill me. I was wrestling with how to pull off this feat of freelancing grannies. I had Gigi's lists before me. She had outlined names of local congregations and the women who had agreed to help us out. I had figured the cost of monthly payroll, and while it was more than I had anticipated, I was certain it was the right thing to do. People were always the costliest part of any successful business, but they were also what made a business thrive. The women in Iowa were the heart of this thing, and I was determined to make it work for them and for their communities.

I was just struggling with the details of how.

How would I manage payroll in a way that didn't make me go insane? How would I structure the pay schedules of the original six women, knowing they were the ones who would bear the most responsibility while I was so far away? How would I coordinate the purchase and regular delivery of new equipment and supplies to all these churches, some of them over an hour away from Silver Creek and none of them near a large city? The logistics were overwhelming me, and

I ran my hand through my hair again, feeling it stay in an upright position even when my hand dropped back to my side.

It was after eight, so the light coming from the windows had just started to soften with the early dusk of a summer's night. I loved summer, or at least I usually loved summer, when I was able to be outside more than I had during the last month. The days were so long, I was just now reaching for the lamp on my desk to switch it on for extra light. Hunched over the papers, I glanced up only briefly when I heard the elevator doors open. James walked toward me with a brisk, efficient stride. He arrived at my desk, but I kept my eyes on the papers, feeling close to a breakthrough and not wanting to interrupt my train of thought.

"Here late again?" James said, dropping a neat stack of paper on my desk. "These are the latest orders. I thought you'd want to see where we stand." He moved around to my side of the desk to see what I was seeing, but recoiled slightly. "Good grief, woman. You smell like a locker room."

I made a face. "Thanks. You really know how to charm a girl."

He tugged at some sketches that were peeking out under my spreadsheets. I kept working on numbers, crunching one series over and over, trying to make them work as I tweaked. Maybe we could hire a runner, a high school kid who could drive afternoons and weekends and deliver fabric and embellishments and other supplies to towns outside of Silver Creek. Maybe that would work more efficiently than UPS, and we could add another job or two to the Silver Creek community. I could ask Gigi. Or Gigi could ask Tucker, I thought with a dip in my heart. Tucker would know the right person, but I wasn't going to be the one to ask. The thought of even pushing his number on my phone caused a sharp pain to ripple through my gut, which was currently empty after hours of neglect.

James let out a low whistle, startling me from my thoughts. I'd nearly forgotten he was still there. I glanced at his face and saw he was shaking his head.

"What?" I asked. I grabbed the sketches, defensive. "These are rough. Don't judge."

He shook his head. "If those are rough, I can't wait to see the finals. Grace, are you even kidding me?" He pointed to the papers in my hand. "These are extraordinary. They're fresh and beautiful and on trend but also iconic in a way. They remind me of . . ." He paused, searching for the word. "They remind me of all the things I like the most."

I laughed at the lunacy of that compliment. "Wow," I said, laying the sketches on top of the numbers sheets and giving them a critical glance. "I feel like that is a gross exaggeration, but I'm tired and hungry, so I'll let you get away with it."

James took his phone from his pocket and started photographing the sketches.

"Hey, now, wait a minute," I said, grabbing for his phone, but he moved too quickly and finished the shot. "I'm not done! You can't have documentation of a work in progress. That's just mean."

"Give me a break," he said, teasing in his eyes. "It's not like they're going on Facebook. I just want to look at them later and remember the level of awe I maintain for you and your design prowess."

I put both hands on my hips, staring him down.

He shrugged. "Also, I want to show them to my new favorite photographer so she can be thinking of where we will shoot your first catalog."

"My first catalog." I said the words in the same voice I had reserved for Justin Timberlake as a tween. "Sounds lovely."

James took the pencil out of my grip and laid it down on the desk. "Yes, but if I might remind you, you don't smell lovely. No offense."

"Offense taken."

He put an arm around my shoulders and guided me to my feet. "Here's what we're going to do. We're going to leave this place because we both need to remember what the world looks like outside these walls. We're trying to clothe that world, after all, so think of it as market research."

I mumbled a protest. "But I'm so close to figuring out logistics. I can't leave now."

"You can and you will." He was already walking ahead of me and turning off lights. "Come to my place. I can justify having a personal chef for once since we'll be there to actually eat what Jean-Luc cooks."

"Jean-Luc?" I asked, draping my bag across my shoulders and feeling muscles creak as I joined him at the elevator. "What happened to Noemi?"

James sniffed. "Noemi became too fond of borscht and not fond enough of flavor. She went on an anti-salt kick and we had to part ways." He led the way into the elevator and I had to scurry to get in before the door closed.

"You're kind of pushy about this," I said, trying to sound miffed but already wondering what Jean-Luc would cook up for us and if the dining room chairs in James's apartment were as luxuriously comfortable as they'd looked.

He punched the code to the underground parking garage. "I'm entitled to be pushy. I'm your boss."

I frowned at him. "Untrue. We're business partners."

He shrugged. "Semantics. But fine. Yes, partners. And as your business partner, I'm going to have to insist you eat. And brush your teeth."

I gasped. "I have deliciously fresh breath. I am compulsive about it, and you know it."

"Point in your favor," he said, and his grin was wolfish as I slipped past him and walked toward his polished Mercedes. We ducked into the smooth leather seats and James started the engine, igniting it to a gentle purr and reversing out of his parking spot in one quick motion. I watched out the spotless windshield as we surfaced onto the city street, alive with weekend traffic and lights coming on to illuminate another steamy summer evening. I closed my eyes as James guided us to Upper Manhattan, ready to move forward, onward, upward, past persistent thoughts of a boy in Iowa who, we had agreed, was best to forget.

twenty-six

By the time James unlocked the door to his penthouse, Jean-Luc was already prepping dinner. We could hear his knife work from the foyer. James called out a greeting to him as I slipped off my shoes at the door, and then he turned to me.

"Follow." He took off down the hallway, pausing only for a quick introduction as we passed the kitchen. Jean-Luc looked up from a cutting board and nodded quickly.

"*Bonsoir, mademoiselle*," he said, and returned his attention immediately to a pile of calamari.

"Not a talker," James said quietly as he steered me to the back of the apartment and the master suite. "But I much prefer wordlessness and outstanding food to unsalted borscht." He opened a closet at the end of the hallway and threw a plush white hand towel at me. I caught it to my chest and inhaled its freshly laundered scent. I knew from his own admission James did not know how to do his own laundry and never had, following a long tradition enjoyed by generational wealth. His mother, he'd once told me, had brought a maid with her to Smith when she was a college girl. She'd boarded her off campus and continued the perks of having her laundry washed and folded, her dresses and blouses pressed, and shopping and errands efficiently performed by a professional, even as she discussed Shakespeare and world history in the hallowed halls of academia.

I excused myself to the restroom to freshen up before dinner. As I reapplied my makeup, I started to hum, pleased that I could feel the dynamic between the two of us shifting this time around. We were on the equal playing field I'd so wanted the first time we'd tiptoed into getting to know each other. No uneasy work-life separations because we would be copiloting this time. I was just as likely as he was to go dark for days, intent on my work, and he would understand that in a way that other people might not. I closed my eyes, shoving out my thoughts of "other people." Tucker had made his choice, I reminded myself again. And I'd made mine. It was time to move on.

When I opened the door to the restroom, the smells coming from the kitchen washed over me. Infinitely better than any slice of pizza I would have nabbed on my walk back to my apartment, Jean-Luc was performing marvels on the six-burner Viking stove.

James opened his arm toward the French doors leading to the balcony and said, "Shall we?"

I followed him to the terrace and a sweeping view of the park and the city beyond. We leaned against the stately brick railing, sipping our wine and watching as the park grew dark and the lights of the city dotted the landscape, rushing to meet the falling night. I took a step back and surveyed the terrace with appreciation.

"James, this is so beautiful with everything in bloom. All the color and the smell of these herbs." I pinched off a basil leaf and raised it to my nose, then popped it into my mouth. "You are a lucky man."

He nodded slowly, eyes on me. "That's absolutely true." He smiled and raised his glass. Walking to the patio table and the waiting bottle, he spoke as he poured. "This really is a great place. Killer view. Something of a tragedy, though, that I don't spend more time out here. I think this is the first, maybe second time this summer that I've eaten on the terrace. Jean-Luc sounded stunned when I suggested it." He winked, just as the chef himself appeared, bearing two beautifully plated appetizers.

"For your pleasure," he said in a thick French cadence, "a sauté of calamari and shrimp, dressed with garlic, coriander, cardamom, and mint, finished with lemon zest. That you may enjoy." He leaned over the table and placed each dish carefully at the two place settings before bowing slightly and hurrying back to the kitchen.

"That was the most words I've heard him say at one time," James said quietly as he pulled out my chair. "I think he has a crush on my date." He leaned over me from behind and kissed me chastely on the cheek.

I smiled as he sat down. "A man of impeccable taste, then." I speared a beautifully crisped ring of calamari and didn't even wait for James to respond before murmuring with fresh-catch pleasure. "This is delicious," I said, putting a shrimp on the end of my fork and feeling another rush of happiness as I bit into the morsel. I shook my head and waited to finish chewing. "I think I'm the one who has a crush on Jean-Luc."

And that was just the first course. The steak-and-tomato salad, with tarragon from James's herb garden, sang of summer, and I told Jean-Luc just that. My words made him blush as he set down a basket of his fresh-made ciabatta, and James raised his eyebrows in amusement. "Now he's just showing off," he said, but he broke the bread with his hands and slathered on chilled salted butter, and I noted he might want me to eat there more often, if Jean-Luc had this kind of reaction.

James laughed. "True enough," he agreed, "though if things at Flyover keep moving in the direction and at the speed they are currently headed, I don't think you'll have any more free evenings for terrace dining than I have."

I frowned, and he tore off another piece of bread as he continued. "Don't worry that pretty head," he said, bemused. "You'll be seeing plenty of other breathtaking views."

I listened as he described the upcoming travel he was booking for us as we followed the plan of expansion. An industry friend in Paris had asked us to visit before the end of fall, James had a contact in Milan who was itching for samples, he said, and a stop in London had already been booked. I thanked Jean-Luc for the slice of raspberry crème fraîche tart that he slid in front of me, and took a deep breath in, letting it out slowly. My parents and I had always dreamed of going to Paris together after my high school graduation.

"Wow," I breathed. "I've never been to Paris."

"You will love it," James said with a smile. "It's very romantic."

James pushed away from the table and came to stand in front of me. He held out his hand. "The City of Love and all that," he said, and pulled me to my feet. "Now I want to make something very clear." I stood inches away, but he didn't take a step back. My breath caught as I stared into his startling blue eyes. He drew even closer to me, his hands tight around my waist. He leaned down and kissed me. It was earnest, intense. I pulled back to catch my breath and searched his face, my thoughts spinning. A smile broke from my lips.

"Who would have thought," I said quietly, "that the whole reason I'm standing here again is because of a group of sweet little old ladies sewing their hearts out in a converted barn?"

Something flickered across James's face, and he stepped deftly out of our embrace and back to his side of the table. I watched him, wondering if I'd said something wrong, and when he daintily speared his first bite of tart, he answered my internal questions.

"Grace, you know the granny thing will need to stop, right?" He took a sip of water.

I stared, still standing where he'd left me. "What do you mean?"

"I mean," he said slowly, "that we love the grannies. We love the *idea* of the grannies. But when it comes down to logistics, the grannies can't keep up."

I could feel my pulse rate start to climb. "I know there are some challenges," I said quickly, "but I've thought a lot about it and I know how to keep production in Iowa."

James's smile was pitying. "Grace, it will never work. The investment in human capital is outrageous if we keep production in the Midwest. That's why things aren't produced in the Midwest. The Midwest is"—he paused, a sad smile forming—"well, flyover country."

I could feel my blood start to boil. "What are you saying?" My voice had raised and I saw

Jean-Luc pass by the soaring patio doors and look outside, concern on his face.

"I'm saying the grannies were the perfect start, and I've kept them in the business as long as I could, but they are simply not sustainable. You had to know that." He waited a moment for me to agree but saw only my fixed stare and set jaw. Hurrying the conversation onward, he put up his hands in surrender. "I know they were important to you, but we have to do what's best for Saffron. And Flyover. You have the next level to think about. The decision is between India or China. You pick." He kept eating his blasted tart, and I gripped the chair in front of me, worried I might just pick up the tart and fling it over the terrace wall to an unceremonious demise on the pavement ten stories below.

"No," I said, shrugging slightly, righteous anger giving my words momentum. "Production stays in Iowa."

James let out a short bark of a laugh. "Grace, calm down."

"Do not tell me to calm down," I said through gritted teeth. "I have worked too long and too hard for this for you to ruin it by cutting corners."

He pushed back his chair from the table and studied me, hands slowly folding his linen napkin into a tidy square. "I'm sorry to disappoint you."

"Well, it's not the first time," I said. I could feel the anger flushing my cheeks.

"Hey, now," he said, and I hated it that he remained so calm, amused even. "No need to get personal."

"This *is* personal. That's the whole point, James. This is incredibly personal. The women in Silver Creek are real people with real dreams and real families and real bills to pay. They believed in this crazy idea long before you came on board." I was breathing heavily by that point, and I paused to catch my breath before continuing, forcing myself to use a more measured tone. "I can't move production overseas. I won't."

"You can and you will," he said with a dismissive shrug. "Perhaps you're forgetting the contract you signed?"

"That contract was a non-compete, a first draft of a larger contract that I have never seen." I narrowed my eyes at him, feeling the adrenaline pulse in my fingertips.

"I'm afraid that's not exactly true," James said. "Consult your copy, but I think you'll find that it's pretty airtight. The ideas, the samples, the relationships with all buyers, Hedda included— those all belong to Saffron, the parent company of Flyover. You may choose to leave, but the rest of it stays. Including decisions of where we continue production."

The terrace, the lights strung in its potted trees, the view of the city, it all swam in my vision, and I grabbed my bag that sat on a nearby patio couch. "I can't be here anymore," I said, stumbling away from the table as the weight and truth of James's words made a tangled mess of my thoughts. I hurried past Jean-Luc and into the living room, my only focus the front door, the atrium, the elevator, the world outside of this room. Somewhere in my brain, I registered the plush white rug that greeted my bare feet as I made my way to the door and my shoes. The feeling made me shudder, remembering a cavalier story of the afternoon James had purchased that rug and spent more than my entire first year's salary from Milano on a stupid piece of carpet. I stopped suddenly, feeling the calamari, the steak, the shrimp that I'd just devoured take a sharp and nasty turn in my stomach. I paused, my hand on the back of James's white leather sofa, my feet rooted to their spots on the carpet. I closed my eyes as the room continued to spin, and I felt sweat form on the back of my neck.

"Are you all right?" James said from his stance in the doorway.

I waited for the nausea to pass, eyes still closed. I saw Gigi, her bright smile as she directed the sewing women in the barn. I saw Goldie, writing a check to her nephew as seed money for his new hardware store. I saw Tucker, his eyes finding mine from across the barn as he placed a Ball jar of flowers on my worktable.

I knew James was nearer to me and I willed

him not to do it, but he placed a cool hand on my arm and said, "Gracie?"

"Don't call me that," I said, right before emptying the contents of my stomach all over his fifty-thousand-dollar rug.

twenty-seven

I clutched my bag to my chest and pushed past the elevator doors as soon as they opened wide enough to let me through to the lobby. I must have looked wild-eyed because James's doorman snapped his head in my direction, worry knitting the brow of his otherwise smooth, clean-shaven head.

"Madam, are you all right?" he asked, taking a step toward me.

I looked at him blankly, trying to locate an appropriate response but only able to blink, stuck on his question.

"Shall I call Mr. Campbell?"

"No," I snarled, finding my voice. Then, more carefully, "No, thank you." My eyes darted to the door and I started to walk.

I stepped onto the sidewalk and headed south on Central Park West, my teeth grinding and my legs shaking as I walked. I would not sit, I would not stop, I would not be still, not until I'd put as much distance as possible between myself and that man.

A cab passed, slowing down like a visual question mark. Did I want a ride? I shook my head and waved the driver on. I walked faster, feeling like someone was chasing me but knowing it was only my desire to escape the conversation I'd just endured. After I'd ruined James's rug, not without a little stab of delight, I remembered taking the napkin offered to me by Jean-Luc and then backing up slowly until I bumped into the front door. I fumbled for the knob and I must have found it and opened it, made my way to the elevator. All I could picture now as I hurried along the sidewalk was the look of disgust on James's face. I'd felt the same revulsion, of course, though not because of any spill to clean up. *Unless you counted my entire life,* I thought bitterly.

Anger bloomed in my chest as I walked, passing the elegant buildings that faced the west side of Central Park. Burgeoning flowerpots, doormen in smart uniforms, tasteful lighting illuminating pristine, monogrammed awnings over spotless entryways—I wondered if all the beauty, all the perfection hid the same emotional bankruptcy I'd just witnessed in James's penthouse.

How could he do that to me? I fumed as I walked. What kind of a person was able to fleece someone he supposedly cared about and then calmly shove bites of raspberry tart into his face as if we were merely talking about the weather or the Yankees' hope for a pennant this year? *He didn't even* see *me,* I thought, adrenaline shooting through my veins as a ferocious additive to the anger already there. He'd never had any real commitment to business partnership, much less to helping Silver Creek or the sewing ladies or to the idea of infusing life back into struggling economies in small towns. He wanted my ideas, my story, just to get the ball rolling with Hedda and her cronies, and then he was done with me. I'd served my purpose, the momentum was sufficiently built, and it didn't matter to him whether I stayed on board or not.

I thought of James's excitement over the new sketches he'd seen in the office just that evening, of the photographs of those sketches that were on his phone right that second. I had to pause, gripping a stately spear on a wrought-iron fence.

James had taken it all.

I was breathing hard, still clutching the fence, as I felt the full weight of my failure start to descend.

James had taken it all. But I was the fool who had let him do it.

I slowly loosened my grip on the fence and resumed my walk, the urgency gone from my step. I don't know when the tears started to fall, but by the time I noticed, my cheeks were wet and my palms hurt from the fingernails I was gouging into their tender skin. I'd let this happen. James was a selfish, manipulative, ego-stroking, elitist piece of work, but I had played right into what he wanted. I'd been so eager to prove myself, so eager to be at the top, so eager to let the fashion world know I was someone to watch, I'd pushed everything else out of the way. I'd ignored common sense, signing those papers and assuming the greater business world operated with the same honesty and integrity as Gigi and her Silver Creek neighbors. I swallowed hard, thinking of how foolish I'd been. I'd dug into my work here, eyes on the prize of recognition and respect and, yes, hoping to help along the folks back home, but always finding an excuse to not actually call those folks, reach out to them, thank them for the work they were doing on my behalf.

And then there was Tucker. A sob escaped my throat, and a man passing took a deep drag on his cigarette and quickened his pace, not looking up to make eye contact with the crazy woman who was stumbling past Central Park after midnight, whimpering like a hurt animal. Tucker, the one who had risked feeling for me again, who had dropped what he was doing to help me build the first foundational steps of this business, who had driven to Omaha on a whim, transformed an old barn into a beautiful work space—that Tucker had been discarded when things got a little complicated. I shuddered as I cried, wondering if I'd made Tucker feel as easily dismissed as James had made me feel tonight.

I walked block after block, not registering where I was, just following the well-lit path in front me, letting it take me past grand apartment buildings on my right, the long expanse of the park on my left. At some point, the apartments gave way to other buildings, businesses closed at the late hour, restaurants still alight with candles and conversation, a club with strains of a jazz standard making it past the darkened door and into the street. My thoughts were muddled, as I thought of Tucker, Gigi, the sewing ladies, the people who were rooting for me back home, and even some who were not. I thought of Natalie, sure that Tucker would have been better off just marrying her straightaway and avoiding the mess I'd created for him and the town he loved. I thought of Hedda and Chase and Eleanor and Moira, of all the people in New York who would wonder about what went wrong with Grace Kleren but who would move on and forget within a week's time. I thought of Isa and Luca and the friends I needed but never made time for anymore.

It was a mess, all of it, and I kept moving as I let the mess overwhelm me.

When I finally paused, forced to acknowledge the blisters forming on both of my feet, I took stock of where I was and my eyes widened, realizing how far I'd wandered. I was in Midtown, miles away from James's apartment, standing near the entrance to Rockefeller Center. My eyes landed on the bronze statue of Atlas that guarded the courtyard, and I sighed, making my way to sit on the ledge that surrounded the sculpture. I sat down heavily, fully identifying with the stupidity of the Greek god enshrined and immobile above me. *Muscles or not,* I thought wryly, *it's not going to end well for you, dude. Holding the world on your shoulders is a fool's errand.* I should know. I'd tried and just tonight been fully demoted to can't-hold-anything status.

I sat with my head in my hands, spent but dry-eyed. I felt an exhaustion I'd never felt before, one that dove deep, past my bones and into my heart. I was so, so tired. Tired of running after approval, tired of running after praise, tired of running after a way to prove myself to my colleagues, my employers, my hometown. Tired of messing up all the things that should be held most precious and dear, like my relationships with Gigi and the sewing girls. Tucker. Tired of missing my mom and dad, I realized with a jolt, and tired of pretending I didn't. I needed help. Life and all its layers and complexities and questions and heartache were too hard.

I shivered as the tears fell, hot and slow-motion this time. All the initial rage of the evening had diminished, leaving only sadness and loss. So much running, so much movement, and none of it had gotten me anywhere I really wanted to stay.

I looked up, letting the tears fall into my lap, and took in a sharp breath. St. Patrick's Cathedral faced me, illuminated and still, its spires reaching up into the dark night. I took in its grandeur, its steadfast beauty, witness to so many years, so many weddings, funerals, joys, sorrows. I suddenly realized what I had to do and who was waiting for me.

I stood and started to walk, not feeling the blisters I'd been stopped by only minutes before. I walked, my eyes on the cathedral, my heart full and aching as I made my way across the street. I startled when a car swerved around me. The driver honked and some remote part of my brain reminded me to be careful, but I only walked more quickly, stepping up the curb and crossing the distance between the sidewalk and the front steps of the church. I stopped at the bottom step and breathed. Tilting my head back, I could just glimpse the top of the building. I felt tears stream down the sides of my face, into my hair, and I closed my eyes. I'd been running so long and it was time to stop.

I took the steps carefully, deliberately, and I kept going until I was standing directly in front of the massive doors. I leaned forward, my forehead resting on the cool bronze surface. I opened my arms, spreading my fingers and gripping the doors, willing them to hold me up, stay where they were, because I was finally here and I didn't want to move. It had taken me ten years to reach this place, this moment, and all I wanted was to step into a love that was ferocious and strong. A love that would forgive and bind up the broken pieces. Not a brokenness, I realized with a hitch in my sobs, that God created but one that He was waiting and able to heal.

Tears dropped onto the pavement below. Leaning into the doors, desperate for the sweet sound of grace, forgiveness, and tender mercy, I closed my eyes and tried what Tucker had defined as prayer. I started the conversation.

"God," I whispered, my words catching on tears. "I'm here."

twenty-eight

My shoulder slumped against the window of seat 23C, decidedly *not* a part of business class this time around. The plane was full, and the woman next to me was snoring. I did my best to give her ample berth, but her head had fallen onto my shoulder three times before I just let it stay there. At least one of us was getting the rest we needed. After my late-night walk across the city, I'd caught a cab from St. Patrick's back to the pied-à-terre and had immediately started to pack, stopping only to book a ticket out of New York and back to Iowa for the following day. Which was actually the same day, if I thought about it, and I didn't really want to think about it.

I watched as the plane banked in a wide arc over Des Moines. The change in landscape from my first visit back home a few months prior was nothing short of miraculous. The long stretches of brown and gray fields had given way to a riot of green, and the beauty was inescapable. We flew over undulating hills, fields planted in neat symmetry, rows of corn and soybeans reaching for the sky. Trees surrounded farmhouses, their various shades of green adding texture and movement to the overall portrait. A series of Grant Wood paintings moved below me, and I sighed, feeling the strange mix of contentment and sadness that was bringing me home to the quiet beauty of this place.

The pilot let down the landing gear, and the sudden clanking jerked my seat partner awake. She lifted her head, strands of her white bob falling into her face before she tucked the hair self-consciously behind her ears. She looked at me and winced. "Did I nap on you?"

My smile was genuine but didn't reach my eyes. "You did. Quite well, actually."

"I'm so sorry," she said, putting a hand to her mouth. "How embarrassing. I'm afraid I had a long night last night, and I didn't sleep well."

"It's no problem," I said wearily. "I understand the long night." I started to gather my things. I'd pulled out a book before takeoff, but it had remained unopened on my lap. I was too distracted by my thoughts and my upcoming apology tour to read with any focus. I tucked the book into my bag and kicked the bag with my toe until it was fully under the seat. Leaning back, I closed my eyes, waiting to land.

"Are you headed toward home or away from it?" The woman's voice was gentle, landing carefully in my heavy thoughts.

I thought a moment before turning to answer.

"Toward," I said, nodding. "Definitely toward."

"Me too." She straightened her blouse and sat up straighter. "I'd expect we will both sleep better tonight."

I closed my eyes and hoped she was right.

Gigi refused to let me heft my bags into the back of the minivan. When I tried, she swatted my hand with her own and glared.

"I know I look old, but I can still lift a suitcase." She nodded toward the front of the car. "You just get in and rest. You look horrible."

I shuffled to the front of the car, knowing she was right about how I looked. After returning from my sojourn across Manhattan and booking my ticket, I had fallen into bed, still in my clothes, only to toss and turn for the waning hours of the night. I slipped into the front seat and glanced at myself in the side mirror. I whistled.

Gigi turned to me when she'd settled into the driver's seat. "What on earth happened?" she said as she turned the key in the ignition. "You aren't due back for weeks. And you have dark circles under your eyes. You are not a fussy woman, Grace, but I haven't seen you without concealer since ninth grade."

I sighed as she pulled carefully out into traffic, making her way to the bypass that would skip downtown and take us to Silver Creek. "Gigi, I ruined everything." I groaned. "Again."

I unloaded my sorrowful tale, my tone dry and unaffected. I'd spent so many tears, I was all out. The miles peeled away behind us as I told Gigi about the rapid rise of Flyover, the meeting with Hedda, the planned photo shoots, catalog, travel. She listened, asking few questions, eyes on the road. Shame burned in my throat as I realized I'd lived the last month in New York in a self-absorbed and self-justified bubble, my texts and calls not nearly enough to paint a full picture of what was going on in my life or in the company she'd worked hard to build.

It was only when I got to the part about vomiting on James's rug that she allowed a small smile. "Atta girl," she said, turning to wink at me before returning her gaze to the road.

I swallowed a lump in my throat as I studied her profile. "Gigi, I'm so sorry." She said nothing so I continued. "I'm so sorry that your beautiful dresses, with their beautiful fabric, are now owned entirely by someone who will discard it all in a heartbeat if that means a bigger bottom line." I gripped the handle of the passenger door, willing myself to say it all. "And I'm sorry I didn't call enough when I was in New York. I thought I'd grown out of all that selfishness, but I can see that I'm not anywhere close."

She shook her head. "I disagree." She covered my hand in hers, stealing a glance at me. "You messed up, yes. You got fixed on a goal that

311

turned out to be something you didn't really want. Gracie, this is the plight of the human race." She smiled at me. "You're not the first and you won't be the last. But you *are* a grown-up, honey. A grown-up with a big, sound heart. The proof is all in front of you: you weren't able to sacrifice your sewing girls on the altar of the almighty dollar."

I listened, holding tightly to her ready forgiveness.

"You know," she said unhurriedly as she exited the interstate and pulled onto the highway that would lead into town. "You're acting like James owns more than he does."

I turned to her. "What do you mean? He owns it all."

"Nope." She shook her head. "He most certainly does not." She set her jaw. "Here's what he owns: he owns the fruit of some long hours of work, some great design fixes, probably some memories you'd like to forget."

My cheeks burned, remembering how not even twenty-four hours prior, I'd been eating with James and kissing him at his table.

"He has that big lofty office in New York City where you worked, and he has lots of deals with lots of buyers. And a really smelly rug. Don't forget the rug."

I laughed, rueful. "Other than the rug, it sounds like he came out way ahead."

She shook her head. "He owns some ideas, but only the ones you've shared with him during the last few months. There are plenty more where those came from, I'm guessing." She slowed as we passed a group of deer feeding in the twilight, careful to watch for their sudden movements until we passed. "Don't let him take more than he has, Grace. You still have all sorts of things. You still have the bright, curious, gifted mind God gave you. You have a hometown full of people who love you. And you have mercies that are new every morning. That's not my promise, mind you. That's a promise from God Himself. New morning, new mercies. That's the deal."

"I know. God and I are on better terms these days," I said quietly, finding the words less foreign on my tongue than I anticipated.

Gigi watched my face and was silent, though I could see her shoulders relax, like a well-worn weight had lifted from her.

The night was midnight blue on the fields around us, and I could see a smattering of lights on the horizon. Silver Creek was straight ahead.

We'd arrived home. The porch light was on, beckoning with its soft, clean light. I could see through to the kitchen, where I knew a small counter lamp illuminated scrubbed countertops and a tin of fresh-baked cookies, probably peanut butter impressed with the tines of a fork and sprinkled with sugar. My eyes filled as I knew

313

again how loved I was in this place, how tenderly Gigi would treat me, even though I'd completely messed up.

She leaned over to kiss me on the cheek, just escaping a fat tear that fell in her wake. "Come on in, honey. Tears feel better in your own house."

I dragged myself out of the car, and Gigi met me, encircling me with her arms as we stood in the driveway. I tucked my face into her neck and she hugged me, waiting for me to feel what I needed to feel.

I sighed. "I think I'll fall asleep before I even turn out the light."

"Just as well," she said as she pushed open the front door to the house that, I knew, would always cushion my fall. "A good night of sleep and fresh mercies tomorrow morning and you'll have the courage to do what you need to do."

I wasn't entirely sure she was right, but as predicted, I didn't have much time to worry about it. The quilt on my mom's old bed was all I needed to close my eyes, hands clutching the worn fabric, and fall into a deep, dreamless sleep.

twenty-nine

Sunlight the shade of buttercream filled the room when I opened my eyes the next morning. I stared at the ceiling, feeling at once disoriented and completely familiar with my surroundings.

Home. The thought came to me unbidden, and I let out a deep, weary sigh. My route had been circuitous and not without some serious pitfalls, but I had made it home. A bit worse for the wear, I noticed, my eyes still puffy and back muscles stiff from all the travel and sleepless nights. But I'd made it, and for the first time in weeks, I felt a lightness in my chest as I thought of facing the day.

Only one thing on the agenda, really, and though the thought of it made my stomach roil, I knew exactly what I needed to do.

I took a long, hot shower, taking care to scrub the last few days away as I caused the small bathroom to steam up. I let my hair succumb to the curls that were impossible to fight in the humidity of late summer in Iowa. As I applied minimal, soft makeup, I paused every few minutes to jot down notes on the pile of index cards accumulating next to me. I pulled on my favorite pair of jeans, an off-the-shoulder top I'd designed myself but not yet taken into the office at Flyover, and a pair of strappy sandals, and I took to the stairs, clutching my pile of index cards.

Gigi was sitting at the kitchen table, Bible open next to her but long done with her morning reading and neck deep in the day's copy of the *Des Moines Register*. She shook her head as she looked up from the news.

"Every day I hope things will get better as I sleep, and every day I find they have not."

I smiled. "What about those new mercies you were talking about? Aren't any of those in the paper?"

She laughed softly. "Not exactly. I look elsewhere for those." She tapped the Bible next to her with one knuckle and rose from her chair, the legs bumping along the wood floor as she pushed them back. "Coffee?" she said, already moving toward the pot.

"Yes, please," I said, and we moved in concert in the tiny kitchen, Gigi with a large pour of coffee with extra cream and I with the toaster, a quickly scrambled egg, and a thick-cut slice of Canadian bacon. I sat down with my breakfast and Gigi pushed the coffee gently toward me.

"You look pretty," she said, smiling. "Your eyes

are bright and clear. A marked improvement over last night."

I swallowed a bite of toast. "Thank you," I said. "My personal goal is to make it through the day without adding red rims to these eyes. Do you think I can do it?"

Gigi paused, a thoughtful expression on her face. After a beat she said, "Not likely. You're rather emotional these days."

I frowned.

"However," she said, one finger up with her addendum, "I've found that it's better to be honest, no matter how horrible you look by day's end."

I raised one eyebrow. "That's it? That's the wisdom you're dropping as I make my way to apologize to the man of my dreams?"

She grinned. "See, now? You're well on your way already." She patted my arm. "And your mascara is still intact. Good work."

I shook my head as I continued eating. I was forcing it, despite the jumble of nerves in my stomach. But after the Calamari Incident, I'd eaten sparingly, and I was grateful to find the bacon and eggs smelled good to me. I sipped the last of my coffee as Gigi asked me about my plan for the day.

"That is," she said, "other than Tucker."

I felt my heart lurch downward, saddened again for my mistake in letting him go. I sat up straighter in the worn wooden chair. "I need to go to the barn, take inventory, see what I can salvage and what I need to sell or dump."

"Dump?" Gigi was indignant. "I should say not. All the garments in that barn are handmade works of art. And they're going with you and me to the flea market this weekend, thank you very much. People around here are already talking about getting Flyover originals before the whole thing goes to pot in China." Her eyes were flinty, and I knew it would make no difference to argue, but I offered a weak objection anyway.

"James will probably want that inventory. We were swamped with orders."

Gigi scoffed. "James can have it if he comes over here and gets it himself. I dare him." She narrowed her eyes at me, both hands on her hips, and I burst into laughter.

"All right," I said, conceding, "I'll let him know your terms. He's never been one for courage, so I'd guess he'll call it a loss and contact his overseas suppliers with an increased order." I giggled. "Though I must say, I would love to see him go up against you and the grannies. Goldie would have her way, I'd imagine."

Gigi sniffed. "Not if I got to him first."

I rose from the table and washed my dishes quickly under the tap. Smoothing my hair, I turned to her.

"All right. I'm off to humble myself."

"Is he expecting you?" Gigi asked, giving me a quick hug before handing me the keys to the minivan.

"Not exactly," I admitted. I leaned against the back door and pushed it open. "But I think I know where to find him."

Tucker's crew had been busy. The farmhouse filled my view as I rolled to a slow stop on the gravel driveway. A few men were working on the roof, but the rest of the house was framed and solid. The long planks of siding had been painted a soft white, and the wraparound porch had floors laid that, I knew, would one day gleam with shiny varnish. I walked slowly toward the bare-wood porch steps, already picturing long flower boxes and a huge porch swing with striped pillows. I squared my shoulders, shaking off the impulse to design a house that wasn't mine and turning my thoughts to trying to repair the mess that was mine alone.

God, please help me get through this, I prayed.

The tall front door, etched glass flanking each side, stood ajar and I nudged it wide enough to walk through. A man was in the light-filled foyer, bent over something that was set up on sawhorses. The saw made a ferocious whine as he finished a piece of baseboard trim. I cleared my throat and he looked up. Removing his safety goggles, he said, "May I help you, miss?"

I swallowed. "I'm looking for Tucker. Is he around?"

A grin spread across the man's face. "I do believe he is. Boss!" he called, turning his head slightly toward the back of the house but eyes still twinkling and on me.

Tucker came around the corner and strode down the hallway, stopping short when he saw me.

"Tuck, you have a visitor." The man made it sound like I was the Queen of Sheba.

Tuck and I were adrift, neither of us saying a word but feeling the silence spread between us. Tucker blinked and then looked at the man working with the saw, who was standing with both hands on his hips, watching us as if we were his very favorite television show.

"Pete, this is Grace Kleren. Grace, Pete Miller."

"Pleasure," Pete said, taking off a work glove to shake my hand. He winked. "I feel like I already know you, Miss Grace."

I bit my lower lip and the nervous smile that was forming.

"That will be enough chitchat from you, Miller. Back to work." Tucker skirted the edge of the sawhorses and opened his hand. "Let's head somewhere a bit more private."

He fell into step behind me as I walked onto the porch. I heard Pete mumble something to Tucker about his need for privacy, and then Pete's bark of a laugh before Tucker closed the front door. He was blushing when he came to stand next to me on the porch.

"Sorry about that," he said, nodding toward the door. "It's a little like junior high over here some days."

I gestured to the house. "It's really beautiful. You've done such great work."

He nodded, turning a critical eye on the porch ceiling, the large picture window next to us. "It's coming along."

"The owner must be thrilled." I was stalling, but my heart was practically leaping out of my chest and I needed a minute to collect myself. After all these years, I still underestimated how weak my knees became when I stood in front of him, close enough to touch his face.

"The owner is, um, not really paying much attention most days," he said, eyes averted.

"Tuck," I said. My heart raced and my hands were clammy but it was now or never. "I have to say a few things. Do you have a minute?"

His eyes were sober. "I do."

"Okay. Good. Okay." I reached into my back pocket for my index cards. Swallowing hard, I began reading. "I'm so very sorry, Tucker. Those are words that would be enough on the playground where we met in elementary school, after I stole your Trapper Keeper or accidentally clocked you during freeze tag. But a simple

'I'm sorry' isn't going to be enough this time."

I pulled the first card off the stack, complete, and moved it to the back of the stack without looking up. "First, I'm sorry for not being clear enough with how grateful I am to you. You helped get the barn into perfect working condition, and you even made it pretty. You took me to Omaha, cheered me on, and flirted with a much older woman, all to help put wind in the sails of my dream."

I looked up briefly as I pushed that card to the back of the pile, and I glimpsed Tucker's face, eyes somber. He'd leaned against the porch railing and was watching my face. I continued.

"Second, I'm sorry for taking you for granted." I swallowed the lump forming in my throat. "I left Silver Creek years ago when I was pretty much a kid, and in my naïveté, I thought there were lots of men like you. Men who were honest, true, strong, and good to the core. I was wrong. There are not a lot of men like you. You are a gift, and I took that for granted, first for the years when we were growing up together, and then, horribly, as an adult who should have known better."

I didn't look up this time, just barreled onward.

"Third," I said, "I'm sorry I mocked you for praying."

Tucker interrupted. "You mocked me for praying?" He sounded confused.

I nodded. "Not out loud, but in my head. I'm sorry about that."

Tucker raised one eyebrow, amused. "You are?"

"Yes," I said, turning back to my cards. "I've been praying some, and turns out, it's not a total waste of time. Turns out," I continued with a sigh, "it can be a kind of a lifeline. And God hears. That's new to me, but I know it to the bottom of me that it's true. He does."

My hands shook a bit when I pushed the card to the back of the stack, and I had to blink away the tears filling in my eyes so I could see the last card.

"Finally," I said, voice trembling, "I'm sorry I let you go. I have recently found out what it feels like to be made to feel like I'm easily replaced. It pains me so much—" I had to stop as I choked back tears. "It hurts me to know that I made you feel like that, not once, but twice." I whispered the last words and then looked up, eyes filled with tears. "And even if you're with someone else now, someone who won't hurt you the way I have, I want to put all my cards on the table. I'm sorry, Tuck. I've learned a lot in the last week, but most of those lessons have hurt you in the process too. I hope you can forgive me."

Tucker barely let me finish the words before pulling me to where he sat on the porch railing. "There's no one but you." He kept his hands on my waist as he looked me in the eye. "And of course I forgive you." He kissed me, gently, sweetly, a lingering kiss that made my head spin. When he finally pulled back, he used his hands to wipe away an errant tear still making its way down my cheek.

"No more apologies, all right?" He spoke quietly, pushing a strand of hair away from my face. "And no more index cards." He bit his cheek but the smile appeared anyway. "I really didn't love AP English the first time."

I frowned. "The last time I made index cards and didn't use them, I got in a heap of trouble. It's good to be organized."

He kissed my cheek sweetly. "No, it's weird." Another kiss, along the line of my jaw. "But I'll tell you one thing."

"What's that?" I leaned into him, worrying that the lightness in my heart and head would soon prevent me from standing on my own two feet.

"Pete is going to be very, very happy you're back." He pulled me close and looked over my shoulder. "You are back, right?"

I followed his gaze behind me and saw a gaggle of workers standing in the picture window. When I turned, they started whooping and clapping, giving us the thumbs-up. Pete looked like he'd just won a heavyweight fight, all fist bumps and high fives to the men around him.

I laughed and waved, totally embarrassed and

totally, ridiculously happy. "Yes," I said, still laughing. "I'm back." I turned to face him. "And I'm totally, finally, all yours."

Tucker planted a kiss on my lips, his hands on my face, and grinned as the guys' cheers escalated in volume.

"Hey," he said.

"Mmm?"

"Welcome home."

thirty

I held her off for a few weeks, but Gigi was relentless. I pulled up the minivan to the back of the familiar tent and shifted into park, switching off the engine and the headlights.

"And I'm back to the very beginning," I said, but there was no rancor in my tone. I turned to Gigi and felt a sleepy smile start to form. "Shall we, then?"

"Yep," she said, and offered her palm for a high five. I complied and then shook my head.

"I'm here, but I still object to the insane hour. I just want that to go on record." I pulled myself out of the driver's seat and stretched my arms to the still-starry sky. Along the far eastern horizon, the inky black was turning to indigo, but it was still ridiculously early in the morning. I gathered my small pile of dresses, fledgling but promising ideas that had taken shape over the last week, and I followed Gigi to the open flaps of the tent.

"It's not that early," Gigi groused. "Any time after five o'clock in the morning is a perfectly reasonable time to start a day."

I muttered a rebuttal of that argument.

Gigi was having none of it as she entered our little booth and started setting up shop. "You millenniums."

"Millennials."

"Millenniums, millennials, same difference," she said, not looking up from her sales table. "People in your age group are utterly confused about how the world works. When you get up early, you get more done. And you don't need to text message or electronic mail or social media every one of your friends every day, all day. You need to look up when you're walking down a sidewalk or you'll miss your life or maybe break a limb."

I rolled my eyes but my smile was definitely making a liar out of me.

"Did you know," she continued, poking the air with a pair of scissors as she talked, "that in Australia they are having an election by mail for some referendum or another, and everyone is worried that the millenniums won't be able to figure out how to mail a letter?" She trained feisty eyes on me. "They don't know how! I read all about it on the World Wide Web." She shook her head, turning back to a stack of blank order forms. "They've made all sorts of instructional videos about what those big red boxes on the street are really for. Can you imagine?" She harrumphed in disgust and I giggled.

"At least you don't sound angry at progress,"

I said, and was rewarded with an eruption of a sigh.

"Progress?" she huffed. "Progress will be when twenty-three-year-old people can place their own prestamped ballots in the mail without needing their phones to show them how."

I was fully snort-laughing now, which was only making Gigi's tirade increase in volume. Right about when she settled into the abominable condition of network TV, I was attacked by a group hug smelling of lavender, hair spray, and cinnamon toast. The girls had found me.

Goldie was in the inner circle of the hug and was cooing the loudest, but I glimpsed Edna, the twins, and even Myrna within the wash of permed hair and nylon tracksuits.

"All right, now, give the girl room to breathe," Myrna snapped, but I caught her eye and saw her grinning. "She's used to crowds in the Big Apple, but there's no need to suffocate her in Silver Creek."

I was surprised to feel my eyes stinging with tears as I gathered in their faces, lined with years and full lives, but still soft and open and brimming with care for me. "Ladies," I said, "I'm so sorry things didn't work out the way we wanted." My voice caught at the end and Goldie and Edna each grabbed one of my hands, squeezing them as the group faced me, tsking.

"We are so proud of you, Grace," Goldie said

with resolve. "You do not need to apologize."

I raised my eyebrows to question how deeply she meant those words.

"All right," she conceded. "It's true you could have called more and sent more selfies. But other than that, we think you should feel proud of yourself for not putting up with that man and his idea of what your company should be. It wasn't right, and it wasn't you."

"Bullies have no spine," Myrna said, chin lifted in defiance to James, who, I was sure, wouldn't care a whit about Myrna Hopkins, but who really, truly should. "I can just imagine that man with his crocodile shoes and his smarmy smile." She wrinkled her nose. "Not half the man of your Tucker, I'll say that."

The ladies cast quick, nervous glances at one another, and I smiled. "I like the sound of that, Myrna," I said reassuringly. No need to worry about where I stood with Tucker Van Es. I was no longer the biggest fool in town. " 'My Tucker.' Sounds lovely."

The ladies nodded, but their smiles were tense. I looked at Gigi for explanation but she had her head down and was industriously organizing a basket of scarves that already looked perfect to me.

I narrowed my eyes at the women and was just about to ask why they were acting so cagey when Goldie's face lit up. She was looking just past my right shoulder and when I turned, my heart flipped.

"We were just talking about you," I said, my pulse quickening just from seeing him. Tucker Van Es was a lot of things. And I was pleased to note, even at an unspeakable hour of the day, one of those things was very, very good-looking.

He zeroed in on the women behind me. "You were, were you? I hope it was all good, ladies."

I looked back at the semicircle of white and gray hair and saw every last one of them nodding, eyes big. I laughed and turned to Tuck. "They've suddenly gone silent, which is a bit worrisome to me."

"Don't worry," he said, pulling me to him and kissing me softly on the cheek. "Good morning," he said, his voice low in my ear.

"Oh, well, that's a little timid, don't you think?" Goldie was scolding us from behind. "That's the best kiss you can dredge up, Tucker?" She tsked. "And people think we're the old people around here."

He locked eyes with me, his face showing mock disbelief. "Is she baiting me? I feel like she's baiting me."

I nodded, suddenly serious. "I believe she is. However will you respond?"

He winked at the ladies and took my hand. "There will be plenty of time for other kinds of kissing," he said with a nod to our peanut gallery. They murmured their approval as I was pulled away by Tuck's strong hand.

"Wait," I said, looking over my shoulder. "Shouldn't I be helping Gigi set up?" But Gigi grinned and waved.

"I already cleared this with her. We're good," he added quietly, and pulled me closer to him as we walked side by side down the lane of booths. He nodded at people he knew, and I could feel them stopping to watch as we passed.

"Good gravy," I said. "I feel like I'm walking with royalty. Guess I'm not the only one smitten with you around here."

He smiled, eyes ahead. "There's just nothing else going on in this town, you know that. Quiet place we live in, Grace Kleren."

"Sometimes quiet is just perfect," I said, and meant it.

I looped my arm around his waist and felt him slow our pace as we neared the entrance to the tent. "Where are we headed?" I craned my neck to try to glimpse the darkness outside. "It's still nighttime out there, you know. Nobody's making doughnuts quite yet."

I looked up at him. He bit his lower lip and met my gaze. "We're going for a walk." He was suddenly very serious, and I felt my heart jump.

"All right," I said, feeling my stomach sink. "You're not breaking up with me, are you?" I meant it as a joke, but my somber tone didn't quite pull it off.

His smile was crooked. "Not exactly." Lifting the flap of the tent aside, he held it for me to walk through.

I breathed in the sweet smell of the last days of summer and waited for my eyes to adjust to the darkness. And then my breath caught in my throat.

"Tucker."

Along the path that wound away from the tent, trees were lit up with sparkling lights. Hundreds of lights, beautiful and lively and dispelling the darkness around them. I started toward them slowly, my footsteps quiet along the thick grass. The lights were coming from within lanterns hung from branches all along the path. The effect was ethereal, and I felt a lump in my throat. I looked at Tucker, who had come to stand beside me and was watching my face.

"You did this for me?"

"I did." His voice was deep and quiet.

I saw movement behind us and realized a crowd had gathered outside the open flaps of the tent. A slow smile spread across my face and I nodded toward the onlookers.

"It appears you've stopped set-up." I shook my head. "Quite a feat with the Midwestern work ethic around here."

He tipped his cap to our fans and then tugged

me toward the path. "Like I said, nothing happening in this sleepy town."

I settled my hand in his, feeling the warmth from it spread. The lights above us danced, flickering and winking as they lit our way. Tucker walked in silence for a bit and I followed his lead, starry-eyed at the transformation of the long line of trees, their full branches lit up and magical against a deep cobalt sky.

"You did this for me," I said again, shaking my head in wonder. "It's beautiful, Tuck."

He cleared his throat, glancing at me quickly before returning his gaze to the path ahead. "I'm glad you like it." His shoulders were hunched a bit and he'd jammed his free hand into his jeans pocket.

"Hey," I said, pulling him back a bit. "Slow down, champ. I want this to last a long time. You're walking too fast."

"Oh. Sorry," he said, and made it about three strides before resuming his pace.

"Listen, speedster, it's not every day a girl—" I stopped my protests abruptly when we rounded the bend, finding ourselves back at the footbridge where we'd stood only a few months before. Small lanterns lined the bridge's walkway on both sides, and more candles and lanterns dotted the shore along the creek. I stared.

"Oh good," he said, relieved. "I was worried the breeze would have done some damage." He smiled at me and pulled me, walking backward as I followed him to the bridge. "I like the look on your face. You're not easy to surprise, Kleren. That control issue and all."

My eyes were roaming, hungry to take it all in. "I'm ignoring that unfounded comment and just basking. Let me bask."

"Bask away," he said. We came to a stop at the top of the bridge's arc. The night was starting to lift and the ocean blue of the sky was a breathtaking counterpoint to the wash of flickering candlelight.

"Really early last spring," I said, "when I'd just gotten back to Iowa, we walked here. Do you remember?"

Tucker nodded, watching me.

"I was so nervous," I admitted. "You were so perfect and handsome and strong, and irritating."

He made a face. "I liked the way that started but the ending was pretty poor."

"You wouldn't even tell me if you were single." I raised one eyebrow in reprimand. "You weren't exactly making it easy on me. Of course," I added, wincing, "you had good reason."

"Grace." He turned me to him and put his hands on both sides of my face as he kissed me, long and sweet. I murmured, "Goldie would have approved of that," and raised myself on my tiptoes for another.

"Wait." He kept his face next to mine. "I need you to hear me."

I stepped back a bit, searching his eyes with my own.

"Here's the thing." His eyes were intent, shining. "I'm not single."

I laughed and the sound rang out in the hush of the creek side. "I'm glad."

He pressed on, his words tumbling out. "I love you, Grace. With a crazy, reckless, exhausting love. I've loved you since I was a kid, when we'd play tag and all I'd want was for you to catch me so I could make Gracie Kleren smile. I've loved you as a moody, heartsick teenager who couldn't hear any pop song or see any movie without getting angry that no girl alive was as beautiful and smart and funny as you. And now." His voice became gravelly, rough. "I love you as a man. A man who can't sleep well when you're miles away. A man who drives his coworkers nuts because nothing and no one compares to the promise of seeing you when the day is done. A man who builds a house, intending it for a buyer . . ."

He paused and I caught my breath as I followed his thoughts.

He shook his head. "But finally having to admit I put every part of it together with your face and laugh and happiness in mind."

My tears were falling freely when he went

down on one knee and looked up at me, eyes trained on mine.

"Grace Kleren, I will love you until I take my very last breath. Will you marry me?"

I didn't wait for him to slip the ring on my finger. I didn't wait to say yes and yes and yes, a word I would never tire of saying for the next weeks, months, and years. And I certainly didn't wait for him to ask again. I pulled him to his feet, wrapped my arms around him, and kissed him through my tears. Because, I reasoned as he lifted me from my feet and turned me slowly, his strong embrace holding me fast, I figured a lifetime of waiting was more than enough.

thirty-one

Tucker used his shoulder to make the heavy front doors of the church give way, and we stepped into the fall sunshine. Myrna was at the organ, pounding out a raucous version of "Great Is Thy Faithfulness" that we could hear even when Tuck let the door shut behind us.

"Hurry and kiss me before all those people find us," he said, framing my waist with his hands and pulling me toward him. "So." Kiss. "Many." Kiss. "People." Kiss on my laughing lips, along my jawline, the tender skin of my neck.

I pushed him gently and made him look at me. "I love you. So much, it's pretty much taking over my life."

He rolled his eyes and starting kissing again. "I already know that part, but thanks. Now stop talking." He commenced kissing and said into my neck, "What do you say we skip the reception? We've seen that barn plenty of times. No need to waste another afternoon there, even if it does look pretty good with all those flowers and lights and stuff." Kiss, along my collarbone.

I pushed him, not as gently, laughing at his

insistence. "We might be missed," I said, pointing to my dress, his suit. "And I didn't make this dress just for a forty-five-minute ceremony. The dress is made for dancing too."

Tucker took me in, head to toe, taking his time. I had to admit it: the dress was a stunner. The design process had been an emotional rush. On several occasions, I'd found myself giddy and humming as I made the fabric come alive from my sketch and to my measurements. Ivory, strapless, with a soft A-line, the dress had a fitted bodice and a lace skirt with pretty, feminine lines. The peplum accent was made of lace from my mother's wedding gown. Gigi had cried when I'd put it on.

Tucker ran his hand along my waist, his strong fingers careful and deliberate on the delicate fabric. I felt a shiver down my spine as he spoke, a wicked twinkle in his eye. "It *would* be a shame not to get to see you in this dress any longer today." He cocked his head, thoughtful. "Unless, of course, the other choice is to see you *out* of this dress."

I felt my cheeks get hot, despite the cool autumn breeze that lifted my veil. "Now, just because you've made an honest woman of me doesn't mean we forsake all other responsibilities." My voice was low. I could hear the voices of friends and family coming close as people filed out of their pews and toward the back of the church.

"Let's forsake." Tucker's voice was more of a growl. "I love forsaking."

The door burst open just as I was seriously considering missing my own wedding reception.

"Mr. and Mrs. Van Es." Erin Jackson was the first to barrel out of the church doors, slightly out of breath. Leave it to Erin to trample little old ladies on her way to being first in line, I thought as I positioned a ready smile on my face. Erin's husband, Les, stood next to her, combing thick fingers through his thinning hair as he shook Tucker's hand. Erin leaned in for an air-kiss.

"It was a lovely service," Erin said, a tight smile pulling apart her fuchsia lipstick. "You look very pretty." She nodded at my dress. "Budget Bridal in Des Moines? I thought I saw one just like this there when I went shopping with my niece last month."

My eyes grew wide and I started to speak but Tucker rescued me. "Thanks for coming, Jacksons. Make sure to stop by the barn for some dinner and dancing." He was practically shoving Erin down the steps after her husband.

"No need for homicide on our wedding day," he whispered into my ear, and I giggled. The man knew me well.

The line was long and full of people we loved. Tucker and I greeted and hugged everyone, sharing lots of laughter. Martin wore a suit coat over a Sturgis T-shirt; Luca and Isa, in from New

York, followed him with compliments on his "edginess." There were high fives from Pete and the work crew, and Miss Evelyn was still blotting her eyes with her handkerchief when she clasped our hands with hers.

"I'm just so happy for you both," she said, lip trembling. "And, Grace, don't you worry one bit about your shipping needs while you're on your honeymoon. I'll take care of everything, even with the extra shipments to your new boutique in Des Moines. Think nothing of it."

"Oh, she won't, Miss Evelyn," Tucker assured her with all sincerity. "I'm glad you reminded Grace that postal matters will just have to wait and that first things will need to come first."

"That's right," Miss Evelyn said, patting Tucker's arm as she walked away and not appearing to notice me nudging him hard with my elbow. The man was shameless.

By the time we gave our thanks to Pastor Simpson for his part in the moving ceremony, the sun was starting to dip behind the sprawling maple tree that lit up the churchyard with red and gold brilliance in its leaves. I was watching the line of trucks and cars snake out of the small church parking lot, headed to our reception, when Tucker cleared his throat. I turned to see the sewing ladies standing before us, arms linked and eyes shining. Gigi held a white box with a wide, sky-blue ribbon. She stepped forward a bit and said, "We have a little something for you two."

Tucker took my hand.

Myrna said, "We talked about giving this to you at your bridal shower, Grace."

"Oh boy, did we talk about it," Goldie said under her breath with a roll of her eyes.

Myrna frowned. "I have strong feelings about etiquette. Things should be done a certain way, especially at a wedding."

"We know," Bev and Madge said in unison.

"But we decided," Edna said in her teacher voice, trying to rein it in, "that this gift was for you both."

"Because you two are a family now." Goldie clasped both of our hands. Her eyes shone with happy tears. "You walk together now, through it all. The good, the beautiful, the tough, the aching—all of it together."

"Just like your mom and dad did, from their first day to their last." Gigi held out the box to me, blinking back tears.

I tugged gently on the ribbon and Tucker held the box while I lifted out its contents. My hands cradled an exquisite, white inlaid wood box. I ran my fingers over the pretty mosaic pattern. Gigi reached out and put her hand on the box.

"Your dad made this for your mom when they were dating." Her voice wavered. "She put all his letters in it. I would see her reading them during quiet afternoons. I can still see her, curled up on her bed and smiling at your dad's indecipherable handwriting, the way her hair caught the light pouring in the windows." Tears fell freely now and I felt Tucker strengthen his arm's hold around me.

Gigi swallowed hard. The other ladies gathered nearer to her, tightening the circle that surrounded her.

"After they were married," she said, "your mom kept adding to the letters. She kept new letters from your dad, even more precious because of how life got busy and he still made time to write. She kept letters she'd written to you but not delivered yet." She turned to Tuck, eyes full of long-earned love and respect. "There are even a few letters with your name on the envelopes."

I heard Tuck draw a shaky breath. Emotion filled his eyes.

"She said once that she was hoping to give the letters to you on your wedding day." Gigi smiled through her tears. "It took no small amount of effort, but I was able to keep it a secret from you. Until today."

"There is one addition your mama didn't know about," Goldie said softly. "The six of us have written a letter to you both," Goldie said. She was holding on to her friends, each hand reaching across and touching as much of their individual hands as possible. She looked at me. "We know you must miss your mom and dad a lot today, kiddo."

I nodded and took the tissue Myrna offered me, pressing it to my wet cheeks.

"But you need to know they would be so, so proud of you."

The ladies murmured in agreement.

"And *we* are so, so proud." Goldie smiled through her tears. "Of both of you."

"May God rain down blessings on your home," Edna said, her voice strong and sure. "He's awful good, so we know He will."

The women nodded. I could imagine the many years of evidence of that goodness represented in this circle alone.

"And we're here for you, if you need absolutely anything." Myrna sounded ready to fight anyone who would disagree with her.

The women hugged us as one, their best Sunday clothes getting all rumpled and crushed in the process. Goldie was the first to emerge and say, "Girls, we're going to need to back up a bit or the rhinestones on my corsage are going to cause an injury to myself and others."

Tucker and I watched them walk away, Gigi looking back and calling to me, "No more tears, now. It's time to party like it's nineteen ninety-nine." She winked at Tucker.

I looked at him. "You did not give her a mixtape."

"I did, and I will do it again. We have a lot of family dinners ahead of us, and I, for one, am glad you'll finally have someone ready to DJ."

I laughed and felt a new happiness at the idea of all those days, all those dinners, all those moments together.

Tucker took my hand and kissed it. He looked at me with tenderness and I hoped my face showed him the truth, that I was perpetually stunned at the depth of my joy.

"You ready, Gracie Van Es?"

I nodded, heart full, and looked toward his truck, festooned with balloons, streamers, and tin cans, ready for our getaway.

Tucker swept me up into his arms as if I were light as air, which was just exactly how I was feeling. He placed me gently into the cab of his truck, and I scooted over just enough to allow him to drive. There was no way I was headed all the way to the opposite window.

He turned on the engine and made all sorts of ruckus as he honked and started away from the church and toward our barn, which was dripping with white hydrangeas, roses, and tulips and full of people who loved us and had made this place our home.

"Okay, beautiful," Tucker said, arm tucked around the fabric of my dress and pulling my legs closer to him. "Ready for the adventure?"

I waved to the smattering of well-wishers

behind us and then turned, lifting my gaze to the crimson maple leaves arching overhead. Before too much road was behind us, I reached up to kiss my husband on the corner of his mouth. I tucked my shoulder into him and took his hand, holding it between both of mine, not able to get close enough to this good, true man beside me.

I smiled, watching the wash of red leaves, the greenest grass, the warm gold of an autumn sun setting over the town I loved. It was the place where I'd learned how to love and be loved, how to forgive, be forgiven, and where I learned about the sheer, breath-catching, truly amazing power of mercy and grace.

"Yes," I finally said, sure to my core. "I am ready."

acknowledgments

Thank you, dear reader, for coming along for this story. I absolutely loved writing this book, and I am honored you would fall into its pages with me. Thank you, too, for being the kind of nerd who reads the acknowledgments page. I am your soul sister.

The fine people at Howard Books deserve all sorts of accolades for bringing *Heart Land* to life. I am particularly indebted to and fond of the bright and thoughtful Beth Adams for her insight, her love of good stories, and her willingness to try the untried in order to get grace (and Grace) into the hands of readers. I am indebted, too, to Anna Dorfman for another stunning cover that tells this story so beautifully. My sincere thanks to you both.

I'm hoping the folks at Alloy Entertainment won't notice if I just move into their offices, hide behind the ficus in the corner, and eavesdrop on their work. I'm honored to have partnered with them on this project. Sara Shandler, thank you so very much for bringing me on, and Laura Barbiea, thank you for hearing my heart, even on weekends. You are an absolute gem.

Chip MacGregor makes everything better. It's true, and even when he's not wearing a kilt. Chip, thank you for your perpetual and convincing argument that I can do this writing gig. You are unparalleled as an agent and also are a phenomenal friend. Thank you.

My writing group endures all sorts of drivel on the way to publication, and I cannot ever repay them, though I'm trying, month by month, with gluten-free baked goods. Wendy Delsol, Dawn Eastman, Carol Spaulding-Kruse, and Kali VanBaale, thank you for providing insight, wisdom, and a razor-sharp red pen.

Thank you to Iowa Writers, a group of smart, brave people who are fiercely loyal to one another and to the craft of writing. I am honored to be in your ranks.

Sarah Dornink Clutts of Dornink knows the real world of design, fashion, construction, and who all those people are at photo shoots. Thank you, Sarah, for making me sound smarter than I am and for not judging me for owning (and, ahem, wearing) multiple pairs of yoga pants.

Speaking of yoga pants, I want to thank my tribe of women who love me and support me and tell me when I'm totally off base. All of these things are rare, and I realize the very good fortune I have in you. Bets, Annie, Deanna, Makila, Sarah, and Sarah, thanks for letting me launch into the injured-cat cry with absolutely no warning. This is true friendship.

Thank you, dear family, hither and yon, for loving me and for reading this book. Thank you, too, to my family members who will not read this book but will fake it at family reunions. I love you, too.

My children, Ana, Mitchell, and Thea, are my most constant and vocal cheerleaders. Thank you for being loud in your love for me, kiddos. I love the loud. Except for at the dinner table. We could be a little quieter there, please.

I am able to write stories about love and grace and passion and laughter-until-it-hurts because my husband lives out those stories in our house every day. Thank you, my dearest Marc, for always, always believing I can and then ordering Thai and praying me through. I love you.

I need, every hour, the bone-deep grace and new mercy that God offers to me. He is writing the story that changes everything, and I am ever grateful.

Center Point Large Print
600 Brooks Road / PO Box 1
Thorndike, ME 04986-0001 USA

(207) 568-3717

US & Canada:
1 800 929-9108
www.centerpointlargeprint.com